THE SEARCH FOR
Sonny Skies

THE SEARCH FOR

Sonny Skies

A Novel by Mickey Rooney

A BIRCH LANE PRESS BOOK
Published by Carol Publishing Group

Fic
Rooney
M.

A Birch Lane Press Book
Published by Carol Publishing Group
Birch Lane Press is a registered trademark of Carol Communications,
   Inc.
Editorial Offices: 600 Madison Avenue, New York, N.Y. 10022
Sales and Distribution Offices: 120 Enterprise Avenue, Secaucus,
   N.J. 07094
In Canada: Canadian Manda Group, P.O. Box 920, Station U,
   Toronto, Ontario M8Z 5P9
Queries regarding rights and permissions should be addressed to
   Carol Publishing Group, 600 Madison Avenue, New York, N.Y. 10022

Carol Publishing Group books are available at special discounts for bulk
purchases, sales promotion, fund-raising, or educational purposes.
Special editions can be created to specifications. For details, contact:
Special Sales Department, Carol Publishing Group, 120 Enterprise
Avenue, Secaucus, N.J. 07094

Manufactured in the United States of America

10   9   8   7   6   5   4   3   2   1

Library of Congress Cataloging-in-Publication Data

Rooney, Mickey.
    The search for Sonny Skies : a novel / by Mickey Rooney.
        p.   cm.
    "A Birch Lane Press book."
    ISBN 1-55972-231-2
    1. Motion picture actors and actresses—California—Los Angeles—
Fiction. 2. Children as actors—California—Los Angeles—Fiction.
3. Hollywood (Los Angeles, Calif.)—Fiction.   I. Title.
PS3568.0632S4   1994
813'.54—dc20   93-44187
                                                                      CIP

THE SEARCH FOR

Sonny Skies

1

Jay Richards turned off Sunset Boulevard and headed up Laurel Canyon. He parked his battered gray 1972 Mercedes 300SL on the downhill side of Kirkwood Drive, eased his bones out of the car, reached into the backseat for a gallon jug of Gallo's hearty burgundy, and looked at his watch. Seven P.M. He was a little early for the poker game, but he thought maybe he could help Tilly Greenberg. Tilly made a fine spaghetti sauce and would brook no suggestions on how to improve it. But she sometimes accepted Richards's offer of help on the salad.

He proceeded along the edge of the street—there was no sidewalk there—cradling the wine jug like a baby and almost tripping over the Greenbergs' calico cat. He caught the jug just before it hit the ground. Then he punched the doorbell, forgetting that it had been broken years before.

The Backstabbers had been meeting every Thursday night at the Greenbergs for the past dozen years. The Backstabbers! Huh! Jay Richards tried to recall how they ever got the name Backstabbers. It was a name they had given themselves; that was certain. Nobody else gave a damn about them or even knew they existed. Unless it was one of the wives—who, except for Tilly, were never invited.

Yeah, maybe it was Tilly Greenberg herself, who, kibitzing one night, watched him, Jay Richards, check and raise and rake in a pretty good sized pot. She called him a backstabber.

One of the other members of the group, maybe Kelley,

said, "You mean 'sandbagger'? The word," he said gently, "is 'sandbagger.' "

Tilly said, "Well, I know enough about poker to know you're all a bunch a cutthroats. Backstabbers is the only word that says it all."

Someone at the table toasted Tilly's originality, and everyone drank to it, and that was that. And so, Backstabbers they were. And Backstabbers they would remain.

Richards waited for someone to come to the door. He was a newspaperman; he had once been bold enough to simply barge in. Now, at fifty-two, buffeted by marital and career misfortunes, he was a shadow of that former self. He had lost his confidence and taken on wimpish ways. He punched the broken bell again.

The Backstabbers had been sources for Jay Richards during his twelve-year romp as a gossip columnist for the *Daily Flick*. History had passed them all by—all of them except Jay Richards himself, who was hanging on to history by his fingernails. But most of them would rather take poison than admit it. Maybe, if life got any more bitter, one of them would take poison. Maybe they'd all enter into a James Jones suicide pact. Death by Kool-Aid.

In his day, Jay Richards had been a big man in Hollywood, if having every press agent in town sucking up to you was a measure of bigness. But now he was a sometime Hollywood correspondent for the *Sun*, England's sleaziest tabloid. He received no salary and no benefits. They paid by the word. He got an occasional phone call from London asking for two hundred words on Julia Roberts's latest fling or, more often, no story at all—just some guidance on the whereabouts of Madonna, Liz Taylor, or Michael Jackson. At which point, they'd assign someone else—a photographer, maybe—to hound the star. He considered himself lucky to have even this pissant job with the *Sun*.

Richards knew that he wasn't big anymore. But if you'd said, "Rich, when you used to be big—" he'd interrupt and tell you, with a wink, "I'm still big. It's only Hollywood that got small." The wink meant that he knew, and he wanted you to know that he knew, that he was paying homage to (not stealing) Billy Wilder's great line in *Sunset Boulevard.* Not Gloria Swanson's line, but Wilder's—because, you see, Richards considered himself a writer, and writers had to stick together and give credit where it was due.

In fact, Richards wasn't much of a writer. He had freelanced a few pieces for the old *Life* magazine, but his bread and butter (and his beer) had come from his steady five-day-a-week column in the *Daily Flick,* one of the town's soaring trade papers back in the days when Hollywood was more than just nine white letters on a hillside. Still, people in the business kissed his ass a hundred times a day because of his column. Maybe that is why the ambitious French actress Susan Genève married him. "Maybe," she told Richards once in a moment of drunken candor, "maybe, dahleeng, zay weel kees my ass on zee way to keesing yours."

Richards used to sit down at his Underwood at four o'clock, sort and balance all his scribbled notes on top of the mess piled around him, then bang out 750 words of pure fiction. He did it every day, Monday through Friday. It wasn't labeled fiction, of course. It was the kind of three-dot journalism once brought to a fine fever by Walter Winchell—99 percent unsubstantiated gossip and 1 percent lies. All of Richards's gossip, of course, focused on the picture business. Few of his items were true. But as Pontius Pilate—and Jay Richards—used to say, "What is truth?"

The kind of gossip one read in "Rich's Rambles" was strategic information: "New Triangle Cinema on the brink of joining the big show with heart-stopping $4 million buy of Missy Gillespie's latest thriller. Hollywood is poised to see how the onetime indie handles the delicate marketing and promotion of 'The Prussy Farm' after an expected boffo opening. That's the ultimate test of any major." Or: "CBS has already inked Olympic skater Nancy Bludorf for prime-time, pre-Olympic feature. To compete, ABC and NBC are already prepping several other Olympic pics, including one on Austria's icy sexpot Mitzy Mall. But even her deal with Spike Eisenberg wasn't controversy-free, as the orphaned skater's guardians brought in an intermediary who aced out Mall's manager, Aaron Smith-Brown, and agent Steve Canyon, who put the deal together. Smith-Brown couldn't be reached, but Canyon opined, 'It's just business.' Spike's telepic is skedded this fall on Fox opposite CBS football." Or: "Susy Cupcake in town for three meetings this week at Myriad Productions. Agent Sy Sipowitz confides Myriad looking for ingenue with hi media visibility as it goes into production next week on sequel to 'Blue Throat.' "

The items were an integral part of the business. Agents and would-be producers fed them to Richards. Richards fed them to Hollywood. And then the whole civilized world— from Cahuenga Boulevard all the way west to Malibu— would know how busy they (and their clients) were. Their actual offices could be as dark as the tombs at Forest Lawn, but if these people made "Rich's Rambles," the world would know that they, the folk who flitted in and out of Jay Richards's column, were working in a town where "not working" was like having seven kinds of venereal disease.

So you didn't look for reality in "Rich's Rambles." Hopes and dreams, that was all. The funny thing was that everybody in the business *knew* that the column was nothing but hopes and dreams—and they read it, anyway. If they weren't reading Richards, they'd be reading tea leaves or paying regular visits to Katherine Kuntz, the chorus girl turned astrologer, or to Gloria Chatham, the numerologist-madam in Topanga Canyon. Richards himself used to pay regular calls on Kuntz and Chatham. He did it in the good old days (when he could afford to buy a new Mercedes) because (1) they always had some good gossip for him and (2) sometimes they had a fresh, new girl in town.

The column was no more. Neither was the *Daily Flick*. It

folded in 1984, after Honey Verdugo won a $47 million libel judgment against the *Flick*—and the appeal as well. She ended up owning the newspaper, lock, stock, and Underwoods, and she celebrated one night by having the thing torched as part of a scenario in *Lethal Doses II*. Paramount paid her $100,000 to let them blow it up and burn it. Verdugo had the satisfaction of watching the whole thing go. Ironically enough, Jay Richards was standing right next to her on a curbstone down the street when Honey spoke its epitaph: "So," she said, standing there brushing her palms while the flames reflected off her sunglasses, "the *Flick* is fluck."

Unfortunately, Richards couldn't report the line the next day because, needless to say, Jay Richards didn't have a job at the *Flick*—or anywhere else, either. (He couldn't even share the line with Susan Genève, for she had left him as soon as the *Flick* folded. That was eight years ago. The destruction of the *Flick* really wasn't a story that Richards wanted to report in public, anyway, because, you see, it was *his* story about Honey that led to the libel suit. No one in Hollywood would dream of hiring Jay Richards after screwing up like that.

Hiring him to do what? Write Hollywood gossip? Hey, any eighteen-year-old kid who could type was quite capable of doing what Richards had been doing for the last dozen years. Typing, that's all it was. No one, not the *Hollywood Reporter*, not *Daily Variety*, needed a Jay Richards. After he had exhausted his unemployment, he almost took a job as a copy editor for the "Calendar" section of the *Los Angeles Times*, but he was saved from that ignominy one day by a call from Jon Applecart, the wire editor of the *Sun*, the tits-and-ass tabloid in London, asking if he'd do a little stringing on Hollywood. "No offense, ducks," he said, "but we thought you wouldn't mind terribly, come out of retirement, as it were, keep you in kippers and all that?"

Richards wondered how the *Sun* got his name.

"Let's see, now," said Applecart. "It was on a card somewhere on this desk. Oh, yes. Seems an actress, a French actress—"

"That's okay," said Richards. "Never mind. I'll do it." Actually, he thought, the *Sun* fit his station perfectly, as did the clothes he wore. When he tried to ring the broken doorbell at the Greenbergs' for the third time, he was wearing his now-standard day-or-night costume: a black-and-white nylon jogging suit made in the People's Republic of China, purchased for $19.95 at K mart's last end-of-the-month sale. The jogging suit was the essence of simplicity. Richards could ramble anywhere in that jogging suit. He could even sleep in the damn thing. And often did.

"Heavens to Betsy Ross," hissed the man who opened the door when Richards finally remembered to knock, not ring. "You ever take a bath?" Dave Benton (sometimes known as "Fat Ben") was recuperating from the aftereffects of an enforced retirement from William Morris as an account executive. He had once specialized in a pretty good imitation of Peter Lorre, and somewhere along the way Lorre's sibilance had taken permanent residence somewhere alongside Ben's bridge. Not only did he end up talking like Lorre; he shuffled his feet and bent his shoulders forward, like Lorre, and rolled his eyes heavenward just before he took in vain the name of the American Revolution's famous seamstress— which he did frequently. As he was doing just now.

"I bathe," Richards said. He avoided Dave Benton's overbearing, hostile gaze and tried to brush by him. "Every Saturday night."

Fat Ben blocked his way and read the label on the jug. "Gallo! Hey, Rich, nice! The cheapest!" Benton was very sensitive about his weight. He carried 260 pounds on a five-foot ten-inch frame, and his best defense was a good offense. He specialized in insults, usually delivered in the manner of Peter Lorre.

"Shut up, cretin." Since he didn't drink anymore, he

didn't see why he should bring anything but Gallo. He said, "You the first one here?"

"Of course not," Benton said. "Kelley's already started on the Beaujolais. The Beaujolais *I* brought." He waved Jay Richards into the foyer.

Richards proceeded to the kitchen, hoisted the Gallo on to a chopping-block table, greeted Tilly Greenberg with a grunt and a hug, and stuck his middle finger in the spaghetti sauce that was simmering on the stove. She swatted him in the ear with a dish towel. "Why don't you just get the hell out of my kitchen?" she suggested. Her tone was not unfriendly.

Richards savored the sauce. "Not bad." Then: "I could do the salad."

She shook her head. "Not tonight. I'm gonna wait and do that later. You made it early last week, and it got all soggy."

He grimaced. "Tom in the den?" Tom Greenberg had been an album producer at Squirrel Records in Hollywood. He had seventeen golds, and at his peak he made at least $500,000 a year at Squirrel. He was now retired, but he kept himself busy playing tennis, dabbling in real estate rentals, and, of course, hosting his poker club.

"Go on in and help him set up."

"Set up what?"

She tossed her head meaningfully. Richards strode into the card room. Fat Ben shuffled in after him. Tom Greenberg was trying to thread an old-fashioned 35-mm projector while Bill Kelley pretended to watch him. Kelley seemed more interested in pouring himself another glass of Beaujolais. "What the hell is this?" Richards asked. "I thought we were going to play poker."

Greenberg paused. "We've been playing poker every Thursday night since as long as you can remember. Why *wouldn't* we be playing poker?"

"So what's with the projector?"

"A gag," said Greenberg. "I got this flick. We aim the projector out this window, we see naked ladies on the neighbor's garage door."

"Huh!" Richards was not amused.

Ben said *he* was amused. "Heavens to Betsy," he said. "What do innocent people do when they come driving up the street and see the dirty pictures?"

Kelley looked up from his glass. "In this town? Who's innocent?"

"That's the whole point," said Greenberg. "We don't know what they're gonna do. We watch and wait."

"Heh-heh." Benton grinned. "We oughta get a rise outta somebody, Betsy's sake."

They got a rise out of no one. The drivers of two passing cars slowed down a bit when they saw the projections of flesh on the garage door. They did not stop. They did not back up. No one else came up the road except the other members of the Backstabbers: Bob Jones, Jordan Bonfante, and Marshall Berger, in separate cars.

"Hey, what's with the broads 'cross the street?" asked Jones. He was wearing a loose-fitting tunic with no collar and Greek frets running up and down its long sleeves. "Oh, I get it," he said when he saw the projector whirring away, with Greenberg and the others peering out another window overlooking Kirkwood Drive.

"Hey, Jonesy," said Jordan Bonfante, "you do something to your hair? And what's with the mustache?"

Damn, thought Richards. He had wondered why Jones looked different. Of course. Jones had dyed his gray hair black and affected a Groucho Marx mustache besides. Made him look younger. Richards wondered whether he should tint his hair.

Bonfante waddled over to Jones and tickled the foliage on his upper lip.

"If I want to get and keep a job as one of the assistant

cooks to a Greek chef," Jones explained, "I gotta *look* a little Greek, right?" He had landed a job in January in the clubhouse restaurant at Santa Anita Racetrack.

"The tunic makes you look a lotta Greek," said Jordan Bonfante.

"No, it doesn't," said Marshall Berger.

"Yes, it does," said Jones in a wounded tone.

"Ah, the hell with this," said Tom Greenberg, giving up on the porn pix. He turned off the light on the projector and put it on rewind. "Let's play some poker."

Seven players. Greenberg slid out six stacks of chips, one stack to each player, each worth fifty dollars. He played out of the bank. "Dealer's choice," said Greenberg, announcing the usual rules as he shuffled a red Bicycle deck. "Aces, straights, and flushes. Dealer antes for all. Pot limit. Three raises. Cut for deal."

Berger won the deal when he drew the jack of spades. He said they'd play seven-card stud, high-low, splitting with the high spade in the hole.

"Betsy's sake, you mean Blue Peter," said Dave Benton. "Whyn't you say Blue Peter?"

"Uh-huh," said Berger agreeably. "Blue Peter." He didn't want to play Fat Ben's intimidation game. He wanted to play poker and smiled when he ended up dealing himself the high hand, a spade flush, including the ace of spades. He was able to build up quite a big pot before he raked it in. "Control," he announced as he apportioned a third of the take to Jonesy, who held the low hand. "Control."

"Betsy's sake," said Dave Benton. Benton's oath—the way he said it—sounded obscene.

"Let's play that game again," said Berger, pushing the deck over to Benton. "Your call."

Fat Ben snarled and snapped two cards down to everyone at the table before he announced, "Seven-card, straight stud."

★ ★ ★

They played for four hours, and at midnight there were no clear winners or losers. Tilly came out of the kitchen and announced that the pasta was ready—"al dente, just the way Tom likes it." The seven members of the Backstabbers Poker Club trooped into the kitchen, heaped their plates high, and returned to the poker table with their plates and their wineglasses while Tom Greenberg examined the labels on some 35-mm movie reels that were stacked on a table against the wall.

"Where'd you get the film?" asked Jay Richards.

"Same place I got the projector."

"Where'd you get the projector?"

"Garage sale up the street. Widow Murphy? Husband used to be a film editor in Culver City? Died a cancer last month. Paid her two hundred bucks for the whole caboodle."

"Oh, yeah," said Jay Richards. "I remember him. Max Murphy. We had him in for poker one night last year. Took him to the cleaners."

"He took himself to the cleaners," said Dave Benton, enjoying his own cleverness too much. He looked around to make sure everybody got it. "Took *himself* to the cleaners."

"Ben," said Tom Greenberg, "it isn't that funny."

"Funny was his losing eight hundred and fifty clams," said Bonfante.

"The sumbitch never came back," said Dave Benton. He smiled with pleasure at the recollection. He had been the big winner that night, taking home more than a thousand, most of it from Maximilian Murphy.

"Well," said Greenberg, "Murphy musta had a thousand rolls a this film. I got 'em now. Here in the closet." He hooked a thumb over his shoulder.

"Why he save all the film?"

"That's for us to find out," said Greenberg. "Who knows what evil lurked in the heart of Maximilian Murphy?"

As it turned out, Murphy had stolen a film treasure—if you happened to be a movie buff with nothing but shit for brains. What he had saved was hundreds of rolls of, mainly, outtakes—stuff that the studio would have thrown away if Murphy hadn't grabbed it first. Paying the widow Murphy less than a dollar a reel, thought Richards, was too generous.

Here was footage of all the M-G-M greats—more stars than there were in the heavens. Gable, Garbo, Pidgeon, Kerr, Kate Hepburn, Jimmy Stewart, Mickey Rooney, Judy Garland, Spencer Tracy; you name them, they were here.

"Jeez," said Marshall Berger. "Judy Garland!"

"Yeah," said Richards, "but so what? What's she doin' here in this garbage? I mean, what's the hook?"

"I already seen a take of Judy Garland outta this batch," said Greenberg. "She was just flubbing her lines, looking scared. Or laughin' too hard."

"That's a find?"

"Well," said Tom Greenberg, lowering his voice, "nobody else has anything like this. Not that I know of."

Berger said, "They don't save it for a reason. It's dreck."

Jay Richards came out of a den closet, bearing an armload of film canisters. "Let's see what this is."

"Hey," said Greenberg, protesting. "I ain't seen that stuff yet."

"So? We'll help you look."

The first of the reels turned out to be a little more interesting than the Garland take. It was one of a batch marked Tests. Just one little word: Tests. What the reels contained—those that the Backstabbers had time to look at, at least—were fifteen-minute segments, mainly of beautiful young women doing "lines." Lines from some M-G-M classics. Lines from Sophocles and Racine and Goethe and Shakespeare and Eugene O'Neill. Dozens of young women. The group moved in closer to Greenberg's portable screen to get a better gander at these faces. Who were these women? Did anyone recognize any of them?

No one did. The group realized that none of them had become household icons. They were, without a doubt, some of the most beautiful young women then existing in America. They had come in from the highways and the byways, from acting schools, from college and university theater clubs, from community theater groups across the land, hopeful as hell that one of them would be the next Lana Turner or the next Deborah Kerr. And none of them ever made it.

Richards thought, History has passed them by, too. "I wonder whatever happened to them?" he said aloud.

"They probably found romance before they went back to Keokuk—or Calgary," said Dave Benton, grinning. "Some studio executives who made 'em think they could sleep their way to the silver screen."

"Hey, what's this?" cried Greenberg. He had just threaded a reel marked Tits. And now, as the film unspooled, the group saw a series of short takes, one after another, of some of the same beautiful, fresh-faced youngsters. Only this time they weren't reading lines. Now they were facing full on to the camera, blouses and bras completely off, saying one line over and over, trying to give that line every shade of emotion possible, enticing, angry, hurt, eager, puzzled. "Kiss me. Kiss me. Kiss me. Kiss me. Kiss me." That was all, as if it were some kind of acting exercise cued by the invisible director just off-camera.

"How degrading," said Tilly Greenberg, standing in the doorway to the kitchen.

"No," said Bill Kelley. "I'm not sure they felt degraded at all. See how excited they are? Look." Kelley walked right up to the screen and made as if to touch one slightly freckled blonde whose young breasts were an architectural marvel. "Look," he said. "See her perky nipples? This is a woman who is aroused. She likes this. She's enjoying it."

Tilly Greenberg's face darkened. Without a word, she turned and retreated to the kitchen.

"By God, Bill's right," said Bob Jones. "Look at this next girl. She looks kinda Greek, doesn't she? Look at the way her breathing starts to get kinda heavy here. On-screen, a brunet was sighing, in a kind of abstracted wonder. "Kiss me. Kiss me. Kiss me."

"Oh, how I'd love to oblige you, baby," said Kelley, talking to the screen. And then, to the group, "How I'd like to bowl a line or two with her. Oh, yes, honey, I *will* kiss you." He did a bump and grind.

"Well, not her, and not tonight," said Greenberg. He stopped the machine and started to rewind it. "This arc lamp is getting dim."

"Aww, party pooper," said Bonfante.

"Spoilsport," said Kelley.

"Betsy's asshole," Benton hissed.

They regrouped in the kitchen. If there was any wine left, these guys would finish it off. And they proceeded to do just that.

All except Jay Richards, who wasn't drinking. He kept noodling around in the den closet, turning over one canister of film after another, trying to read the labels. Some were completely faded. Other cans had no labels at all. Finally, he emerged with one canister marked Tests. Kids.

"Hey," said Richards, coming into the kitchen and confronting Greenberg. "Let's see this one, huh? Let's just see this one."

Greenberg examined the can. "Kids. Yeah, this is the label I found on the Judy Garland reel. This may have some value. These 'Kiss me' girls? They were never nobody. But M-G-M had some great kid stars."

"And you wanna see their screen tests?" demanded Benton. "I didn't know you were a freakin' historian."

"Yeah," said Richards. "Well. Maybe I am."

Greenberg looked over at Richards. His wife, Tilly, had

been sitting on his lap, blowing in his ear. Apparently, the boob footage and all the "Kiss mes" had turned her on despite her outward disapproval. It was obvious she was in the mood for a game of Hide the Salami—right now—with her Tom.

"Go on," said Greenberg. "You watched me thread those reels. You know how to do it. Go on. Go ahead and do it. Just that one, though." He hunched his shoulders in pleasure as Tilly kissed him on the side of his neck.

Jay Richards had the reel up in a minute or two. He was as jaded as the rest of this group, maybe more so than most of them. But for some reason he was fascinated with the prospect, maybe, of seeing, maybe, Mickey Rooney or Freddie Bartholomew in a screen test.

All of a sudden, there is an eight-year-old kid up on the screen. He has a Buster Brown haircut; he is wearing an Eton jacket, blue velvet pants, and shiny black shoes. An assistant director comes in from the side with a slate that says Sonny Skies. He claps the clapper and says, "Take one, Sonny Skies. Action."

And then Sonny is on, looking directly into the camera. It is a crappy, scratchy piece of film. And the sound isn't much better. The director's kindly voice, off-camera, comes on next. "What's your name?"

The kid says, "Sonny Skies." His voice is strong, unwavering, his gaze into the camera unafraid.

"What can you do, Sonny?"

"Oh, I can smile real good. I can sing. And I can dance."

"All right. Sing, Sonny."

Sonny looks around as if for an orchestra or at least a man with a piano. There is nothing. No music. He makes his own. "Bumpa, buh, buh, buh, baaaaa," he hums. And then, in a thin, small, soprano voice:

Every little bluebird flies by,
I say what's your name?

Every little bluebird flies by,
Lands on my windowpane.
You're a naughty little bluebird
You better learn to do what I do . . .
Mr. Bluebird, bluebird fly, and bye-bye.

The kid has a far-off look in his eye. Then he regards the camera lens with a steady curiosity. "Okay," says the director off-camera. "You can dance now."

Sonny, still supplying his own music, bumpa, buh, buh, buh, baaaaa, goes into a little spin and then a buck and wing.

Jay Richards was fascinated. But Dave Benton's whiny voice broke the moment for him. "What shit!" he said.

"Shut up, Ben," said Richards. "This ain't shit."

"Betsy's sake, you wouldn't know if it was or if it wasn't, Richards."

"I said, 'Shut up.' " In fact, Richards felt like a bum who had just found a wallet filled with bills. Now all he had to do was see if they were for real or counterfeit. Then, who knew? Maybe he could sell the footage to somebody, some film-history buff, maybe. This piece of footage of Sonny Skies had something special about it, something sad. At the very least, maybe he'd get a finder's fee for discovering this piece of celluloid. Maybe he'd split the fee with Greenberg. Then again, maybe he wouldn't. Greenberg was a multimillionaire. He was broke.

Richards stopped the film, proceeded to rewind it, put it back in the canister, tucked it under his arm, and repaired to the kitchen, where the Greenbergs had their heads together at the sink, rinsing the dishes and putting them in the dishwasher.

Benton had preceded him, and he and the Greenbergs were trading stories about what had happened to all the old kid stars. "Freddie Bartholomew got a job on one of the networks."

Tilly said, "Shirley Temple—"

Benton interrupted her. "Shirley Temple Black. She did okay, too. Became a U.S. ambassador."

"Mickey Rooney's still working," said Tom Greenberg. "And Jackie Cooper, too. I think he's working."

Richards said, "As a director. Cooper didn't do too bad. He directed some of the M*A*S*H episodes on TV."

Benton said, "Yeah, but Judy Garland OD'd, and Scotty Beckett committed suicide. Most a the kids who didn't get outa the business in time went down the toilet."

"Look," said Richards to Tom Greenberg. "I got this can a film." He showed it to Greenberg, then tucked it back under his arm. "Give you five bucks for this one."

"Naw, I don't wanta do that," said Greenberg. "None a these reels are for sale. Not right now."

Richards took Greenberg aside. He said, "Look, you don't know, but things haven't been so good for me lately. I think I might be able to parlay this footage into something."

"Into what?"

"I don't know. Something."

Greenberg shook his head. "I don't know, Rich."

Richards raised his voice. "Look, we'll go partners. You get half of what I get. I'll do all the shopping it around."

Tilly heard that. "What is it?" asked Tilly. "The 'Kiss me' reel?"

"Tilly," said Richards with reproach.

Tom Greenberg tried to pry the canister away, but Richards wouldn't let it go. Then Greenberg saw the label: Test. Kids.

"Sonny Skies!" said Greenberg. "This the Sonny Skies reel?"

Richards nodded. "Whaddya say?"

Tom looked at Tilly. He was still a little horny. Then he looked back at Richards. He certainly didn't feel like wasting time with Richards, dickering over a five-dollar reel of old film. "Aw, what the hell," he said to Richards. "Why not? Just be careful with it. Fifty-fifty? Right? Fifty-fifty?"

"Absolutely," said Richards.

"You'll be sorry," Benton said to Tom Greenberg.

"And so, Mr. Know-it-all," said Tilly to Benton, "what happened to Sonny Skies?"

"He fell in a bucket a shit," said Dave Benton, "and the hogs ate him."

★ ★ ★

On the way home to his tiny apartment, Jay Richards noted a glow in the skies south of the city, and he heard sirens—too many for this hour. The clock on his dash said 2:00 A.M. He switched on his radio, but all he got was static. He reminded himself to get the damn thing fixed soon. Once home, he snapped on the TV in his bedroom. First, a lot of confused footage about a city in flames. What? Where? Why? He invested a few minutes in front of the tube, switching from channel to channel. All the TV guys were trying to deliver the same story. That afternoon, a Simi Valley jury had acquitted the cops that everybody in the world saw beating Rodney King. Now, to get even, the people of South Central L.A. were burning their own neighborhoods to the ground.

He turned to his answering machine. Only one message. It was Applecart, from the *Sun* in London. Would he mind, old chap, filing four hundred words on the riot in Los Angeles? "Sorry, ducks, but Alison Carberry is out of town. By two P.M., Greenwich Time, if you could?" Well, thought Richards, it's nice to know the *Sun* thinks it can count on me when its regular correspondent is out. But Applecart was only giving him three hours.

Thank God for television. During riots, earthquakes, fire, and flood, the TV guys in L.A. did what they did well: They showed what things looked like. Sometimes they even collared a cop who could sum things up. In between times, they chattered and asked dumb questions of their on-the-scene reporters and speculated about things they shouldn't have been considering on the air. It wasn't so much news as it was a chronicle of a process; viewers got to see the news being made. But it suited his needs. He was a burned-out columnist trying to earn an extra three hundred dollars by producing a quick account for a London newspaper. He'd let the boys from Channels 2, 4, 5, 7, 9, and 11 and 13 be his legmen. TV was perfect. And he didn't have to put himself in harm's way, either.

Richards made himself a pint of iced tea, grabbed a legal pad, fluffed up the pillows on his bed, and settled down for a night of news reporting. Let's see, he said, let's try one of the independents first. Let's try Channel 5. Jane Fonda demonstrating a treadmill. How about 13? Yes. Now he was up in the KCOP chopper, high above the Coliseum, heading toward Florence Avenue, where the fires seemed to be burning the brightest. . . .

He filed his copy by modem at 5:15, some forty-five minutes before his deadline in London. He decided to lead with the kids. The kids of this L.A. riot, he told English readers of the *Sun,* were not like rioting kids in other places. These rioters were a law-abiding sort. He led his story like this: "When Luis Peinado, Cesar Gonzalez, and Conchita García pulled up in their truck outside Ralph's Market near Slauson and Normandy in Los Angeles yesterday to join the looters inside, they carefully avoided parking in spaces set aside for the handicapped." His piece had a wry tone, and it wasn't likely that the gentleman from the *Times* of London who was reporting from L.A. would even think to include this note. He pulled the Mexican-sounding names from thin air. But old Applecart wouldn't be upset—even if he found out that Richards had fabricated them. The *Sun* wasn't interested in truth so much as the larger Truth. Or maybe just circulation.

That done, Richards told himself he really needed a drink, but he wasn't going to blow off months of sobriety in AA. He took a hot shower, brushed his teeth, plopped facedown on his bed, and dreamed about a little kid with a Buster Brown haircut.

2

Richards awakened at ten, padded into the kitchen, drank a large glass of water, and downed two vitamin pills. Then he went to the bathroom, splashed some cold water on his face, and regarded himself in the mirror. His eyes looked a little tired, a little bleak. Ah, what the hell, he told himself, for him, *life* had been a little tired, *life* had been a little bleak. Taking it "one day at a time," as they always kept saying at AA, was beginning to take its toll. He had to have something to look forward to tomorrow, and the week and the month and year after tomorrow.

What he needed was something new. He prayed for a writing project, to fall in love, inherit $3 million, win the California lottery. Then he remembered his dream: Sonny Skies was standing atop a jet airliner, singing his head off.

He went to his door, opened it, and picked up the *Los Angeles Times*. Most of the front section told the story of what the *Times* chose to call "an insurrection." A dozen stories. Lots of pictures. The hell with that. He'd already seen better pictures on TV than they had in the *Times*. He climbed back into bed and turned to the sports section. He was disappointed when he didn't find a column by Jim Murray. He liked Murray, but Murray was writing less and less these days. He flipped to the "View" section and started to skim a feature story about a group of Southern Californians who had just returned from a successful treasure hunt in the Bahamas. It was a good story, one that made him feel that he was a part of the treasure team.

The phone rang. Probably Applecart in London, he thought. But it was a woman with an Irish accent who identified herself as Elle McBrien, from HMO (Home Movie Office), the cable-movie company.

"Dublin?" he said to her.

"If you're referring to my accent, I come from London."

"But you're Irish, aren't you?"

"Indeed I am. I was born in Ireland, my parents were Irish, and my friends were Irish. Are Irish. But I loved in London most of my life. I mean lived." She giggled.

"Your slip is showing," he said.

"So what?" Now she wasn't so giggly.

Richards wondered what she wanted. She told him she was a documentary producer for HMO, that she was thinking about doing a feature on Sonny Skies, to help commemorate D day.

"D day?" he said. "When's that?"

"June the sixth, 1944."

"But today is May first, 1992."

"This isn't a newspaper piece, Mr. Richards. This is a serious film. We have a long lead time."

"And how can *I* help you?" asked Richards.

She said she'd been tracking some footage and some outtakes at M-G-M and had just come from an appointment with the widow of a film cutter at M-G-M who was supposed to have some archival footage—only to find that this woman had sold her husband's film collection to a neighbor in Laurel Canyon.

"Would the neighbor's name be Tom Greenberg?" asked Richards.

"The very one."

"I see," said Richards. He didn't really see. He only assumed that the widow Murphy had sent Elle McBrien to Greenberg and that Greenberg had referred her to Jay Richards. When he learned that his assumption was correct, he asked, "Now what's the connection between Sonny Skies and your documentary on D day?"

"Sonny Skies was the only American movie star killed in World War II. And he was killed parachuting behind enemy lines in Normandy. On D day."

"I see." Richards hadn't remembered this history on Sonny Skies when he had conned Greenberg out of the footage. He had only been intrigued by it because there was something engaging about this eight-year-old's screen test. It was an early look at a kid who would soon rocket to fame in a day and an age when the movies were remaking America. But now that HMO was interested in the footage, he complimented himself on his foresight. Maybe he'd even make a buck. "And you'd like to buy this footage, right?"

"Buy it, lease it, license it, whatever is right," she said. "But I'd like to see it first." She suggested he send it to her.

"No," he said, stammering a bit. "I couldn't let it go just like that." He didn't tell her why—that the film had been stolen by the recently deceased film cutter. "I mean, I don't know you."

She processed that thought and didn't much like the implication. "You snatched those words right out of my mouth," she said defensively.

"Huh?"

"I don't know *you*, Mr. Richards."

What could he say? Give her his resumé over the phone? Hardly. He wasn't proud of his old job on the *Daily Flick* or of his role in scuttling the publication. And he didn't see the utility of telling her he now worked for the *Sun*. If Elle McBrien was from London and knew the *Sun*, she'd probably remember it mostly by the half-page nudes they ran every day on page 2. But it wasn't his trustworthiness that was an issue here. It was hers. How did he know she wasn't going to rip him off?

"Well, look," he said, "I'd like to help you. Suppose I

bring it over to HMO? We could look at it together. Then we can make a deal."

She said she'd like that. When could he come over?

He pretended to look at his calendar. "Really jammed all next week," he lied. "How about week after next? Maybe Wednesday?"

"Wednesday, May thirteenth?" She sounded a little disappointed, which pleased Richards. The delay might make her want the footage a little bit more. "All right, then," she said.

Richards had long ago learned the ways of Hollywood. You never agreed to meetings just because you wanted to do so or because you were free. You scheduled them in accordance with the laws of negotiating and the art of the deal. The main thing was to seize control and keep the upper hand. In order to approach this negotiation, he decided he'd better test the market on the Sonny Skies celluloid.

He tried to make some inquiries by phone and soon learned there was no market at all in Sonny Skies futures. The name Sonny Skies drew blanks almost everywhere. Well, jeez, Richards told himself, why should that be so surprising? Sonny Skies had died almost exactly forty-eight years ago. Most of the people in the L.A. media business seemed to be about twenty-four. How would they know anything about him? Much less be interested in doing a documentary about his heroism in World War II? These kids weren't even sure when that war began. Sure, they knew World War II had to come sometime after World War I. But since they didn't know when World War I happened—well, the kids of Hollywood were dummies when it came to history.

He was able to speak with an executive secretary at the Arts and Entertainment (A&E) channel. She must have been ancient, at least forty, because she remembered Sonny Skies. She was kind enough to consult a list of film personalities scheduled for film biographies on A&E but found there were no plans to do anything on Sonny Skies. She told Richards to check with HMO.

Now Richards began to panic. Suddenly, he felt stupid for putting off Elle McBrien. Maybe he'd blown the deal already. So he decided to just drop in on this McBrien woman. He'd do it by trumping up a scouting trip to HMO on behalf of the *Sun,* visit HMO's press agent, find out what films they had in production, and ask whether any deals had been struck for English television. It was a ruse. But if it got him in to see Elle McBrien . . .

✯ ✯ ✯

HMO's offices were in the office complex of fairly new buildings just north of Hollywood, through the Cahuenga Pass, within walking distance of MCA-Universal. There Richards found HMO's press agent, a friendly sort, a young kid just out of the USC film school, trying to shoehorn himself into the movie business. Richards feigned interest in the kid's career and demanded to know where he had come from and what he wanted to do with his life. After he told Richards his life story, *he* said *he* found Richards fascinating. To him, Richards was fascinating because Richards seemed to be interested in *him.* After that, he couldn't do enough for Richards.

That included showing him the way to Elle McBrien's office. She wasn't in. But the press agent quickly found her in a nearby editing room, hunched in the dark over a Movieola. She looked quite busy. "Miss McBrien?" said the press agent. "Just wanted you to meet a friend of mine." Friend? Richards couldn't even remember the kid's name. But what the hell. For some reason he was glad to hear she was a miss.

"I found some white space on my calendar, Miss McBrien," said Richards, interrupting the press agent's introduction and trying to explain his sudden presence. He peered through the relative darkness.

"Footage on what?" She didn't look up. Then she swiveled around in her chair and peered at Richards. "And who might you be?" In person, the Irish accent was even more pronounced.

The press agent attempted again to make the proper introduction. Again Richards interrupted. He didn't particularly care to have Miss McBrien know of his affiliation with the *Sun*. "I'm Jay Richards. Talked to you on the phone this morning about Sonny Skies."

She was still sitting at her editing bench, a soft fluorescent glow hitting one side of her face. Richards noted that she had nice cheekbones. "Oh, yes. Sonny Skies." She seemed a little flustered. "You caught me on a little deadline, Mr. uh—"

"Richards."

"Yes. Richards. I have to get this finished by five o'clock today, for the Fed Ex pickup." She looked at her watch.

"Oh, I'm sorry," he said, backing off. He could see she was eyeing the film canister he had under his arm. It was obvious she was curious about the film. So he exercised the old used-car salesman's ploy—the take-away. You offer the car, and then, when the prospective buyer hesitates, you tell him you just remembered that there was someone else wanting it. In this case, he wanted to be more subtle. "I can come back. I can see you on the thirteenth." He started to back out the door.

"No. Oh, no," she said. She looked at her watch. "We could talk for a bit."

Richards wanted more than a little bit. But since he had her attention, he was bolder than he thought he could be. He surprised himself by suggesting lunch. She surprised him by switching off the Movieola and accepting.

The three of them left the editing room together. The press agent went one way; the two of them, another. In the light of the corridor, Richards saw her as very definitely Irish-looking, dark brown hair in a feather bob, fair skin, light freckles, slim. She had almost no hips, and she was no kid. She was wearing Levi's and Keds and a green knit shirt with a Ralph Lauren logo near the pocket. He began to feel better about snatching the film. This morning he had uttered a kind of prayer—though to whom or what he wasn't at all certain—that maybe his life would take a turn for the better. And already it had.

They walked to a nearby diner, Richards's choice, the M&M Sweete Shoppe on Ventura. M&M stood for Maisie and Michael—Richards never knew their last names—and they had run the place for years. Then Michael moved on— Richards never asked why—and Maisie stayed with it. Maisie herself was at the counter today, wearing a blue-and-white-checked jumper, cut low to emphasize her assets. Twenty years ago, they were the best mammaries money could buy. On her today, at age fifty-five, they looked phony. At fifty-five, breasts *should* sag a little. "Hey, Maisie," he said.

She gave him a twisted smile and asked if he wanted the usual. "No," he said. "I'm here for lunch with a lai-dy." His voice fairly sang.

With a frank regard, Maisie nodded at Elle. "Take a booth in the back?"

They did, and as soon as they were seated, Elle McBrien said, "You're a regular here?"

"Yes," he said. "I only live a couple blocks away."

"Then maybe that explains it," she said.

"Explains what?"

"I think I know you. Maybe I've seen you before, in here?"

He said, "You live near here?"

"Not really. I live on Franklin in Hollywood. But I come here for lunch sometimes."

"Well, maybe you've seen me here. Coulda been." He looked at her more closely. "Seems to me, now that you mention it, I know you, too." He tried to imagine where or when. Then it came to him. "Tell me, do you know Bill W?"

"That's it," she said, snapping her fingers. "AA. I've

seen you at AA meetings. Tuesday nights? Hollywood Presbyterian?"

He laughed and said he sometimes went to Hollywood
Presbyterian's AA meetings on Tuesday nights.

"But you don't use 'Jay,' do you?"

"My friends call me Rich."

She peered at him. Maybe she was a little nearsighted.
"Aha," she said with a cry of recognition. She pointed at him
and repeated the AA formula—greeting and response: " 'Hi,
I'm Rich. I'm an alcoholic.' 'Hi, Rich!' "

"Well—" Richards laughed. "You can call me Rich anytime. Someday, I hope, you can call me rich with a small r."

She said, "Yes, yes, I remember you. I remember the
night you gave your pitch. You told about your notorious
screwup on the Honey Verdugo items. The way you told it
was funny, losing your job and then—watching the *Flick* blow
up in your face."

He chuckled. "Yeah. Literally. I watched the whole
building come down."

" 'And so,' " she said, quoting Richards quoting
Verdugo, " 'the *Flick* is fluck.' "

"Yeah," he said. "Pretty damn funny. It really was. Even
though the destruction of the building kind of stood for the
destruction of my career as a columnist, too."

"By the time you told your story at AA," she said, "you'd
learned to laugh through your tears."

He nodded. That's the way it was at AA. One man's
history was everyone's history lesson. But he was amused and
a little pleased that she had remembered his story. He had
wondered now if and how they might hit it off. Did one alcoholic need another? Of course, he had remembered her, too.
He recalled that her drug of choice had been a combination
of cocaine and booze—Stolichnaya, to be specific—and that
her marriage, to some kind of stockbroker type, had exploded over it. "I remember you, too," he said. In fact, he
even remembered that she had a daughter—recently re-

turned to her custody by the court—and the daughter's name as well. "How's Gremmie?"

That gave her some pause. "You remembered my daughter's name?"

"It was easy," he said. "Not too many kids get the name Gremlin. Hard to forget that. How is she?"

"She's okay—now. Just fine. She's quite precocious for eleven, but she's fine."

"You're trying to raise her in Hollywood?" he asked.

"Yes. And so what can you expect, trying to raise a kid here?" She shrugged. "When I went off to treatment, she was with her grandparents for a while in the Valley. They sent her to Catholic school. Now she's in her first year of junior high, a public junior high in Hollywood. And I'm not sure I want her to continue there." She stopped herself. Why was she babbling? "But I came here to talk to you about Sonny Skies. What have you got for me?"

"Well," he said, "I've got this footage on Sonny Skies. And you're interested in Sonny Skies."

She explained that she'd once told her boss at HMO—Charlene Burr—that she'd had a crush on Sonny Skies. "When I was ten years old. I thought the sun rose and set on him, I did, until I realized that the telly was just playing his old movies. Next thing I knew, HMO had given me this project."

"And how far you into it?"

"Frankly," she said, "I've just begun to do my research on Sonny Skies." She could have hedged, played a game of let's pretend. But she was straight with him. She told him that she had been a producer at HMO's Hollywood operation for less than a year. She had little or no power. She had been a cameraperson at Channel 2 and then, wanting to improve her lot, persuaded HMO to let her do documentaries —write, direct, even do some camera. Thus far she had been executing other people's ideas. But her boss wanted her to start coming up with her own ideas.

"But why Sonny Skies? And why now?"

"Well, I've already told you about the fiftieth anniversary of D day coming up in two years. Plenty of time to do a smashing documentary on Sonny Skies. And it's gonna be a big deal, you'll see. The French government is already planning some ceremonies. They expect President Bush to be there. The place will be crawling with media. And that's why I've been able to sell the people at HMO."

"Hmm. Yes. Yes, I see." Richards was impressed, not so much with the idea as he was with Elle McBrien. Undoubtedly, the powers at HMO saw the same thing he saw: an inner intensity that animated her external beauty.

"Charlene Burr a kind of mentor for you, Elle?"

"I did some freelance for her a couple years ago. She liked my work, got me into Women in Film. Finally hired me. And told me to see if I could come up with some unusual film biographies. Not the obvious people. People whose lives would make people think—not about Hollywood but about themselves. Since then I've thought of some other things. Like, there's no reason why I can't produce a feature film someday. I think that's what Charlene wanted to hear."

Her account was clear and honest, thought Richards. That's the way it was with a lot of people who had spent some time with AA. They had long passed the bullshit stage, with themselves, with others. He wasn't sure he had—yet. He felt a tinge of envy. It would be nice if he weren't so damned cynical and had more of this, well, this optimism, that he saw in Elle McBrien.

Elle looked pensive. "What I really want to do is come up with a good story line on Sonny Skies."

"What's a good story line?"

"Surprises. Not just a rehash of the fan magazines of the forties."

"Well," said Richards. He hardly thought there would be many surprises ahead for anyone who wanted to look into the life of Sonny Skies. Unless his screen-test footage demonstrated that there was something more to Sonny Skies than met the eye. Or less. If you looked at that footage critically, you might think the kid was retarded. "I think your documentary really has to go into all those movies he did."

Yes. She said she realized that. She had been a fan of Sonny Skies when she was ten, didn't he remember? She knew that for thirteen years, from the age of eight until he was almost twenty-one, he had been a headliner at M-G-M. And for three of those years, 1941, 1942, and 1943, the number-one box-office attraction in Hollywood. Sonny Skies's pictures sold tickets. Wholesome family pictures.

Richards said, "Well, you'd want to show some clips of those old classics. I mean, all those 'Billy Bunting' movies! Those pictures taught me how to be a teenager." Together, they recalled some of Sonny's other hits.

She remembered *Young Bert Einstein.*

He remembered *The Last Grizzly.*

She remembered *Pennies from Hell.*

He remembered *The Master of Ballantrae.*

"Oh, yes," she said. "I loved that one. He won an Oscar for that. And almost won again with *Kentucky Derby.*"

"Then there was *Huck Finn's Little Brother.* And don't forget the musicals he did with Noelle Sparks—*Swing Time in the Minarets* and *Two Hearts at Ruidoso.*"

"Then came *The Aeneid.*"

"How about *Alabama Cotton?*"

"And don't forget *Pearly Grave,*" he said.

"Yes, the Pearl Harbor story. His last picture."

Richards said, "Uh-huh. And then he was drafted into the U.S. Army and went off to fight in World War II." He finished the last of his Reuben sandwich, grunted with satisfaction, and wiped his lips.

She said, "And this is where the story gets good. With Sonny Skies going off to fight, we have something of a mystery story. Which means that we don't have to do the kind of film biography that everyone does all the time about the old stars. We can go beyond old film clips. I think our documentary could well be about patriotism. Your young Americans—I'm not sure they realize what a sacrifice their grandfathers made for them in World War II."

Richards was pleased to note that she, too, was using "our." He was suddenly struck by the thought that he could pull some extra work out of this if he could only wangle something from HMO. Even some freelance work would be okay. "Then what we really have to do is interview some of the men who knew Sonny Skies in the army. People who can tell us great war stories about him. You know? The kind of people Warren Beatty found for *Reds*."

"But won't that be a problem? Finding people who knew Sonny Skies? Aren't most of them dead?"

Richards said, "They're some still around, somewhere."

She said, "It'd help me with the money people at HMO if I could line up some good, colorful, quotable people before I turn in my treatment. Like, maybe, some army buddies, survivors of D day, maybe?"

"I might be able to help you," said Richards.

"You think you can help me find some colorful, quotable folks who knew Sonny Skies in the army? You have time for that?" Her tone said she'd be grateful. And that maybe that's all he'd get, gratitude.

But then he found himself trying to step up the tempo on his sell. "Hey, I've been a journalist most of my life. This is what I do."

"Well, Rich," she said, "it isn't what I do. Frankly, I don't have much patience with journalists. They're an unattractive bunch, always trying to get people—as cynical a bunch as there is in the world. So maybe I need somebody like you." She lowered her eyes.

"Somebody unattractive and cynical, like me?"

She laughed as she lifted her eyes again to his. Then she looked away again, an indication, he thought, of her ambivalence, getting into new waters.

For the first time, Richards noted that she had extraordinary green eyes. He felt a momentary tightness in the crotch of his Levi's. Jeez, he thought. What in hell was this? Since he'd lost his job at the *Flick,* he hadn't gone out with many women, hadn't had that many sexy thoughts. He looked at Elle now with new interest. She was ten, fifteen, years younger than he was. He wondered if she could, or would. "Well, yeah," he said. "And don't forget that little piece of footage, Sonny's first screen test, far as I know."

"Tell me how you found it?"

He wondered how much to tell her. He took her back to the poker game the previous night with the Backstabbers. And explained how he came across all this junk footage in the closet at the Greenbergs', racked up this reel labeled Kids, and found Sonny Skies's first screen test. "He was eight years old. He sang a cute little song about bluebirds. He danced a little bit. And he came off like a four-year-old."

"You're saying there was something wrong with him?"

"Well, there was something really simple about this kid," he said. "Something very, uh, innocent at least."

"Naturally enough," she said. "When did he do the test? —1930, '31?"

"The clapper said 'June 8, 1932.' "

"Uh-huh. *Everybody* was innocent in 1932. The world's a different place today. My daughter's eleven. She knows more now than I did at twenty-seven. Just by watching TV, she's visited every country in the world, and outer space, too, going boldly, with the Trekkies, where no one has dared go before. My god, when she was five, she asked me what a lesbo was."

"Whatcha tell her?"

Elle finished the last bite of her fruit salad, put down her spoon, blotted her mouth with one of Maisie's large paper napkins, and regarded him with amusement. "Wouldn't you like to know?"

She was kidding. But he didn't see the twinkle in her

eye. Instead, he felt he'd gone too far and looked foolish. "Not really. Not if you don't want to say." He was sorry he had asked. "The thing is, I think this footage really belongs in your story." He was really being sincere now. He wondered what was happening to his cynicism.

"You don't think that there weren't more screen tests done at M-G-M? Or at other studios that wanted him on loan-out?"

Richards shook his head. "You know Hollywood. You know about the studios. They were making history. But they didn't know it. Over at M-G-M, in the seventies, they dug a big pit on the lot, took all their files—they didn't know enough to call 'em archives—and dumped 'em in the hole. Buried their history."

"What do you mean, 'history'?"

"Correspondence. Contracts. Stills. Film. Negatives. Prints. Architects' renderings. Set designs. Everything. You name it. No. If I have a reel of Sonny Skies's first screen test, I probably have the only copy. It's just a happy accident. A happy accident for you."

She blinked. To him, it was, all of a sudden, a sexy blink. "You'd give me that rare footage?"

"Sure!" he blurted out. But then he felt foolish. He was pretty damn generous, giving Elle something that wasn't even entirely his. "Look," he said, "I don't own the rights. But I can get 'em for you. M-G-M probably has the rights. But M-G-M doesn't own this footage now. Ted Turner does, and Ted Turner couldn't care less about a piece of film— especially if he thinks it's worth maybe a quarter."

"You mean." she said, "twenty-five dollars?"

"I mean twenty-five cents."

She lowered her eyes. "Well, it may be worth more than that."

"So? How much more than a quarter? Double? Ten times? One hundred times. Big deal." She laughed. "If HMO likes what we're doing with it," said Richards, "we can buy the rights from Turner."

"*'We?'* Whaddya mean, 'we,' white man?"

For the past fifteen minutes they'd been talking "we." Now Richards couldn't tell if she was kidding or serious. He said, "I was thinking maybe we could work on it together." He was surprised that he could come right out and say that.

Elle smiled. "You want to work with *me?*"

He hesitated. Did he really want to do this? But he was emboldened by her smile. "I could do that. Sure, why not?"

"Well—" She reached over and touched his elbow to take the edge off her letting him down. She wanted to do it lightly. "As I said, I don't have a budget—yet. I don't even know if I have a project yet."

He returned the touch. "Doesn't matter, Elle. I'd like to do it gratis, help make sure you get a chance to start doing what you want to do."

"Did you say gratis, Rich? No. No way. I couldn't let you work for nothing."

"I don't mind," he said. "Right now, I'm between projects." How many times had he written "between projects" to describe some poor son of a bitch who wasn't working? He hadn't set out this morning to work for free. But suddenly it seemed right to him. If they worked together, he could get closer to her. And he really wanted to do that.

She said, "Well, maybe. Let me think about it. I want to talk to Charlene Burr." She stood up, offered him her hand, and gave him the kind of full handshake men give other men.

He laughed.

"Why're you laughing?"

"Oh," said Richards, "nothing." He was laughing at the thought that, with a failed marriage behind him, he might be falling in love again. But he told Elle McBrien, "I was just thinking that doing a documentary—with you—might be fun."

She surprised him by saying she thought it might be fun for her, too.

He watched her go. She had a nice figure. He wondered if she slept in the nude.

3

The next day, Saturday, Elle McBrien phoned Richards and told him that Charlene Burr had given her some extra development money for the Sonny Skies project. "Not a lot," Elle said, "but enough to cover our expenses."

"What do you mean, 'our' expenses, white girl?" He chuckled so she'd know he was only twitting her.

"Oh, I guess I didn't tell you," she said, all businesslike. "I decided I *would* like you to help."

"Well, now." He had been hoping she'd say yes, but his cynicism told him she wouldn't. Now his heart skipped a beat. At fifty-two, it was nice to know he still had a heart that could skip a beat. "When do we start?"

She said she was going to be tied up all day in one thing or another. But she wondered if he was going to try to make an AA meeting that evening. He said he was considering it. She said, "You ever do the Saturday nights at Malibu?"

He said, "I've heard about the one at the community center. Lot of screenwriters and producers and actors?"

"That's the one we heard about in *The Player*. Place where writers who aren't alcoholics come looking for work? Apparently it's true."

"Okay. We could go there."

Elle said, "I could meet you there." She said she had to drop her daughter off in the Valley first. "Gremmie's going to spend Saturday night with her grandparents."

"I thought your parents lived in London."

"They do. These are Gremmie's other grandparents."

Nice, thought Richards, that Elle and her ex's folks were on such good terms.

At the AA meeting in Malibu, Richards tossed his wallet on the seat next to him, to save a seat for Elle McBrien, and, half-turned in his chair, nodded to her when she entered, only a little late, from the back patio. She was wearing Levi's and boots and a kind of military shirt, and a big leather purse was slung over her shoulder. He indicated the space next to him. She shook her head and stood in the back of the hall.

A famous songwriter was there as the speaker of the evening. He charmed them all with the story of his own redemption—from Myers's rum and Coke and his own bad self-image to sobriety and a brave life one day at a time. At the halftime break, Richards expected to talk to Elle McBrien, but she apparently knew two other women in the group, and she schmoozed with them while he waited off to the side. He filled the time by sizing up the upscale people who were there.

He noted that the women didn't flaunt their place on the scale by getting all gussied up. The men dressed down even more than the women. They wore shorts and polo shirts and moccasins, with sweaters tossed casually around their necks. But he had never been to such an AA meeting, one where they served a sumptuous fresh-fruit buffet at the halftime break, provided a coffee bar besides, with urns of Starbucks coffee lined up in several different flavors, and offered valet parking, too. Well, he thought, drug and alcohol addiction was certainly an equal-opportunity spoiler. It hit the high, it hit the low, and it hit the people in between.

After the meeting, the drunks seemed to pair off and group up for dinner at one or another of the Malibu restaurants. Or for coffee. AAs were great coffee drinkers. He understood they had been great smokers, too, until the past few years. Talk about smoke-filled rooms! Now they had special meetings for smokers only—and there weren't too many of those. He didn't really get to talk to Elle until they were both in the parking lot, waiting for the kids to bring their cars. While they waited, he wondered why she had arranged for her daughter to be away this particular Saturday night. Was it too sanguine for him to hope that—No. He wouldn't hope. She probably had a boyfriend, anyway.

"Where to?" she said when her car was delivered.

"Polly's Pies in Santa Monica?"

"You want pie?"

He sucked in his stomach. "No." But they ended up at Polly's Pies, anyway, where he ordered something called a Black Bottom: chocolate pie crust, topped by chocolate ice cream and chocolate sauce. Elle had coffee, decaf, cream, no sugar.

For more than an hour, right there in a booth at Polly's Pies, the two of them put their heads together over her Macintosh 180 laptop. She keyed in the names of people who might be able and willing to talk about Sonny Skies. Elle had Xeroxed a minibio of Sonny Skies from the *Film Encyclopedia* and handed it over to Richards. He scanned it and saw little there that he didn't know except to note that Sonny was born Homer Brownlee, the only son of two vaudevillians, Edna and Edgar Brownlee, who did their act on unicycles. They balanced on their cycles while playing Chopin on the violin. For encores, they balanced on their heads while they played Gershwin.

"Let's see," said Richards. "Edna and Edgar would be more than ninety years old if they were alive today."

Elle shook her head. "Not to worry about that. Somewhere I have a piece that says Edna died in 1944. The old man had already made his exit."

"I'm not surprised," he said. "In fact, I'd be surprised if there were too many others still around—people who knew Sonny Skies."

In fact, Elle McBrien surprised him by coming up with a good many people who, according to her research, were very much alive. Her list was long on aging actresses and short on aging actors. But Sonny's agents were long gone. And so, according to Elle, were all the people at the studio who had shaped the kid's career.

"Except maybe Nigel Parrish," said Richards.

"Nigel Parrish?" She gave him a blank look.

He didn't tell her she should have known that. But he was glad that he knew and she didn't. If he was going to nail down an assignment from HMO, he had to know things she didn't. "Louis B. Mayer," he said pleasantly, "gave Sonny Skies his own PR man, somebody who'd keep the kid's goody-goody image well polished. Nigel Parrish was that man. He turned out to be more than a PR man for Sonny Skies. He was a mentor. Almost a father figure. And I re-member that one of my sources—who was it?—told me a couple years ago that Nigel Parrish was still around. Some-where."

"Well, see?" she said brightly. "Already you're earning your keep. I didn't know about Nigel Parrish. You did. Good for you."

"You want to go looking for Parrish?"

"You do what you can, if you want," she said. "I have an all-day tomorrow with Women in Film." She added quickly, before he could utter the invitation he was about to offer, "Gotta get to bed early tonight. Our program starts at seven-thirty in the morning."

"Uh-huh." So the evening was almost over. Richards had long ago learned that if something was too good to be true, it was usually not true.

"You want to copy some of these names down?" She dug into her purse and fished out a large spiral notebook and a ballpoint.

He didn't really want to do that. He did it, anyway, cop-ied some of the names off her computer screen, tore off the page, folded it lengthwise and did so again, and stuck it in the breast pocket of his shirt. He might have been folding his hopes, too, for an interesting Saturday night. Folded, but not forgotten.

They drove all the way back to Hollywood on Santa Monica Boulevard, each in their own cars, stopping at some of the same lights, winking at each other in the rearview mirrors on three successive stops until finally, Richards felt, she grew tired of the game and sped on ahead of him. Back at his apartment, a stray cat was meowing at his front door. "No free lunch here, kitty," he said. He tried to kick the cat, but it was too quick for him and took off with a screech.

Inside his apartment, he didn't turn on the TV, as usual. He pulled Elle's list from his shirt pocket, studied it, scribbled some phone numbers alongside some of the names, brushed his teeth, and went to bed. He dreamed of lions, female lions, and he didn't even dream of kicking them, because he was frightened of lions. And lionesses.

First thing Sunday morning, Richards played doubles at Beckwith Park with Tom Greenberg, Dave Benton, and Jordan Bonfante, Backstabbers all. He told them nothing of his new friend and nothing about his interest in Sonny Skies. He hustled home in time to see the last half of the Lakers and the Trailblazers, then showered and shaved and started phoning people.

He tried to remember. Who the hell had told him about Nigel Parrish? Hmm. Well, somebody would know. He proceeded to make eleven phone calls. They took way too long. He had to make small talk before he asked them what they knew about Sonny Skies or about his long-gone Hollywood era. He finally said, "Bingo!" when Charles Champlin, the former entertainment editor for the *Times,* told him that

Nigel Parrish was living in a rest home in Chatsworth. Champlin thought it might have been called Buddha West.

It wasn't Buddha West. But, after almost a half hour of funny, friendly, free-associating conversation with a playful information operator for Pac Bell, Richards figured it out. The rest home was called West of Nirvana, as he (and the operator) reckoned. He was able to confirm that guess with one more phone call—to West of Nirvana itself, where the operator put him right through to Nigel Parrish.

Yes, Parrish said he remembered Jay Richards and the *Flick* with fondness. He'd be pleased to see him and his colleague on Wednesday morning at eleven.

Hot damn, thought Richards. He left a message on Elle McBrien's answering machine, telling her about the Wednesday appointment, if she was free. He rang off, then drove down to the Boulevard to see a movie at the Chinese—*Groundhog Day*. Pretty good movie. And for him, a message movie: Life is a rondelet. You keep repeating your life until you get it right. Maybe this time he'd get it right.

4

West of Nirvana had an expensive look about it. Management took care of the place, and there was a good gardener at work here, judging from the trimmed hedges and bougainvillea that graced the railings of the sunny terrace where Parrish received them. It may have been 94 degrees on that deck, but Parrish had a blanket around his knees and a colorful Mexican serape over his shoulders. He had a flowing white mane, like Buffalo Bill's, a handlebar mustache, and an Oxford accent.

Parrish didn't seem to mind talking on videotape. In fact, he chuckled when Elle clipped a lavalier microphone to the serape folded over his chest. And when Elle set up her minicam on a tripod and said, "Action," he seemed energized.

"Let's see," said Parrish. "I do believe the studio put Sonny in my charge when he was about nine or ten. Yes, ten. He'd just done—what was it? *Albert Einstein*. No, *Young Bert Einstein*. Got great reviews. Big box-office hit. That's when Mr. Mayer decided the kid needed special protection."

"Protection?" Richards knew what he meant, but he wanted Parrish to say it on videotape.

"From the press," said Parrish. "I had to coach him what to say to Louella and the others. And what not to say."

Richards asked, for the record, "You were his press agent?"

"Uhh, Mr. Mayer preferred calling me Sonny's press secretary. Actually, I was much more than that. I was his keeper, too. If the kid wanted to go to the racetrack, I handled his bets for him. If he wanted a massage, I phoned for the masseuse. If he'd wanted his ass wiped, I would have done that, too, I expect." He said the last with a chuckle at the camera. Did he want to shock Elle? Probably. But so what? Richards told Elle she shouldn't hang back but ask questions of her own.

Elle asked Parrish, "You know how he got the name Sonny Skies?

"No. No. I knew his real name had been Brownlee. But the change came shortly before I happened along. I think it might have been just about the time he made his first screen test at M-G-M."

"Tell us about Sonny," said Elle. Richards could see what Elle was doing. As a TV producer who had to worry about cutting this interview and melding it in with everything else, she didn't want Parrish to answer yes and no questions. She wanted him to talk. See if he had good stories to tell. And if he knew how to tell them.

"I was Sonny's tutor," said Parrish. "As such, you might reasonably expect that I'd want to give you a report on what kind of student he was. Well, I can tell you this—that for almost six years he had the docility of a four- or five-year-old and a quick memory that one would only associate with genius. For those early years, the kid was an absolute delight."

Elle said that she didn't want a detailed account of those years. Later, maybe. Now she wanted to cut to the chase. "Tell us about the later years."

"About sixteen, he started getting snotty."

Elle contained herself. Richards laughed.

"Yes. Snotty. Hell, I'd been like a father to the kid. Taught him how to play tennis and golf. Got him into my club and all. The Riviera in Brentwood. And then, all of a sudden one day, he told me to go fuck myself."

"What was that all about?" asked Richards.

"We were getting ready for a big event in his career.

Center court at Grauman's Chinese Theatre. He was joining
the ranks of the immortals. Hands and feet in the concrete,
not far from Clark Gable and Mickey Rooney and Judy Garland. I was just telling him that maybe he'd better not talk to
anyone who showed up with a microphone and—"

"Why couldn't he talk? Why shouldn't he?"

Parrish said, "Wrong time. Wrong place. He'd been
stopped for speeding along the Pacific Coast Highway the
night before. I had managed to keep the thing out of the
papers. Fixed it with the L.A. County Sheriff's Office in
Malibu. But some bloke in the substation must have tipped
the AP. I got several calls the next morning. AP, UPI, *L.A.
Mirror,* Louella's leg man. Told them I knew nothing about it
but I'd check it out."

"You check it out?"

He shook his head and laughed. "I never checked these
things out. I had my orders. I just lied. I called the boys back.
'Nothing to it,' I said. 'Stop by the office next time you're at
the studio. I got a bottle of scotch the other day that I can't
stand.' "

"You really did have a bottle of scotch?"

"Johnny Walker. A whole case of the stuff, which I used
to hand out to the boys on the studio beat. Kept 'em under
control with Johnny Walker. And for the right kind of favor
—generally keeping something out of the papers, not getting
something in—I could get a guy a date with a starlet."

"A starlet! My-my!" Richards was egging Mr. Parrish on
for the education (though perhaps not the edification) of Elle
McBrien.

"Well, it was never a starlet. Truth to tell, it was always a
hooker." Richards was watching Elle. "A nice *young* hooker,
mind you. That way, there'd never be any trouble with the
studio and all. For a while there, I had a nice stable of fillies."
Parrish grew silent, ruminating, perhaps, about some of the
fillies he had saddled up for members of the press. And perhaps girls that he rode himself—to maintain quality control

and all that. Or maybe he wasn't ruminating. Maybe he was just dozing there in the sun.

Thus far, Parrish was a great interview, as long as they could keep him on track or keep him from going to sleep. "Mr. Mayer didn't object?" asked Richards.

Parrish opened his eyes and blinked. "Mr. Mayer? Object? Oh, heavens, Mr. Mayer never knew. Didn't want to know. Not that he didn't have his own stable of girls. That was an open secret around the lot at Metro. Mr. Mayer's philanderings. But with his stars he was a terrible Puritan. He was easier on himself. But he would have resented the hell out of it if he knew that anyone else knew."

Richards suspected that Elle was squirming inside. It was she, at any rate, who tried to get Parrish and Richards back to the scene at Grauman's Chinese Theatre. "So here you are at the Chinese, and you are telling Sonny to stay away from the press?" prompted Elle.

"And," said Richards, also trying to prime the pump, "he didn't cotton to that?"

"Cotton?"

" 'Like?' Didn't like that?"

"Oh. Oh, no, Sonny didn't like it a bit. He said if he was old enough now to go all the way with girls, he was old enough not to need coaching with the press."

Richards said, "He'd started to diddle girls? At sixteen?"

Parrish rolled his eyes. "Oh, my, yes! But not little girls."

"Starlets? Hookers?"

"Neither one. He was very partial to lady tennis players."

"Tennis players?"

"The tennis club was one place Sonny could meet young women who weren't fans. On the streets of Hollywood and Beverly Hills, he couldn't go anywhere without having girls throw themselves at him. That bothered him. But the young women at the club. That was different."

"Women, not girls?"

"At least ten years older than he, they were. Lean, tanned, muscular young women. Experienced, athletic creatures who weren't about to be dazzled by a sixteen-year-old kid who happened to be in the movies. But it turned out they liked him enough to teach him all about fellatio."

Richards glanced over at Elle McBrien. She had on her professional face. No look of shock or surprise—or loathing for these sleazy reporters' questions. Maybe a shade of interest. "Uh, Mr. Parrish?" she said. "Mind if I ask how you knew that?"

He threw back his head and laughed. "Oh, it was my *business* to know. And I had my ways. I had my ways." He shook his head and chuckled over some fond memory. Parrish must have been at least ninety, he was in a wheelchair, and his mind tended to wander. But when he focused on a given question, he seemed quite lucid.

Richards asked him if he knew Sonny Skies's parents. Parrish said that Sonny's mom died of acute alcoholism in 1944, shortly after Sonny went off to the army. She and Sonny's dad had been divorced since Sonny was six, and he, too, was long gone. Parrish was sure about that. In 1939, he had found Sonny's dad, a red-nosed comic in baggy pants, playing the Roxy Burlesque down on Main Street in L.A. Parrish had gone to Sonny and asked him if he wanted to see his dad.

"The kid wasn't interested," said Parrish. "Not a bit. Can you feature that? Coupla years later, his dad was dead. I was the one brought Sonny the news."

"How did the kid take it?"

"He said, 'Yeah?' Cool as a cuke, he said it. 'Yeah?' And then, without a beat, 'Now, Mr. Parrish, about that trip to Caliente this Saturday? We're all set to leave at nine, aren't we? I don't want to miss the first race or the double.' "

"So," said Richards, "this kid had two kinds of fever. Women and horses?"

"No. He liked women. But he *loved* the horses, and he

loved betting on them just as fiercely. That's why he needed me, to lay the bets at the mutuel window, and to collect his winnings, too. He wasn't old enough to bet, you see."

"He won, did he?"

"Won a lot more than he lost," said Parrish.

"Uh, Mr. Parrish," said Elle. "Back to that day that you were headed for Grauman's Chinese? He told you to go, uh, eff yourself."

"Yes."

"Then what happened?"

"Well, I was very stern with him. I told him that if he didn't follow my leads with the press, I'd tell Mr. Mayer. And he was, at that time, hoping for a big, new contract."

"This about the time he won his second Oscar nomination? For *Kentucky Derby?*"

"Yes, yes, I think it was. So, after he told me to go fuck myself and I chastised him, he did exactly what I'd advised. He mugged furiously for the cameras the day he put his footprints in the wet cement at the Chinese. But you'd think he had a case of laryngitis. In fact, he *sounded* like he had laryngitis. Very froggy voice that day. All he could say to members of the press was: 'Hiya. How are ya?' Croaky he was. Good little actor. Always a good actor."

"You think he didn't want you to give Mr. Mayer a bad report on him?"

"Exactly. Sonny Skies may have been crazy, but he wasn't stupid. Still and all, from that day on, Sonny Skies got harder and harder to control. He was growing up, I guess, and he didn't enjoy having the studio—meaning me—telling him how to part his hair any longer."

Elle asked him if Sonny had had any friends his own age. "Yes, yes. He had a stand-in type. Kid who lived with him and his mom in Studio City. I've forgotten his name."

Elle said, "Gee, we need that."

"Let's see." Parrish closed his eyes in concentration. "I know. His name will be in the credits in two of Sonny's musicals, *Swing Time in the Minarets,* and *Two Hearts at Ruidoso.* Sonny was able to get him bit parts in both of those musicals. His name was Billy Something or Other. McShane. McSorley. Dolan. Something like that. Irish kid who used to rollerskate."

Elle flashed on that. "Irish?" she said.

"Well, American kid with an Irish name. He was a kind of constant companion, valet, gofer, stand-in, whatever. Frankly, I was overjoyed when I heard that Sonny came home with him one day. Met him at the roller rink. When Billy Whatever-his-name moved in with Sonny and his mom, I breathed a big sigh of relief. Now, you see, I didn't have to be so much of a gofer any longer. This Billy kid took over a lot of that. I still handled Sonny's press, mind you."

Elle said, "Tell us about Sonny and Frances Farnsworth."

Parrish smiled. "Well, that's a long story. Short marriage but a long story."

"You know why they broke up?"

Parrish had a far-off look in his eye. He blinked hard two or three times. Then he said, "They were both very young. And she grew up faster than he did. Pretty soon they had little in common."

"But," said Elle, "even after they split, didn't he try to help her with her career?"

Parrish gave Elle a look that was somewhat condescending. "Sure, Sonny tried. But he couldn't help her like some other people could. Powerful people." He shook his head, as if the recollection were too much for him.

"What people, Mr. Parrish?"

A nurse came into view, all starch. Her name plate read MS. WELLSPRING. She motioned for Elle to stop the camera. Then she leaned over to Parrish and shouted in his ear, "Time for your lunch now." Richards hadn't noted that Parrish was hard of hearing. Maybe Ms. Wellspring shouted at every patient in West of Nirvana. In any event, that signaled the end of the interview, for now. This was the understanding Richards had struck with the management. Mr. Parrish had a nap every day after lunch. Nothing could get in the way of that. The home had a vested, financial interest in keeping Mr. Parrish well.

"Uh, just one more thing," said Richards. "Tell me what you know about Sonny's being called into the service. Wasn't it a little strange that he wasn't assigned to some entertainment unit?"

Parrish didn't understand the question. Maybe he didn't want to.

"I mean," said Richards, "I don't think there was an actor in Hollywood assigned to combat in World War II. Maybe Jimmy Stewart. And he was a flyboy. But Sonny Skies? They sent him to the infantry. And he went in on an early wave in Normandy, where they knew the casualties would be very high. How do you explain that?"

Parrish seemed to bristle at the question. "How would I know, young man? Don't ask me. Ask the military." He shook his head and glared at Richards.

Ms. Wellspring scowled at Richards and intervened again. "Mr. Richards, Miss McBrien, I am going to ask you to stop right now."

Elle, obedient to authority, even if it was to that of Ms. Wellspring, had shut off her minicam and was starting to pack her gear.

Now Nigel Parrish was grumbling at Ms. Wellspring. He had been enjoying this interview, and now she wanted him to stop. "In a minute," he said to Nurse Wellspring. "Okay? In a minute." Then he motioned for Richards to come closer and whispered, "Say, young man, you wouldn't happen to have any grass, would you?"

Richards was startled, and he didn't do a very good job of concealing his surprise. He was more startled to be called a young man than he was to be asked about the grass. He said,

"No. No. I don't." Not only didn't he have any marijuana. He didn't even have a connection who could get him some.

Elle had hovered, waiting to remove her Lavalier mike from Parrish's serape. She had heard his whispered request and, much to Richards's surprise, said to Parrish, "But if we come back, we'll bring you some good Colombian. Won't we, Rich?" She winked at Richards. And Parrish beamed at her.

Richards was sorry they hadn't got that look on videotape. But he was surprised and a little disappointed that Elle had promised to get him some grass. "You can get your hands on some Colombian?" Richards asked her when they got into the car.

"Yes, if that's what he wants. Yes, some good weed."

He shrugged. As a member of AA, one who had had her problems with drugs, she was the last one in the world, he thought, to be someone's connection. He said nothing, and they drove for a while in silence.

She may have intuited his discomfort. "Well," she said finally, "after all, the guy is near ninety. A little toke isn't going to do him any harm—stuck in a wheelchair. He wouldn't be driving anywhere, that's certain. No menace, then, to society."

He nodded. Maybe grass wasn't good for her, but she'd let others make their own decision about using or not using. "Parrish was a very good interview, wasn't he?" he said.

"Yes," said Elle. "All we need is a few more colorful geezers like Nigel Parrish and we'll have a good start.

Richards smiled. Already Elle McBrien was beginning to think more like a reporter.

✯ ✯ ✯

Elle drove through Laurel Canyon and over the hill on to Fairfax, then took a right turn on Sunset. They had lunch on the sidewalk at a place called L'Oreille—"The Ear"—at Sunset Terrace. "I like to lunch here when I can," she said.

"I used to come here a bit," he said as she was parking the car in a rear parking lot that had a breathtaking view of the city. He didn't tell her it was a favorite spot of his ex-wife's. "Why do *you* like coming here?"

"Research."

Richards nodded. He wondered what kind of research —talent for the circus? The people who lunched at the Terrace were out of a freak show. Braless young women with silicone boobs. Thin, young gays, with spiked blond locks, wearing leather shirts and leather pants stuffed in the crotch. Musclemen, who could have been bouncers at the Whiskey A Go Go, wearing thin cotton sleeveless undershirts and tight Levi's and boots. A bearded old man who was wearing a gigantic red top hat, like the Mad Hatter's in an illustration in *Alice in Wonderland*. A good many foreign-actress types, many of them speaking French. A number of young men, dressed like bankers, holding hands. "Watching these people is research?" he said.

She giggled and examined her menu. Richards thought that maybe he had this woman wrong. At times, she seemed awfully straitlaced. At other times, she seemed full of mischief. "I'll order," she said. "Then I want to go phone a friend at the Academy Library. She'll get me the name of Sonny's friend and stand-in." She told the waitress, a stunning black girl in a tight white jumpsuit, that she wanted a Cobb salad. Then she was off to the pay phone.

"Same for me," said Richards to the waitress. "Cobb salad. And put a chocolate soufflé in the oven for me, okay?"

When Elle returned, she was shaking her head. "My friend's out to lunch. I'll have to call her back."

Richards nodded but was soon distracted by a woman who was taking a seat at a table to their immediate left. It was Gloria Chatham, the numerologist-madam. She didn't have the appearance of your classic madam. Although fifty, she looked to be in her mid-thirties and was wearing an expensive, tailored, pinstriped pantsuit. But then Richards knew that Gloria plied her trade mainly in Beverly Hills and Brent-wood.

She recognized him immediately. "Rambling Rich!"

"Hi, Gloria. How are tricks?" He chuckled.

She responded by opening her palm to two young hook-ers, obviously girls who worked for her, judging by the way they sat down with Gloria, uninvited. "See for yourself," she said. "Best tricks in town." Rich could see for himself. They were slim, well-scrubbed, well-dressed types. They could have been Ford models.

Richards coughed, gave a sidelong glance at Elle, and proceeded to introduce Elle to Gloria—"my numerologist and a prime source on who's dinging whom in Hollywood."

Elle smiled at Gloria and nodded to the two younger women. Gloria introduced the two of them. "This is Marvel. And this is Tiffany."

"Hi, Marvel. Hi, Tiffany," said Elle. "I'm Elle McBrien." Richards mumbled a greeting, too.

They didn't carry on a cross-table conversation. Elle and Rich turned back to their task of the moment—getting a line on the friend of Sonny Skies, the young man with the Irish name that Nigel Parrish couldn't remember.

Gloria Chatham gave it to them. "Couldn't help over-hearing, dearie," she said to Richards. "Could it be that you're looking for Billy Dwyre?"

"That the stand-in for Sonny Skies? The blond kid who played in a couple of his musicals?"

"The very one. Yes. Billy Dwyre. I think he's still around —somewhere. Used to be a member of the sheriff's posse in Oxnard, as I recall."

"Uh, you wouldn't happen to have his number, would you?"

"His phone number? You know I couldn't give it to you even if I had it. Which I don't. That would be very unprofes-sional. You should know that, Rich."

"Sorry," he said. "I'll go stand in the corner."

Gloria Chatham reached over and tapped him lightly, first on one wrist, then another. "No need to stand in the corner. Consider your wrists slapped, okay?"

"It's okay," said Richards. "I can call the sheriff's office in Ventura County. We'll find him."

"You mean," said Elle, "if he's still around."

"Well, yeah," said Richards. "Unless you can get Shirley MacLaine's channeler to put us in touch." When she ignored that remark, Richards told himself he had to go easy on the sarcasm with Elle. He didn't want to belittle her. He wanted to bed her.

The waitress brought Jay Richards's soufflé. When he sighed at first bite, Elle said, "You're a choc-o-holic, right?"

Richards shrugged. "Well, you know the AA personality. Addictive. And if it's not booze now, which it isn't, and if it isn't cigarettes, which it isn't, then it's gotta be something that hurts me a little bit." His smile served as a kind of coda to the confession.

She smiled, too, with a look of what he hoped was understanding but was probably more like pity.

"Let's go," he said. "I want to see if we can find Dwyre."

She let Richards off at his apartment. "Call me if you get anything," she said. "I'll be at HMO till seven or so." He blew her a kiss. This time, she smiled.

5

As cub reporters in the 1960s, Dan Morley and Jay Richards had worked the police beat together on the *Arizona Republic*. And they played poker together at the Press Club, up in the old Westward Ho. Then they each began the kind of odysseys common to many reporters in those days. Morley went east, first to the *Worcester Telegram,* then to the *New York Daily News* before he finally was hired for the enterprise team at the *Washington Post*. Sometimes Richards wished he'd gone east, too.

Instead, he had gone to La La Land and was just unlucky enough to be hired as a reporter for the *Flick*. After seven years at the *Flick,* his editor, the late Jack Carey, who owed him $1,441 in poker debts, made him the *Flick's* gossip columnist. Since this was one of the softest jobs in town, one that allowed him to chow down free almost any night of the week at any of a number of Hollywood screenings, Richards forgave the $1,441. Which was probably what Carey had in mind when he gave Richards the job.

Richards hadn't talked to Morley in years. "Hey, Rich," said Morley when Richards got him on the phone. "You still married to that actress? What was her name?"

"Nope." Richards didn't phone Morley to elaborate on his failed marriage.

"Don't get mad at *me*. You knew better. You once wrote a piece for *Playboy* called "Never Marry an Actress." That was *before* you married Susan Genève. Yeah, I remember now, Susan Genève. French actress. Nice bod."

Richards ignored the sally and said, "Dan, I need a favor." He told him about the Sonny Skies documentary he was working on and some questions that had come up about his military service. "We'd like to see what we can find in his military records. Can you try to get Sonny Skies's file pulled in the Pentagon?"

"You know his rank and serial number? You got any discharge papers?" Richards reminded Morley that Sonny Skies wasn't discharged but killed in action. "Oh. Oh, right." Morley asked, "Got any budget for this from HMO?"

"Maybe. Depends on how far we go with it, I guess. But, Dan, I thought you were my friend."

"Yeah, Rich. Sure. But if there's a budget for this. I mean, Hollywood and all."

★ ★ ★

According to one of Richards's sources, a longtime secretary at the Screen Actors Guild, Billy Dwyre hadn't worked in years. But the source had a lead that almost confirmed Gloria Chatham's recollection. "There's a note in his file here says he moved on to an investigator's job at the Ventura County Sheriff's Office."

That made it easy. Almost. A call to the personnel office there met with a clerk who wanted to stonewall Richards. He tried to sweet-talk the woman; then he gave up and hung up and redialed for the sheriff himself. Sheriff William B. (Pork) Macomber was a genial type who brightened when Richards identified himself as a columnist—paper unspecified—and he didn't mind giving Billy's phone number to Richards. "Billy always did like the press. And they liked him. He had quite a scrapbook, Billy did. Lotta stories about him and his cases in the local papers. He solved our 'Headless Model' case, you know—1957."

Richards didn't know. But he remembered reading about the grisly Oxnard beach murder in 1957. Despite the

sheriff's generous memory, it was one of Hollywood's un-
solved mysteries. The Case of the Headless Model—a beautiful young body, washed up on the beach one morning, nude,
with no head. For days no one stepped forward to identify
the corpse until a sad couple from Nebraska named
McQueen showed up in Ventura with pictures of their
Lorna, who had taken a Greyhound to Hollywood to become
a star.

✴ ✴ ✴

Richards and Elle McBrien paid their first call on Billy
Dwyre at the Citrus Bowl, an upscale trailer park on a well-
landscaped three acres just east of the beach road in Oxnard.
Richards had phoned ahead, told him he was working on a
film bio of Sonny Skies, and wondered if he would care to
reminisce a little bit about Sonny Skies. "Sure," he had said
breezily.

But when the two of them sat down with Dwyre, not far
from his double-wide, at a poolside table under an umbrella,
all Dwyre wanted to talk about was the Case of the Headless
Model.

"Yes, sir," said Dwyre, "that was probably the best work
I ever did in the sheriff's office." Well, if he wanted to talk
about it, what the hell. Richards shrugged at Elle. She nodded—meaning she agreed that it was best to let him go
ahead. Let Dwyre get more comfortable with them—and
with her minicam.

He did get comfortable. In fact, he had a tendency to
babble. But when she turned off the minicam, he stopped
talking. So she turned it back on. Tape was cheap. And she
had batteries to burn. As he droned on, Richards let his attention wander. A voluptuous teenager, wearing a white
bathing suit hardly bigger than three postage stamps, was
sunning herself on a nearby chaise. He was enjoying the sight

of her, and the scenario that started to play in his head, when Elle kicked him in the shin.

"Ooof!"

"What's that?" said Dwyre.

"Nothing," said Richards, shooting a look at Elle. "I just hit my funny bone on the arm of this chair here. Heh-heh." He rubbed his elbow, wishing he could rub the hurt on his shin.

Eventually, Dwyre wrapped up his tale of the sex crime in Oxnard and asked them what he could tell them about Sonny Skies.

"You know how he got the name Sonny Skies?"

"Naw. I think he got it from Mickey Rooney. The Mick suggested it even before the kid took his screen test."

"At M-G-M?"

"Yeah. I think the Mick figured you couldn't expect to make it in Hollywood 'less you changed your name. I think I heard him say once, 'How far do you think Cary Grant would have gotten with the name Archibald Leach?'"

"So Sonny Skies really worked with Mickey Rooney?"

"Well, they were never in a picture together. Oh, yeah. They were. *Huck Finn's Little Brother.*"

Elle turned to Richards and nodded vigorously. He understood her to mean that they had to put Rooney on their list. Well, sure, thought Richards, they had to see Rooney. But would *he* see them? Rooney was a busy guy, he was doing movies all over the globe, and he was becoming something of an entrepreneur. Richards had heard that Rooney had just made a killing in Mexican oil.

"Did Sonny hang out with Rooney?"

"No way," said Dwyre. "To Rooney, Sonny was just a nice little kid."

"Who did Sonny hang out with? Boyfriends? Girlfriends?"

"Sonny was pretty shy around girls. When I started living at his house, anyway."

Elle seemed disappointed to hear that. "So how did Sonny live his life?"

"Hey, he was working. Every day. We had to be at the lot by seven A.M., Monday through Friday. Sometimes we didn't get home till ten at night. We'd have something to eat. Then we'd go to bed."

"I read somewhere," said Elle, "that he played the drums and had his own little band."

"Well, yeah, he played the piano a little. By ear. And the sax. I guess he was best on the drums. But he couldn't read music. A few kids in the neighborhood would come over to fool around a little."

"You mean 'rehearse'?" asked Elle.

"Uh-huh. Sonny's mom had a pretty good sized place in Studio City. Nice game room where we could play. She had it soundproofed for Sonny. One kid used to come with a sax. Another had a clarinet. There was a kid named Nutsy Nutley who played the piano in our game room downstairs. He went on to become a pretty good songwriter. In fact, he wrote some of the songs in *Pennies from Hell*."

Richards said, "You play in this band?"

Dwyre said, "I played the trombone. But we were just foolin' around. We never played any gigs anywhere. We just did it to amuse ourselves."

"How old was Sonny Skies when all this was happening?"

"Oh, fifteen, sixteen."

"That about the time he started playing tennis?" Richards was thinking of Parrish's tales about Sonny Skies and the tanned young women in their twenties initiating Sonny Skies in the joys of sex.

Dwyre looked away and said nothing. Richards wondered where Sonny played tennis. O'Dwyre said he didn't know. "He play at the Riviera Country Club in Brentwood?"

"I'm not sure," he said. Dwyre, who had been such a

spigot of information, had suddenly gone dry. It was obvious to Richards that he didn't want to talk about Sonny's sex life.

"You were always pretty loyal to Sonny, weren't you?" said Elle.

Dwyre smiled. "The faithful valet. That was me."

"You still feel the same sense of loyalty?"

"Oh, I don't know. Last time I saw Sonny was, let's see, I think it was 1944. That was a long time ago, a long time."

Richards did a mental calculation. Yeah, forty-eight years ago. Richards was four years old then. Sonny Skies was twenty. "The occasion?" Richards asked. "When did you last see Sonny Skies?"

"Well, let's see," said Dwyre. "Sonny got married in the fall of 1943. He'd just finished doing, you know, that movie about the heroism at Pearl Harbor—"

"Pearly Grave?" prompted Elle.

"Yeah. *Pearly Grave*—with Robert Taylor and Herbert Marshall and Sonny Tufts and Frances Farnsworth."

Elle McBrien looked over at Richards and nodded. Frances Farnsworth was the ingenue Sonny married six months before he joined the U.S. Army. "Could you tell us some stories about Sonny Skies and Frances Farnsworth?"

Dwyre shook his head no. "I don't think I can tell you much." Then he paused, caught up in thought. Richards wished he could see the pictures that were playing across the man's mind. Then, at length, Dwyre looked up and pleaded, "But you know, it wasn't a very long or a very happy chapter in Sonny's short life."

Yes, Richards thought. The news clips and Frances Farnsworth's own autobiography, ghostwritten for her in 1984, had said as much. They were just two kids. He was nineteen, and she was seventeen. They were married before a judge in Tijuana. They spent a three-day honeymoon in Acapulco, where, according to press accounts, he was seen playing a lot of tennis and she was seen doing a lot of watching.

And then Sonny was off to do a movie about the Royal Mounties in Vancouver, Canada, a movie that was never finished because Sonny Skies had gone off to war—while Frances Farnsworth was signed to a long-term contract by Orpheum Pictures and sent to upstate New York to do the ill-fated *Oneida* with Orson Welles. Welles never finished the picture, about a Utopian community that practiced group marriage—every man the husband of every woman, every woman the wife of every man—but work on it kept the newlyweds apart almost until Sonny was drafted.

"Is it true that Sonny and Frances never even had time to get a place of their own?" asked Richards.

"Right. The little time they spent together here—maybe a month—was with Sonny's mother in Studio City. I'd gone to Vancouver, as Sonny's stand-in, but when we got back, I moved my things out just as Frances was moving her things in. Then—it wasn't more than a week—she moved out. Couldn't stand living with Sonny's mom. She found a house of her own somewhere on the West Side."

"You mean she and Sonny found a house together?"

"No." He looked away.

"Then you're saying she left Sonny?" asked Elle.

Dwyre hesitated. "Well, uh, yeah. She left him, all right. That story—that she didn't get along with Sonny's mom—was just the story the studio's flacks told the press. Fact was, she'd been away from Sonny for months. It was almost like, when they both got back from shooting their movies—she was in upstate New York, he in western Canada—they didn't know each other anymore.

"Did you get along with Frances Farnsworth?"

"Did before. We'd been friends. Used to laugh a lot together when she and Sonny first met. But then—"

"Where'd she move to?" The interruption was from Elle, and Richards frowned at her. You don't interrupt a subject when he's about to tell you something he's already shied away from.

"She got her own house."

"Where?" Elle persisted. "Hollywood?"

Dwyre shook his head. "Westwood? Santa Monica? I'm not sure."

"Let's back up a minute," said Richards. "Tell us more about Sonny Skies and Frances Farnsworth."

Dwyre smiled. "Oh, their courtship was a beautiful thing. Before Frances came along, Sonny had had a lot of girlfriends. But with Sonny they were out of sight, they were out of mind. Then *she* visits Stage Seventeen one morning in June, just a slip of a thing, wearing a little nothing of a silk shirtdress, unbuttoned in front, down to here. It was obvious she wasn't wearing a bra. She didn't need one. Nice knockers. Nice nipples, too. You could see 'em. They stood right up, real perky. Well, I was impressed. I'd never seen such a beautiful body before—tiny waist, perfect legs, a real dollface. When her press agent, name of Jeremiah, asked me to go back to Sonny's dressing room and tell him this new girl from Oklahoma wanted to meet Sonny Skies, I said, 'Sure!'

"But then Sonny said when I told him, Sonny said, 'Hey, Billy, you know I do not have any kind of a thing at all for starlets. Anyway, I'm waiting for a call from my bookie.' "

"So I went back and told Jeremiah that Sonny was involved in a very important business thing—a three-way call involving his stockbroker in San Francisco and somebody in New York City. I could hardly look at the girl, she was so beautiful, but I knew she was listening when I said Sonny was busy and on the phone and all. And then, all of a sudden, he is there in back of me, smiling and holding out his hand to her."

"He was right behind you?"

"Yeah. I think he must have seen some kind of light in my eye or something, and he followed me out. Anyway, there he was. And from that time on I don't think he had any spare moment when he wasn't with her, thinking about her, talking about her, calling her on the phone, sending her presents, composing songs for her, writing poems." Dwyre paused and shook his head, as if the memory were too much to bear. "I think he persuaded Mr. Mayer to cast her in *Pearly Grave*. Convinced him there wasn't an actress on the lot could play the role of Helen, the virgin whore, like she could. And he was right. She was terrific, as you may remember.

"Well, that was all Sonny needed, just needed to be close enough to woo her, and being on location with her in Hawaii gave him all the chance he needed. They saw each other every night. I got the hell out of the way, and when the picture was in the can, they came back and went to Mr. Mayer and said they were going to get married and could they have his blessing?"

Richards said, "Mayer didn't give his blessing, did he?"

"Nope. Tried to talk 'em out of it. Soon as *Pearly Grave* was released, Frances was a sex symbol all over the world. She get married, first thing you know she'd be pregnant. And there goes your Hollywood sex symbol."

Elle McBrien coughed. Richards kicked her—gently—in the shin.

Dwyre was really wound up. Richards and Elle let him go on. "And Sonny Skies? He was Mr. Mayer's biggest moneymaker, with all those Billy Bunting movies, made for cheap on the back lot, with Sonny Skies playing everybody's favorite wholesome small-town teenager."

"What you're saying, Billy, is that Metro had nothing to gain if these two got married?"

"Exactly," said Billy Dwyre. "But Sonny got his back up. Said Mr. Mayer could fire him if he wanted to, but they were going to find the biggest church in America and get married in it. Maybe they'd get married in the Mormon Temple in Salt Lake City. From Mr. Mayer's point of view, if they *had* to get married, then a church wedding, with music by the Mormon Tabernacle Choir, was the worst way they coulda done it." He paused. "Oh, I guess it woulda been worse if they'd gone to Rome and been married by the pope. But far as Mr.

Mayer was concerned, less said, seen, or heard about the wedding, the better.

"So Mr. Mayer, he just up and said he'd give Sonny a bonus of fifty thousand dollars if he and Frances eloped to Tijuana. If they eloped, mind you. Quietly. No press advance, no interviews with the press afterward.

"I can remember Sonny and Frances coming back to his dressing room after that meeting and Sonny telling me what the old man said, fifty thousand dollars, and what would I do?

"I asked Sonny how much he was making now a year. 'About that,' he said. 'Fifty?' says I. 'Uh-huh,' he says. 'Take another fifty,' says I. And so he took it. Later, I found out he was only making forty.

"He invited me to the wedding. Weren't only about six or seven of us there in Tijuana. Nigel Parrish was there, of course, to make sure there was no press coverage, even if he had to hire all the hookers in Tijuana to buy the press off. Nobody else from the studio. Director Sam Glover came. Dead now. You remember, he'd directed Sonny in *Young Bert Einstein*. Hortense Blake, the lady who'd played Sonny's mom in all those Billy Bunting movies. She was more of a mother to Sonny than Sonny's mom. Howard Jeremiah, Ms. Farnsworth's agent. Her older sister from Oklahoma, big horse-faced gal named Bethany. Sonny's mom. And that was it."

Elle, behind the minicam, was shaking her head in disbelief. Richards, too, had a frank admiration for Dwyre's recall. "How'd you remember all those names, Billy?"

Dwyre reached into a brown leather briefcase that was sitting at his feet and pulled out a photo album. "I saved a few pictures," he said. He opened the book and flipped the pages until he came across the picture he was looking for. A group photo taken at the Tijuana wedding. He pushed it across the table toward Richards. "It's kind of a dark photo. I took it myself in the office of the justice of the peace, or whatever they call him down there. There we are. Count 'em. Six of us. Plus Sonny and Frances. And the justice of the peace. Or whatever he was."

Richards studied the photo, and Elle leaned over to scan it with her minicam. "I never knew Frances Farnsworth had a sister," said Richards.

"Bethany Farnsworth?" said Dwyre. "She didn't stick around after Frances started seeing Howard Kenelly. Went back to Oklahoma, as I recall."

Richards was riffling through the album, pausing over one picture, then another. "I don't suppose," he said, looking up at Dwyre, "that you'd let us take this album and make some copies of these photos?"

"Wait a minute," said Ellen. "Did you just say Howard Kenelly was dating Frances Farnsworth?" Elle kept her minicam running, but she couldn't let the name of Howard Kenelly get passed over in this conversation. "When did Howard Kenelly and Frances Farnsworth start, uh, as you say, dating?"

Dwyre gave Elle a blank stare. Richards felt foolish. He had gotten distracted by the photo album, and without Elle's intervention, he would have let the name of Howard Kenelly pass unnoted. For many a year Howard Kenelly was just about the biggest man in L.A. When World War II broke out, he owned half of the airframe business in Southern California. He had his hands in a dozen other pies. His overpaid scientists had done the earliest pioneering work in undersea boats, in satellites, radar, and rockets. He had taken a fancy to the movies, bought himself a studio, even tried his hand at directing a movie about a hero of his, Pancho Villa. He built the fastest plane in the world, a long-range two-seater, which he tried to fly around the world. He thought it was common knowledge that Howard Kenelly and Frances Farnsworth had had a romance. But it was, obviously, news to Elle McBrien.

"Well," said Elle to Dwyre, "do you know or don't you?"

Dwyre said he couldn't remember.

Elle persisted. "Was it after Sonny's death?"

"Well," he said, "what does your research say?"

Elle said that shouldn't matter to Billy Dwyre. "All of the research I can do in some archive isn't worth one good memory by someone like you." Dwyre looked flattered, but Elle wasn't trying to compliment him. She was serious.

"Well?" prodded Richards.

"Couple years after Sonny went off to war, I heard Mr. Kenelly started seeing Frances. It was in all the trades. Two glamorous people. Hell, they were in *Life* magazine."

Richards said, "You're sure Howard Kenelly wasn't seeing Frances Farnsworth when Sonny was off to war?"

"Oh, no, no, no, no. Nothing like that." Richards looked over at Elle. She'd been fiddling with the focus on her lens, and for some reason, she had a puzzled look on her face.

"Billy," she said evenly, "you ever meet Howard Kenelly?"

"Oh, no. Nothing like that."

Elle turned and looked at Richards and shook her head.

"Getting back to the pictures," said Richards. "You think you might let us borrow some of those snapshots?"

"Not a chance," said Dwyre. "My memories? They're all I got now. I had my years with Sonny Skies. I had my years with the sheriff's office. Good years. My albums. They're all I got."

"What would you say if we came back with a nice still camera? We could take pictures of your pictures."

Dwyre didn't reply. He was thinking. The two of them let him think. He shook his head yes but said, "No. I don't think so. Why would I want to do that?"

"Well, we don't actually need 'em," said Richards. "But it'll help us make a better documentary record."

"Well, then, if you don't need 'em—"

"Of course, we'd have to reimburse you for the right to use them," said Elle. "HMO has a budget for that."

Dwyre smiled. "Well, whyn't you say so? You weren't going to hold out on me, now, were you, Mr. Richards?"

Richards almost blushed. He wasn't going to offer Dwyre a damn thing—unless he asked. "Absolutely not! I assumed you'd know—"

"You heard the old saying, Mr. Richards. 'A-S-S-U-M-E makes an ass out of you and me.' "

"Heh-heh. Yeah. I remember that."

Elle took the play away from Richards. "So maybe we can work something out?" said Elle. "I mean about the pictures?"

"Naturally. I don't live on air here."

Richards nodded. And then he was startled when the teenage nymph in the eensy-teensy white bikini rose from her chaise about seventeen steps away and walked toward him with a bottle of suntan lotion in her hand. She had her eyes on his, and the look in them was bold. She's coming to me? he thought.

"Billy," she said, turning abruptly away from Richards and moving to Dwyre's side, "I need you to put some of this Coppertone on my back." She looked back at Richards with a mischievous grin.

"Oh, sure, honey," said Dwyre. He turned his chair away from the table to face her. She knelt down in front him, handed him the brown plastic bottle, flipped her blond locks off her back and over the top of her head, and put her face in Dwyre's lap. He untied her bra in the back and started pouring the oil on her shoulders with one hand and smoothing it down her back with the other. When she put her face in the crotch of his trousers, Richards almost toppled over backward in his chair.

Elle kept her cam running. In fact, she pulled back on the zoom lens to get a long shot of this teenage fellatrix at work.

Dwyre laughed. "You okay, Rich?" He laughed again and said reassuringly, "This is my daughter, Timmi Tyler."

Richards thought, Oh, in that case, it's all right, then. Instead, he said, "Uh-huh." Brilliant. But the look on Richards's face—disbelief—was an invitation to Dwyre to explain. He did—after Timmi had been properly oiled and after she rose to return to her chaise, holding her still-untied bra in front with one hand. "You see," Dwyre said, "me and my recently dear departed wife adopted Timmi almost ten years ago, when she was six. She's my foster daughter. But she's legal and all."

"Uh-huh," said Richards again.

Elle turned to Richards and winked. "I'm almost out of tape." She wasn't out of tape. But he knew she'd only scheduled four hours for this trip. She wanted to get back to HMO for a 5:00 P.M. meeting. But why reveal that to Billy Dwyre?

It was a good time for one last, Colombo-type question from Richards. "One more thing," he said. This time Elle left the minicam running. "Tell us about Sonny's service career."

"What about it?" said Dwyre.

"Seem strange to you he went in the infantry?"

"Naw," said Dwyre. "I took him down to the induction center, and just before he went in, he said he was going to ask for the infantry."

"He signed himself up to die? You know why he did that?"

Dwyre was direct. "He'd just broken up with Frances Farnsworth. He was suicidal, anyway. He really loved that girl. When she left him, there was nothing more to live for."

"You didn't try to talk him out of it?"

"Sonny? There were times when you couldn't talk to Sonny. This was one of 'em."

And you never saw him again?"

"Oh, yes."

"When was that?"

"After a few months in the service, Sonny came home. He'd been at Fort Huachuca in Arizona. Got a furlough to come for his mom's funeral. She passed away in May. Then Sonny returned to his unit."

"You saw him at the funeral?"

"Yes. I was with him the whole time. Met him at the church. Went to the cemetery with him. Forest Lawn."

"Was Frances Farnsworth there?"

"No."

"Who was there?"

"Just Sonny and me and the preacher and a couple guys worked for Forest Lawn."

"And then what happened after the ceremony?"

"And then Sonny took off."

"How did he take off?"

"Let's see. I, uh. I think he was driving a rental car. Planned to leave it at the Santa Monica Airport and take a charter to Fort Huachuca. That's the last I saw him."

Richards was disappointed. Somehow he expected something more off the wall from Dwyre. "Okay, thank you, Billy. I guess that's a wrap for today." He nodded to Elle. As she switched off her minicam and started to pack her sound equipment, Richards tried to pin down Dwyre for a return visit.

"I gave you a lot today," said Dwyre. "You got enough."

"You were terrific today," said Richards. It didn't take him more than a moment to think of a good, sellable excuse to return. "But we didn't get into Sonny's musicals. You had a role in some of them, didn't you?"

Dwyre smiled. "Well, yeah. Two big roles."

"Well, then you're one of the guys who can tell us a lot—maybe more than anybody—about Sonny and Noelle Sparks." He was, of course, referring to the bubbly star who had done all those great musicals with Sonny.

Dwyre smiled and allowed that, yes, he probably could. "Sonny and Noelle, they were the cutest kids together. But never any romance there. Brother and sister, they were."

Richards held up his right hand, like a traffic cop. "Hold

it, Billy. You just save that for when we come back. When we have a lotta tape. We *can* come back, can't we?" Richards was nodding and smiling. Tools of the reporter's trade, nods and smiles.

Dwyre said, "Yeah, I guess. That'd be fine." He turned to Elle. "And, uh, Miss McBrien? Be sure and bring that still camera, too, so's you can take some pictures a my pictures. I've got some pretty good ones a me in *Swing Time in the Minarets,* and *Two Hearts at Ruidoso.*"

✷ ✷ ✷

"Well," said Richards, "two good interviews. What next?"

They were on their way down the coast. Elle was at the wheel of her Volvo. Elle said, "One good interview—with Parrish. And one load of bullshit from Billy Dwyre."

Richards was surprised—as much over her using the word bullshit as he was at her negative judgment about Dwyre. "You don't think he was telling us the truth?"

"About half the time. Then I suddenly realized he was covering up."

"Who was he covering for?"

"For Howard Kenelly."

"No!"

"Yes! He was lying."

"How do you know he was lying?"

"He had a 'tell.' I didn't notice at first. We'll be able to see more when we review the videotape. Once I realized what Dwyre was doing, I tried to get it on tape."

"Doing what? Get what on tape?"

"Every time he lied, he lifted the heel of his right boot."

Richards looked over at her with a mixture of admiration and disbelief. "Raising a heel? That was a 'tell'?"

"I realized it when he volunteered the information about his so-called daughter. 'She's legal and all,' he said.

You didn't believe it. And I didn't believe it. And I was in a long shot then, and I think the camera saw him lift his right heel just before he delivered the line."

Richards was nonplussed. In all his years as a reporter, shooting the breeze with reporters, drinking with reporters, he had never heard of such a simple truth test. "Where'd you learn this little trick?" he said.

"A Gestalt-therapy workshop. Up at Esalen. Met a genius up there named Dr. Leiter. He demonstrated how it works with all of us. When we lie, our bodies give us away. A lot. We all have 'tells.' Different people have different 'tells.' The trick is discovering which ones."

Richards nodded. He knew how some poker players gave themselves away. Some bluffers raised their voices a bit; others lowered theirs. Some smiled. Some were unusually sober. Some touched their noses just before they said, "I'll raise you five." And nine times out of ten, the touch of the nose meant they were bluffing. But he wasn't sure Elle was right about Dwyre. "Frankly," said Richards, "I was surprised Dwyre told us as much as he did. Parrish, too. He was very open with us."

"Sure," said Elle. "These people are movie people. They love my minicam. That means they'll talk. It doesn't necessarily mean they'll tell the truth."

"You have a point."

"So," said Elle. "You asked me just now where we go next. I think everything's pointing to Sonny's breakup with Frances Farnsworth. We need to find out more about that. Then his joining the U.S. infantry, for god's sake. And his brave death on the beach at Normandy."

Richards nodded. He was quietly pleased. The fastidious Elle McBrien, who had expressed her distaste for reporters' nosy questions, was becoming a snoop. "And if you're right about Dwyre, we also have to find out more about Howard Kenelly. Find out where he fits into this picture."

"We're going to be busy."

"Yes, and we may need help." Richards told Elle that he'd already put out some feelers in Washington through his old buddy Dan Morley. "If Morley comes through, we'll know more about Sonny's army days. Where he was killed, exactly, and how. We oughta be able to find some of the men who survived. They oughta have a story or two to tell. We don't even have a picture of Sonny's grave. We're gonna have to find his grave."

"Yes, that. And we've got to get to Frances Farnsworth."

"Frances Farnsworth? Definitely. But she's going to be a problem."

"Yes," said Elle. "She isn't going to talk to us about Sonny Skies. Through her entire career she's never gone on the record with anyone about Sonny Skies. Or about any of the other men in her life."

Richards nodded. After her brief marriage to Sonny Skies, Frances Farnsworth became one of the most sought after beauties in the history of Western civilization. "She had affairs with Ernest Hemingway, Howard Kenelly, Frank Sinatra, John Kennedy—"

"Well, everybody had an affair with John Kenn—"

"—the prime minister of England, half the matadors in Spain."

"But you have to give the old girl credit. After retiring from the movie business—"

"She didn't retire," said Richards. "Nobody in Hollywood retires. They just find they can't get work anymore, and they give up."

"Well, okay. After she finds she can't get any more movie work, she starts up this chain of health-and-diet places."

"The Farnsworth Health Centers."

"And then she gets her own TV talk show."

"Featuring, mainly, former fat people who have gotten a grip on their personal problems, problems that made them overeat." Richards shook his head. "You've got to give her credit. She's making more money now than she ever made in the movies."

"Trouble is," said Elle, "she's notoriously unavailable to the media. How do you explain that?"

Richards said, "I can't." Both he and Elle knew that Farnsworth got her high daytime ratings on TV by exposing others. She was right up there with Oprah and Donahue and Geraldo. But Richards was sure that many viewers knew little about her movie career and even less about her current private life.

"So how do we get to her? She can tell us a lot about Sonny Skies."

"Can but won't."

"How can you be so sure?"

"She did one of those as-told-to autobiographies a dozen years ago. She disposed of her marriage to Sonny Skies on a single page."

Elle said she had forgotten about that book. "Who helped her with it?"

"Arthur Markstein."

"You think he knows more about this chapter in the life of Frances Farnsworth?"

"Knows more? Certainly. But will he tell us? Not very likely."

"And why is that?"

"Because he's a schmuck." Elle frowned. "Someone who, if he had all the money in the world, wouldn't give you a nickel. Someone who, if he had the entire *Webster's Dictionary* committed to memory, wouldn't tell you how to spell *syzygy*. Someone who—"

"All right. All right. I get the picture. But we have to at least make a try to see Frances Farnsworth. And if that fails, we go to option B."

"Which is what?"

Elle shrugged. "Find friends. If she has any."

"People like Frances Farnsworth don't have friends. They have employees."

"Meaning?"

"Meaning they only trust the people they pay."

"Must be a lonely life."

"Yeah," said Richards. "But the hills—the Hollywood hills—are full of these people."

Elle pondered that for a few moments. "We'll just have to play it by ear. Try for a interview with Frances Farnsworth. If we fail, we start looking for somebody who knew her way back when—when she left him and he went in the army. "I wonder if the sister of Frances Farnsworth—what was her name? Bethany?—if Bethany is still alive. I have a feeling about her."

"Why is that?"

"The ugly-duckling sister who never became a swan? While her sister was acclaimed by some as the most beautiful woman in the world? Maybe Bethany would welcome a chance to even up the scales of justice."

"Uh-huh." Richards, an only child, professed not to know much about sibling rivalries. He had another idea. "Or maybe I could go on the Frances Farnsworth freak show and confront her there."

Elle laughed. "You could qualify, Mr. Chocolate. On the fat front. But what particular perversions does your eating disorder drive you to? You going to get on the show with 'Fat Boys Who Sleep With Their Mothers'?"

Richards smiled. "That show's already been done."

"Not really?"

"Yep. Saw it a few weeks ago."

"You're kidding."

He laughed. "Yes, I am. But don't be surprised if you turn on the TV someday soon and see 'Fat Boys Who Sleep With Their Grandmothers,' courtesy of Frances or Oprah or Donahue or Geraldo. Or somebody. I can't keep track of all the freak shows anymore."

They rode for a while in silence. Finally, Richards said, "How old do you make our friend Billy Dwyre?"

"I figure he's got about fifty years on her."

"Yeah, I'd say Dwyre's in his late sixties. And she's maybe sixteen."

"He sure was right," said Elle, "when he said he didn't live on air. Neither, apparently, does Timmi Tyler. You believe he adopted that kid?"

Elle said she didn't know what to believe. She quoted Dwyre. " 'My memories? They're all I got.' Yeah, right, just his memories and his own Lolita."

Richards whistled a few bars of an old tune. "Nice Work If You Can Get It."

Elle took her eyes off the road for a moment to look over at him and hoot. "C'mon, Rich. I saw you lusting after that nymph soon as we took our seats out there at the pool."

"Who, me?"

"You don't remember taking a kick in the shins? I remember giving you one. That *was* the toe of my boot. I *thought* that was your shin."

"Okay. Okay," said Richards. He didn't want to remind her about his gentle kick to *her* shin. He wasn't in the mood for a feminist lecture on sex and Hollywood, which he was fully expecting to get any day now.

Elle pulled off the Santa Monica Freeway at La Brea. It was perhaps ten more minutes to the offices of HMO. "I'm going to be in time for my five o'clock meeting," she said. "But it isn't going to take more than a half hour. Why don't you pick up some Chinese food and come over for supper with me and Gremmie."

6

$\mathbf{G}$remmie was a latchkey kid, but as far as Richards could tell, a pretty darn good one—if it meant anything to come into Elle's apartment on Franklin and find the kid studying a history lesson without the TV on or anything. Richards had arrived at Elle's with the Chinese food at the same time she was checking her mailbox at her apartment's entryway. "She gets good grades," Elle said to Richards as she cuddled her daughter with her left arm while sorting through a stack of mail with the other. "Don't you, honey?"

She nodded. Gremmie must have been born with her dad's genes, for she didn't look at all like her mom. Gremmie was tall for her age, brown-eyed, and very, very blond.

"Honey, Gremmie, this is Mr. Richards. He's the nice man I told you about. He's working with me now at HMO."

She came over and shook his hand, looked him right in the eye, and said, "Hello, Mr. Richards."

Richards and the girl talked for five minutes or so while Elle zapped the Chinese in the microwave. He had no trouble drawing her out; then she had her turn. She discovered he was a newspaperman and asked him a number of good questions about the life of a reporter. Precocious? he asked himself. Yes, he guessed she was. And he was very pleased that Elle had introduced him as the nice man she was working with at HMO. He had only been to the headquarters of HMO once, and he certainly wasn't working there. For her daughter's benefit, Elle was making him into a solid citizen and, stretching it a bit. A colleague at work. He liked that.

He had been attracted by Elle's good looks and her earnestness. But now something else was growing. A kind of regard for the way her mind worked. She was intuitive, and despite her dislike of snoops, she herself had the instincts of a natural-born reporter.

After the three of them had pitched in together to clear the dinner table, Gremmie excused herself—"to take my bath and get some reading done for tomorrow." She kissed her mother, shook Richards's hand, and said good night. Then Richards went over near the front door, where Elle had deposited her Macintosh laptop, picked it up, and brought it to the kitchen table. "I've noticed you think better with your trusty Mac in hand," he said to Elle, who was finishing her coffee. "So, let's review what we have here."

She smiled at him, touched his arm gently, and opened up the Mac. He liked her touching him. Maybe she was beginning to have a regard for him, too. "Okay," she said. "First, we have a good story. It's a real Hollywood story, of course."

"What do you mean by 'Hollywood story?'" asked Richards.

"You know. Moom pitchuhs. Big names. Big money. Beautiful dames. Greed. Power."

"Incest." He laughed.

She laughed. "I'm not so sure Billy Dwyre will allow us any more footage of his Lolita."

"Yeah. Especially since you already got some footage of her nibbling in his lap."

"But," she said, "we've got some photogenic characters. Maybe they won't all be as colorful as Nigel Parrish and Billy Dwyre. But if these shows depend a lot on the right talking heads, then I think we've got some pretty darn good talking heads."

"Two, anyway."

"Yeah. But two out of two isn't bad. It's a proper start. And maybe more than that. I think there might have been something sinister going on here." Richards's silent nod indicated he wanted her to go on. He wasn't sure she was right. But he wanted to hear more. She said, "Consider the pieces of the story." She scrolled up and talked through her notes, typing occasionally as she thought of something to add.

"Item One: Sonny Skies, who has all the sex he can handle, suddenly falls head over heels in love, then marries this poor little ol' stunningly beautiful country girl from Oklahoma against the wishes of Louis B. Mayer, the most powerful man in Hollywood. But only days later he's sent off on location. He goes off one way."

"And his bride," said Richards, "goes off another."

"I'll put that down," said Elle McBrien, "as my Item Two: While he's on location, Orpheum Pictures—that's Howard Kenelly—just happens to buy up Metro's contract with this poor little ol' stunningly beautiful country girl from Oklahoma."

Richards added, "Howard Kenelly, one of the nation's richest men. He owns the biggest airframe business in Southern California, holds one hundred percent of Kenelly Aircraft, the majority stock in the A & P, Liggett & Myers, and BBD&O, a big chunk of Standard Oil, and—"

"He also owns Orpheum Pictures."

"Which," said Richards, "he bought because it was the best way in the world, at that time at least, to buy his way into the bedrooms of the world's most beautiful women."

"Then Frances Farnsworth makes her debut in *Pearly Graves*. And then Orpheum buys her contract."

"And then?"

Elle said, "That's my sinister Item Three. This bride of maybe a week or so ends up in upstate New York, way off nowhere, to work on a picture that's never released, even if it is made, which maybe it never was. My guess is that nobody has ever seen *Oneida*. My guess is that there never was an *Oneida*. I think it was only a way of taking Miss Frances Farnsworth out of circulation until Howard Kenelly could pull enough strings to get Sonny Skies into the army."

"No!" Richards said no, but he was telling himself: What a helluva story if Elle is right.

She plunged on. "Sinister Item Four. Sonny Skies has been eligible for the draft since it began. He's never called up. He keeps on making movies for Metro. Then suddenly he's drafted in early 1944. Why then?"

"It's a good question," says Richards. "But it doesn't necessarily have a sinister answer."

"It is sinister in light of my Item Five. Where does Sonny Skies end up? In Special Services, the home of practically every entertainer who ever entered the military? No, he does not. He's assigned to the U.S. Infantry, where he becomes a paratrooper. His outfit is among the first to hit Normandy, in the middle of the night, before the dawn of D day. They're behind enemy lines, they take horrendous casualties, and, poof, all of a sudden, Frances Farnsworth is a widow. On D day."

"A dramatic note. But what's so sinister about it?"

"Did you forget about Howard Kenelly's affair with Frances Farnsworth?"

"Far as we know," said Richards, "that affair didn't start until 1950. If there was an affair. I never really believed the rumor. It was just fanzine talk. Or maybe just a rumor planted by a studio flack or by the Kenelly competitors in the aircraft business.

Elle said, "By a studio flack in the same studio owned by Howard Kenelly? Come on. I can believe the Kenelly competitors in the airplane business. But not the studio-flack thing."

Richards conceded that the Howard Kenelly–Frances Farnsworth connection needed exploring.

"Absolutely," said Elle. She walked into the living room, knelt on the floor, fiddled around with her minicam, then plunked a cassette into her TV. "Let's take a look at Billy

Dwyre's lies." She settled into a kneeling position on the floor and rewound the last part of their interview with Dwyre. Richards took a seat on the couch. Elle got to the point where Dwyre's Lolita was nibbling in his lap. "Here, now," she said, "I pull back from my close-up on Dwyre so the camera can take in what she's doing. And now, coming up, he's telling you—"

They watched the tape. Here was Dwyre: "You see, me and my recently dear departed wife adopted Timmi almost ten years ago, when she was six. She's my foster daughter. But she's legal and all."

"You see?" said Elle. "You see him lift his heel?"

"No. I didn't see it."

"Look again." She reversed the tape, then hit the play button again. "You see, me and my recently dear departed wife adopted Timmi almost ten years ago, when she was six."

"Right here, coming up now. He's going to lift his heel. See it?"

By God, thought Richards, she's right. Here was Dwyre: "She's my foster daughter. But she's legal and all." And he was lifting his right heel.

"Now," said Elle, "let's go back a couple minutes on the tape. Here's Billy Dwyre on Frances Farnsworth and Howard Kenelly. "Couple years after Sonny went off to war, I heard Mr. Kenelly started seeing Frances. It was in all the trades. Two glamorous people, hell, they were in *Life* magazine."

"See," said Elle, hitting the pause button on her VCR. "His feet are firmly on the ground. Then here you are." She hit the play button. Here was Richards now, pushing Dwyre a bit: "You're sure Howard Kenelly wasn't seeing Frances Farnsworth when Sonny was off to war?"

And then here came Dwyre's answer. "Oh, no, no, no, no. Nothing like that." Elle hit the pause button. "Now look at his right foot." She was right. Elle had caught him with his right heel raised an inch or two.

"Now," said Elle. "There's more. Watch." She hit the

play button, to catch her own words: "Billy, you ever meet Howard Kenelly?"

And here came Dwyre's reply. He paused. Then he lifted his right heel. Then: "Oh, no. Nothing like that."

Elle looked triumphant. Richards saw now what she meant. And the look on his face told her that he believed she was right. "So," he said, "Dwyre knew Howard Kenelly."

"And if Dwyre knew him, my guess is that he knew him because of Sonny Skies. I think he knows a lot more about Howard Kenelly and Sonny Skies than he wants to tell us."

"But why won't he tell us?"

"I haven't the slightest idea. And neither do you. And we won't know," she said, "until we put together some more pieces of the puzzle."

"I'm intrigued by this tape," he said. He looked over at the screen. The tape was on pause. Billy Dwyre was looking a little ridiculous, caught in the middle of a word, with his mouth open. "Can you go to that place in the interview where Dwyre says Sonny drove himself to the airport in a rental car?"

She nodded and fiddled with the buttons. She spun the tape backward. "No," she said. "I guess it's further ahead of this point." Finally, she found it. Here was Dwyre. "Yes. I was with him the whole time. Met him at the church. Went to the cemetery with him. Forest Lawn."

Richards voice: "And then . . . ?"

"And then Sonny took off."

"So far," Richards said to Elle, kneeling there in the living room with the VCR controller in her hand, "so good. His feet are still."

"Right," said Elle. Now here's your key question: "How did he take off?"

"Let's see. I, uh. I think he was driving a rental car. Planned to leave it at the Santa Monica Airport and take a charter to Fort Huachuca. That's the last I saw him."

Elle stopped the tape here. Billy Dwyre had his right heel in the air.

"So," said Richards, "if your 'tell' is right, Billy was lying. That wasn't the last time he saw Sonny Skies!"

"Exactly! But we can't just go back to Billy Dwyre and tell him we think he's lying. If he's got a reason for lying today, he'll still have the same reason tomorrow, or next week."

"Right. We have to confront him with some other facts, then try to get him to tell us more."

"What other facts?"

"I don't know. I think we just have to keep probing. Try to find Frances Farnsworth. Or find some of Frances's old friends. Maybe see if her sister's still around."

"You want to check out her sister, or should I?"

"You take it," said Richards. "I have some other trails to travel."

Elle was rewinding the tape. When she had finished, she rose from her knees. "I'm tired of this. You want to see a movie?"

"Where? Something on the Boulevard you want to see?"

"No. Here." Elle dug out an old Hitchcock movie, put it on her VCR, then came over and sat closer to him on the couch while the two of them watched. It was *Foreign Correspondent* with Joel McCrea, a thriller with a nice climactic Hitchcock ending in an eerie windmill in the Netherlands. After the film, she said, "Coffee?"

He shook his head, reached over, and pulled her closer to him. He kissed her neck and then her cheek, and she kissed him on the lips. But when Richards started to put his hand inside her shirt, she said, "Not now, Rich." She nodded toward the door of Gremmie's room.

"I understand," said Richards, rising from the couch.

She smiled. "Don't go away mad."

" 'But do go away?' " he said. "Okay."

7

Richards was having his morning coffee and chocolate doughnuts at the M&M Sweete Shoppe and reading Jim Murray in the *Times* when he heard some commotion at the front of the shop. He paid no attention. Murray had a funny column about Charles Barkley and Hakeem Olajuwon pounding the boards (and each other) in the NBA Playoffs in Phoenix. Murray had some amusing things to say about basketball, a winter game when it was invented a century ago by Dr. James Naismith, now being played on the first day of summer. Richards was laughing at Murray's gentle chiding of the multimillionaires when Dave Benton squeezed into his booth with a cup of coffee and his copies of the *Times,* the *Hollywood Reporter,* and *Variety.*

Richards looked up at Benton. "That you making the fuss up front?"

Benton didn't answer.

"How much you win last night." At the Backstabbers Poker Club, Ben always won, sometimes a lot.

"I broke even. Where were you?"

"Had something else going," said Richards. He went back to Jim Murray. Benton read, too. Maisie came by twice to give them refills on the coffee. Finally, Richards said, "How's life on the I-way?"

Richards knew that Benton had turned into a computer nerd after he left William Morris. For Ben it was a good move. He had a lousy, negative personality that wasn't much enhanced by his looks. He was overweight, his unending imitations of Peter Lorre were annoying after a very short while, and he dressed like a racetrack tout. On the Internet, however, no one could see him or hear him, and he came across as a very informed, if opinionated, source on any number of topics. Furthermore, he was becoming more and more involved with a group of hackers, who were teaching him how to break into corporate computer systems for the thrill of it all.

Ben had told the Backstabbers all about it one night after poker, bragging from too much wine. "I got into MCI's E-mail system," he confessed. "The stories you see on E-mail! Beats television all to hell."

"You still sit up nights looking in on everybody's E-mail?" Richards asked.

"Oh, heavens to Betsy Ross," Benton said. "I can't be bothered with that. I'd never get anything done if I did that."

"Ben," said Richards, "what else would you do? No woman would ever look at you—"

"My mother looks at me," he said.

"Have you had a date recently?"

"Betsy's asshole!" he said. "Who even uses that word 'date' anymore? I see women all the time. Naked women, too."

"Hookers?"

"None a your business." Benton went back to reading his *Hollywood Reporter.*

Richards went back to his *Times.*

When Maisie came by to give them refills on their coffee, Benton said to Richards, "You been missing a lot of meetings of the Backstabbers." It was true. It had been seven weeks since he met Elle, and in that time he had been to the Backstabbers only twice.

"Something the matter?" asked Benton.

"Nope," said Richards. "I've just had something else to do."

"Yeah, that's what Tom and Tilly were saying last night.

Tilly told me in the kitchen that you got away with something of theirs, something they want returned to them."

Richards didn't miss the menace in Benton's voice. Maybe it was just the tone of his voice, that goddamned Peter Lorre voice. But what if the Greenbergs started to make trouble for him? No. It couldn't be. Not over a little piece of film, a bit of celluloid not worth more than five dollars to the Greenbergs but worth a lot more to him. Richards tried to sound unconcerned. "And what's that?"

"They said you'd know what it was. Tilly says you should call her."

Richards shrugged.

Ben stood and put on his best Peter Lorre. "And we want to see you next week," he said. "The Backstabbers miss you."

"Yeah, sure, Ben. Mind if I keep this?" Richards was studying Benton's *Reporter*. Benton shook his head and shuffled off.

Richards turned back to the magazine. He and Elle had reached a kind of impasse in their search for Sonny Skies. They had decided to pass up possible interviews with other contemporaries of Sonny Skies. What they really needed was a way to get to Frances Farnsworth. He wondered if someone at the *Reporter* could help. Well, as far as he could see, there was no one on the staff that he knew well enough to ask for help. Maybe he'd call his ex-wife. They hadn't parted as good friends. But, then again, they hadn't parted as enemies, either.

He walked home and dialed Susan Genève's private phone number and found it had been changed—to a 457 number, probably Pacific Palisades. He got her machine, her unmistakable voice, and a bilingual message, first in English, then in French. He didn't catch the nuances of her French. But her message in English was haughty. "Leave your name and number at the beep," it said. "I *may* call you back."

When she called back, she was both friendly and

haughty. Friendly at first, until she learned that all he wanted was some advice on how to reach *another* actress. "No, *cher,* I don't know *how* you can get to Frances Farnsworth. I knew her slightly. I did *The Snows of Tibet* with her, as you may recall."

"Oh, yes, yes, I do." He hadn't recalled. But now that she mentioned it, he remembered that *Snows* was Susan's American debut. It was directed by Huston and shot mostly on location in India.

"But all I can suggest is to call the guy who used to be her agent."

"Who is?"

"Wally Winter. She was with him for years. Goodbye."

That was a little abrupt, thought Richards. But what the hell. He really didn't want to renew old acquaintance with Susan. He thought of Elle. He was going to see her Saturday night. No meeting her at AA this time. For the first time, he was going to drive with her. She intended dropping Gremmie off at her ex's parents in the Valley, then they would head out the Ventura Freeway to Malibu Canyon Road and drop down to the meeting in Malibu.

He phoned Wally Winter. Winter was out. Or maybe Winter was just screening his calls. He left word. But wouldn't you know it? He saw Winter a few hours later at the Malibu meeting. The agent was sitting way up toward the front, so Richards waited for him in the patio, with Elle at his side, during the fresh-fruit-and-Starbucks-coffee break.

"Wally Winter?" he said. He tried to look friendly but not too eager. He didn't remind Winter that he had left a message. That would imply a rebuke, which wasn't going to get him anywhere.

Winter had already lit up a cigar. He took a nice puff, then shook Richards's hand and gave Elle the trace of a nod. "What can I do for you?"

Richards tried to explain about the documentary they were doing for HMO.

Winter gave him a respectful hearing. But then, agents, aging ones like Wally Winter, couldn't afford to insult people. After you got to be a certain age in Hollywood, you were nice. By then you had learned the wisdom of Wilson Mizner, the Broadway wit, who once advised, "Be nice to people when you're on the way up, because, sure as shooting, you'll meet them again when you're on the way down."

Winter was warm, but he was not a bit encouraging when he learned that Richards wanted to see Frances Farnsworth. He shook his head, looking sincerely pained. "She hasn't talked to a reporter in the last ten years," he said. He leaned toward Richards conspiratorially. "You see, with her health clubs and her TV talk show, she's got go-to-hell money. That means she doesn't need the press anymore. Hardly ever needed the press. That's why she got Nigel Parrish to be her press guy. To keep stories *out* of the papers."

Richards and Elle tried not to look surprised. Richards said, "But maybe if I could just talk to her on the phone?" He reminded Winter that he had done a not-bad story on her once, freelancing for *Life*. "She might remember that."

Winter said, "But if you know she's not going to ever step in front of your camera, you should also know that she's not going to be much use to you. Just a chat on the phone? How can that help your documentary? Assuming that she has anything at all to say about Sonny Skies? Which I doubt."

"Whyn't you just give it a try. We just want to clear up a couple of little bits of history. Two or three."

Winter took a long puff of his cigar. "I'll think about it. But don't count on anything. No, I won't call you; you call me." He handed Richards his card. "Like on Monday afternoon?"

Some friends of Richards were standing there schmoozing as they waited in line for their car. He introduced Elle.

They wondered if the two of them wanted to join them for coffee near the Malibu pier. He looked to Elle. She said that she had a headache and thought she'd just rather go home. Richards said to his friends, "Sorry. Ask us next time."

"I don't really have a headache," Elle told him with a smile when they climbed into her Volvo.

"I'm glad," he said.

They talked about their project as they drove south on the Pacific Coast Highway, then eastbound on Interstate 10. She said she'd checked the clips at the Academy archives. Kenelly and Frances Farnsworth didn't become an item in the gossip columns until the early 1950s. But Elle pointed out that since they already had Dwyre's unconscious give-away that Howard Kenelly was seeing Frances Farnsworth when Sonny went off to the army, the gossip columns only proved that Kenelly was very, very careful.

"Well, yes, and those were different times," said Richards. "Hedda and Louella didn't dig up dirt on the Hollywood mogul types, which Kenelly was when he owned Orpheum Pictures. Or, if they did, they were very careful about publishing it. And if Hedda or Louella happened to find anything on a guy like our friend Howard, they'd just put it out as a blind item—like: 'What Hollywood biggie was seen making goo-goo eyes at what actress last night at Ciro's?' "

"That figures," said Elle. "I guess these gals had nothing to gain by alienating men like Louis B. Mayer or Harry Cohn. Or Howard Kenelly."

"And a lot to lose," said Richards, who knew a little something about the gossip-column business, where a studio big shot could get an item yanked just as quickly as he could plant one. He knew that Kenelly was very close to the Chandlers and the Hearsts.

"I dug up one Hearst–San Simeon clip dated 1945 that mentioned Howard Kenelly among the guests. It didn't mention Frances Farnsworth. But I'll bet he had Frances Farnsworth there with him."

Richards reached over and touched her shoulder. "That's one bet I won't take."

When they got back to Hollywood, Elle drove directly to his place, stopped in front by the curb, and turned off the key. That was a surprise to him. He thought they'd be going right to her place. Gremmie wasn't there. The coast was clear. That's why he thought Elle had taken her to her grandparents in the Valley. "Rich," she said, "we have to talk." She put her right knee up and tucked her right foot under her to get comfortable.

Uh-oh, he thought. What now? She liked him. He knew that. Moreover, she liked working with him. They'd been working together for almost two months. And they'd both shared their life stories. Elle had told him all about her therapy sessions with the brilliant Dr. Leiter, the psychologist she'd once met at Esalen, and he, Jay Richards, had had three sessions with Dr. Leiter himself. Two of them were hypnotic regressions to his early childhood, and they'd led Richards to dredge up a lot of suppressed hostility toward his own mother. He'd even been emboldened to tell Elle all about those memory trips, and he found she was not only fascinated by the story but impressed that he trusted her enough to share some pretty intimate stuff. Now, by the sober look on Elle's face, he could see that something was the matter. The tension inside the car was almost unbearable. He opened the car window on his side and waited for her to speak.

"Rich," she said. "We're both AA. Neither of us has been in the program that long. Eight months for me. How many for you?"

"In a few days," he said, "it'll be six months."

"Well, see? They say no one in the first year of the program should enter into any kind of love relationship."

He felt his old cynicism taking over. A defense against

the kind of feelings that were welling up inside him now. "Yeah, I've heard that. But who said anything about love?' What's the matter with simple lust?" He laughed. But his laugh was full of phlegm, and that gave him away.

She caught the feeling. "You don't mean that."

He quickly agreed. "No, Elle. No, I don't. But what are we going to do? I want you. And I think maybe you want me."

"I don't know if I do or not. Maybe I do."

He sat up straighter. "Well, then—"

"And maybe I don't." He sagged. "But I believe in the program. It's a very, well, it's a very spiritual thing. And I think that if we're each going to make it, we have to follow the rules."

"Well, hell," he said with some heat. "Who made the rules? Bill W? *Father* Dowling? A Jesuit! What do they know?"

"Hey," she said. "I doubt they made these rules. AA members have found, by trial and error, what works and what doesn't work. Over the years. Many years."

He said nothing, but tried to look deep into the windows of her soul. She looked back, into his. She blinked first, then started to laugh. "I mean it," she said.

"Sure," he said. "That's why you laughed."

"I laughed because you make me laugh."

He sat up straighter. "I do?"

"You know that. But that doesn't mean I love you."

"But, Elle, I love you. I've loved you from the moment I first laid eyes on you."

"Yeah. Well, I kinda knew that. And that's what worries me. When I entered AA, I promised myself I wouldn't be getting intimate with drunks."

"But that's a double standard."

"How so?"

"You expected that maybe someday you'd meet someone special?"

"Well, yes."

"But that someone special. What if he'd made the same resolve—not to date a woman with a drinking problem or a drug problem or both? Then *he* wouldn't be seeing *you*. That's what I mean by a double standard."

"Yes," she said. "I guess it is. And it's embarrassing. But the guy I end up with—I want him to be stable."

"How do you define stable?"

"A guy who wears shoes."

He laughed. "What does that mean?"

"You know, shoes? Florsheim? Bally? Bostonian? Shoes-shoes?"

"Well, I don't exactly go around barefoot, you know." He lifted both feet from under the dash.

Now she was angry with him for being so dumb. "Nikes? That's what I mean! Take a look around at our next AA meeting. Most of the men are bums, and you can tell it because they're all wearing Nikes. Or Adidas. Or Topsiders, for God's sakes. Little boys' shoes! These guys are all little boys. They've never grown up. And I wonder whether you have, either."

"Gee."

"There! See? 'Gee.' That's what little boys say. 'Gee, Mom, buy me some Snickers, Mom, huh, will ya? Gee!' "

Richards had nothing more to say, and his body language showed it. She had reduced him to a tomato. A three-day-old eggplant. A carrot that had gotten lost in the back of the refrigerator for a month. He had his Nikes up on the seat, heels under his behind, and he was clasping his knees.

Once Elle saw him tucked into a ball, she realized she'd gone too far. "Look, Rich. I like you." She paused and smiled when his face lit up as she added, *"Really* like you."

He nodded, suddenly chastened by the honesty of her feeling. "Even though I haven't grown up?"

"Yet," she said. "Haven't grown up yet. But you will."

Richards thought, This woman is good. And suddenly

he no longer felt lustful. "Okay," he said. "I can wait if you can."

Suddenly, she was in his lap. She had almost leaped at him, and now she was kissing him, lips closed at first, but fierce, then open-mouthed. "All right," he said when he was able to come up for air. "But now I feel like a yo-yo."

"Oh, dear," she said, moving back into the driver's seat. She shook her head as if to clear her mind. Then she said, "Men!"

"Yeah," he said, glad she didn't say, "Boys!" "And I guess I can say, 'Women!' "

"Okay. Okay. Why don't we both just say, 'Good night,' huh?"

"Absolutely." He opened the car door, climbed out, then put his head back in the window. "This may be the most important night of my life. Good night. I'll call you in the morning."

She nodded. She said nothing. But her eyes were glistening.

☆ ☆ ☆

It was 11:30 P.M. when he let himself into his apartment. There were three messages on his machine. Tom Greenberg. He was wondering about tennis tomorrow. Ditto the message from Marshall Berger. Nothing from Wally Winter, much less from Frances Farnsworth. Dan Morley's voice came last, and Richards thought he detected a note of excitement in it. "I realize it's been a while since you asked, but I finally got something good," said Morley. "I'll be up till midnight. Otherwise, try me in the morning."

Too late to return anyone's call. It was almost three o'clock in D.C. He'd phone Greenberg and Berger in the morning. He'd like tennis; yes, he would. But he couldn't wait to talk to Morley, and at 6:00 A.M. he was awake and found himself punching Morley's phone number in Washington.

"Okay, buddy boy," said Morley, getting right to the point when he recognized Richards's voice. "Here it is. Sonny Skies's records were out at the Pentagon's documents warehouse in Suitland, Maryland. But I have a new friend who works there. Didn't have to go through any Freedom of Information lawsuit. Just told my friend I wanted everything they had on Sonny Skies. And she got it for me."

"Thick file?" said Richards.

"Thin. Very thin. Five items in it."

"Namely?"

"Let's see. Let me read it to you. Inducted January 1944. Basic training at Fort Ord. His form 4058 showing his first orders, as part of the Eighteenth Cavalry at Fort Huachuca on February 28, 1944."

Richards interrupted. "Cavalry? You mean 'Infantry'?"

"No. It says 'Cavalry. Eighteenth Cavalry.' Citation for sharpshooter's medal, April 17, 1944. Copy of a six-day furlough. Copy of a 'regret to inform you' telegram to Frances Farnsworth Skies, 533 Tilton Drive, Los Angeles, California, on June tenth, from Washington, D.C., telling her Sonny was killed in action with the Eighty-Second Airborne Division, June sixth, at Omaha Beach. Buried at Ste.-Mère-Église. Then there's an insurance form, a receipt or something, signed by Mrs. Skies. That's all."

Richards asked him, "You got the location of the grave site?"

"Yes. Looks like it, right here. Some numbers and some letters." He gave Richards the coordinates. DD-114 in the cemetery at Ste.-Mère-Église. "But there's something doesn't figure," said Morley. "There're no interim orders. He is with the Eighteenth Cavalry at Fort Huachuca. Then he's killed in action with the A Company, Thirty-Fourth Battalion, 508th Parachute Infantry Regiment, Twenty-ninth Infantry Division. I did some checking on this outfit. Most of the guys in that battalion were from Virginia. And here, all of a sudden, here's Sonny Skies from California. How'd he get from the Eighteenth Cavalry into the 508th Parachute Infantry Regiment? That doesn't figure, does it?"

"I guess not," said Richards. "But see? This was my hunch. Somebody pulled some strings and got him transferred to the 508th. What's the date on the transfer?"

"There's no transfer orders."

"No orders?"

"Missing, I guess. But that's normal enough in the army."

"Is it?"

"Well, I mean there are snafus in the army all the time. Lost paperwork."

"Yeah," said Richards. "Can you send me the whole file? It's a copy, isn't it? Your friends didn't steal the original file for you, did she?"

"Naw," said Morley. "These are Xerox copies. I'll fax 'em to you right now."

Richards thanked him, then said he didn't own a fax machine. "So don't fax the stuff. Send it by Express Mail on Monday, okay?" He wasn't too sure he wanted the Kinko's people down on the corner to be reading his faxes from Washington, D.C.

So Dan Morley expressed it, and Richards had it on Tuesday afternoon. After he had studied it and a hurriedly scribbled note from Morley that was stapled to the top document, he phoned Elle at HMO. She was out. That was okay. He hadn't seen her at all on Sunday or Monday. They both wanted to cool it. But they had decided to meet Tuesday night at AA in Hollywood.

After rechecking the documents Morley had mailed to him, Richards could see that Sonny Skies's last furlough orders were dated May 25, 1944, at Fort Huachuca, Arizona. It was a six-day furlough. By rights, he wasn't due back to Fort Huachuca until June 1. Now how the hell could he get from

Fort Huachuca to the staging area of the paratroopers of the 508th in southern England by midnight, June 5? According to Morley, it was at midnight, June 5, that the men of the 508th had boarded a C-47 for their parachute drop behind German lines on the plateau just above Omaha Beach. And, thought Richards, there's nothing in Sonny Skies's file about training as a paratrooper. Now, all of a sudden, he's a paratrooper.

There was something wrong here, something very wrong.

8

Richards phoned Morley in Washington and proposed a deal: a collaboration between HMO and the *Washington Post;* joint investigative reporting, joint stories, TV and newspaper exposés. Richards didn't have any right to speak for HMO. Morley couldn't speak for the *Washington Post.* But they knew they could make this deal stick. All they had to do was get the story.

"Okay, let's shake on it," said Morley.

"You got it," said Richards. "But how do we shake on it on the telephone?"

"Trust me."

"Heh-heh."

"What?"

"You know how they say, 'Fuck you,' in Hollywood?"

"How?"

"What you just said. 'Trust me.' "

"Shit!" said Morley with a growl. "I'm not in Hollywood. Hope I never am!"

"You may have to come out here."

"Why is that?"

"To pick up your Emmy."

"On 'Sonny Skies?' "

"Exactly."

"Your lips to God's ears, Rich. 'Bye."

✯ ✯ ✯

When Richards played tennis with the guys on Sunday, he decided it was best to lay things out very plainly for the Greenbergs. He said nothing to Tom Greenberg during the match, but after it was over, he asked Tom if he and Tillie would join him and his new girlfriend for dinner at Chasen's on Wednesday night.

Greenberg smiled. "New girlfriend? First one in a long time, isn't it, Rich?" He said he didn't know if Tilly had anything already planned for Wednesday. He'd have Tilly phone and confirm.

Tilly was on the phone to Richards an hour later, effusively pleased that there was a woman in his life.

There's nothing women like more, Richards thought, than a new romance. Too bad he didn't really have one. Yet. But even before that really happened, Richards was eager to show his friends that there was someone in his life. They didn't have to know what stage he and Elle had reached, did they? "Well," said Richards, "now you know why I haven't been coming to meetings of the Backstabbers. But you also know, Tilly, I don't ever want to lose touch with my old friends."

✯ ✯ ✯

Wednesday night at Chasen's. Not too crowded. Jay Richards still had enough clout to get a table in the front room. (Maybe the maître d' at Chasen's was living in the past. Or maybe business was bad. He hadn't been to Chasen's in a long time.) The Greenbergs seemed to approve of Elle McBrien. Indeed, what was not to like? Tom asked her what she was doing at HMO.

Elle said, "It doesn't have a green light yet," she said, "but I'm gathering some material on John Garfield."

"Hmm," said Tom Greenberg.

"Hmm," said Tilly Greenberg.

"Not such a hot idea, huh?" said Elle.

"John Garfield's a pretty dark story," said Tilly.

Tom said, "I'm not sure people, these days, will want to watch it. I mean, John Garfield? Half the population, maybe more, doesn't even remember John Garfield. He made a few pictures. Then he was dead. OD'd, didn't he?"

Elle nodded. "You may be right. Maybe HMO won't do it."

No one wanted to speak. Richards was sure the Greenbergs knew there was something else on the agenda. They weren't there just to meet Elle. Somehow he didn't feel quite ready to tell them about Elle's documentary on Sonny Skies. And neither, apparently, was Elle.

Tilly Greenberg took the bull by the horns. She said she understood that he and Elle were working on a documentary together about Sonny Skies.

Richards tried not to look startled. But he did. "How'd you know?"

"Benton told us."

"How'd he know?"

"Beats me," said Tilly. "You probably told him."

"You aren't pissed?" asked Richards.

"Why would we be pissed?" she said. "Tom, you aren't pissed, are you?"

Tom Greenberg was telling the waiter how he liked his steak. " 'Course not," he said.

"Well," said Richards, "however you learned this, it doesn't matter. This has been bothering me for some time. But I have to tell you that I have every intention of expropriating that footage of Sonny Skies's first screen test. In fact, I have already given it to Elle as a gift, my first, to her."

"But it's mine," said Tom.

"Not really. I sought legal counsel on this one. It's stolen property. Buying it from the widow Murphy doesn't change that situation. My lawyer tells me—"

"Well, excuse me," said Tom, "but fuck your lawyer and fuck the horse he rode in on."

"Boys! Boys!" said Tilly.

Elle excused herself to go to the ladies' room. Tilly said she'd join her. When they left, Tom Greenberg and Jay Richards came to a quick decision: to agree to disagree. Tom had reason to believe he owned the film. Richards had reason to believe that the real owner was M-G-M. But since possession was nine-tenths of the law, at this point Elle McBrien had at least 90 percent of it. And Richards said he'd tell her (and his lawyer would tell her) she had every right to use less than a minute of it for any goddamn reason she pleased. "Lawyers call that 'fair use.' "

"This piece of film hardly runs a minute!" said Greenberg.

"Precisely! That's why it shouldn't matter at all. *De minimis non curat lex.*"

"Day what?"

"It's an old legal expression. 'The law doesn't worry about minutiae.' "

"*Shmegegge!*" said Greenberg. "Why don't you speak English?"

"Why don't you?"

"I am."

"*Shmegegge?* That's English?"

"It's Yinglish," said Greenberg. "Nobody speaks it but American Jews in New York and L.A. You've heard it a hundred times. You know what it means."

"Idiot. Like you."

Greenberg waved his hand impatiently. He said he could cite some law negating Richards's position. Hollywood had already made some very good law that had stood up in the appellate courts: People couldn't rip off a Hollywood movie without getting certain rights and permissions.

"But we're not talking about a movie," said Richards. "Just a goddamn screen test. One minute's worth." He looked up to see that the girls were returning to the table.

Greenberg saw them, too, and he was enough of a gentleman to know that their battle had upset Richards's new squeeze. "Rich," he said, "let's just drop it for now, okay?"

Richards gave him a grateful look. "Okay."

Tilly said, "Elle tells me you met through an ad she placed in the *Times.*"

Richards didn't have the slightest idea what she was talking about.

In 'Dateline'? You know? 'Where the Best Connect'?"

Elle kicked him under the table.

"Oh, yeah! In 'Dateline.' In the *Times.*"

Tom Greenberg laughed.

"Hey, why not?" said Elle, advancing the put-on. "You don't want to leave these things to chance anymore. So you advertise."

"How'd your ad read?" asked Tom Greenberg.

Elle frowned. "Let's see. What was it? 'Slim, petite, perky DWF, into film, books, beach, kids, good cook with specialty in soufflés, ISO DWM with same interests.' I listed 'L.A.' and gave one of those code numbers."

"It was the soufflés drew my interest," said Richards, getting in the spirit of Elle's tall tale.

"You sampled her soufflés?"

He looked at Elle and grinned. He didn't even know she did soufflés. "Oh, yes."

"What's her best soufflé?" asked Tilly.

"Oh, chocolate, I guess," Richards said, looking embarrassed.

"Must be a helluva soufflé," said Tom Greenberg.

"In fact," Richards said, "just talking about desserts makes me want to flip over to C. C. Brown's for one of their hot fudge sundaes. Join us?"

"I'll pass," said Tom.

"Not tonight," said Tilly. "You guys go ahead."

When they got into Elle's car, she said to Richards, "You're not serious about C. C. Brown's tonight?"

"I'd rather have your soufflé, Elle. Your *chocolate* soufflé."

She said, "If you play your cards right, buster, you shall have my chocolate soufflé. For the time being, however, we'll both have to make do at C. C. Brown's."

"All right," he said, "one hot fudge sundae at C. C. Brown's coming up."

"With two spoons," she said. "Then I have to get home. Gremmie's home alone."

☆ ☆ ☆

They had taken Richards's car that night. He saw her to her door. She asked him in. Gremmie was still up, in a pink nightgown and lavender robe. "Mom," she said, "Charlotte Burr called. She wants to see you at seven in the morning. In her office."

"Oh, dear," said Elle.

"I think it's good news, Mom. She said HMO is gonna want you to go to Normandy."

Elle wondered why Gremmie didn't let Charlotte call back and put the whole message on her answering machine.

Gremmie said that was the only message Ms. Burr wanted to leave. Anyway, she was quite capable of taking a message—and getting it right, too.

"Honey, I know you are. I know."

After Gremmie excused herself and said good night, Richards made a move to leave. "No, wait," said Elle. "Let's talk a minute."

"About?" Richards felt that HMO's decision to send Elle to Normandy—without him—was premature. He was angry. And when he was angry, he was curt.

"About the Normandy trip, of course. What do suppose got into the people at HMO?"

"Does it matter? You're going. What difference does it make to ask why?"

Elle was subdued. "I don't know. But I'd like you to come with me. And I'm going to ask about it tomorrow." "Good," he said. "You do that."

★ ★ ★

As it turned out, Elle didn't even have to ask. When she appeared in Charlene Burr's office early the next morning, it was apparent that her boss had already been there for some time. Charlene Burr's desk was piled with files, and she was sorting them and packing some of them into her briefcase. She was a large, buxom woman and wore her long blond hair in a bun.

"I want you to take your friend Richards with you to Normandy," she said to Elle.

Elle thought that was very abrupt. But she realized that Charlene was in a hurry. "What's happening?"

"The world's biggest media mogul, Foster Kane, has just bought HMO, and we're scrambling to make HMO over the way he wants it. He wants to expand our scope—a lot. No more 'just movies.' He's convinced there's a big, new public appetite for news. 'Reality-based programming,' he calls it. For us, that means more movies that spin out of real life. That also means hot, compelling, fearless documentaries. One of Kane's lieutenants in New York phoned me at home last night and gave me the word. If I want to keep my job, I have to go to New York. Today. With as many new ideas as I can bring to the table."

"Where do I come in?" asked Elle.

"That documentary on Sonny Skies? If you and Richards are on the right track with it—and I think you are—you're not only going to have a great documentary. You're going to make news with it, too. That's just what Kane wants."

"You think we're right about Howard Kenelly? That he

had Sonny sent off to die in Normandy so he could have his way with Frances Farnsworth?"

Charlene nodded. "Prove it and we'll both be sitting pretty with Mr. Kane."

"So that's why you want me to move fast?"

"That's not the only reason. Seems that Mr. Kane has been charmed by three wealthy Australian widows. He comes from Australia, you know. Well, the husbands of these widows were among the few Australian soldiers in Normandy on D day. Apparently they're big fans of Sonny Skies. And even though this is two years before the official D day commemoration, they're determined to dig up the body of Sonny Skies."

"Wait a minute. Let me get this straight. They're Australians, but they want to exhume the body of Sonny Skies?"

"Well, not exactly. They want the U.S. Army to do it. In fact, the army has already agreed to it."

"Why on earth would the army want to do that?"

"It's Mr. Kane. This has been in the works for some time. And Mr. Kane has persuaded the Pentagon that Sonny Skies, the only Hollywood star to die during combat in World War II, deserves a proper new burial, with honors, at Arlington National Cemetery."

"How could he do *that?*"

"Apparently he shamed a top aide to the army chief of staff. He took the man to a wet lunch at the Palm in Washington, and when Kane asked him what the U.S. Army was going to do to commemorate D day. The guy said, 'Nothing that I know of.' Kane whaled into him. Wondered where the man's patriotism was. Right there in the middle of the Palm, in front of God and man and everybody. That was the right button to push, I guess, because, next thing anybody knew, the Pentagon had a letter on Mr. Kane's desk telling him they were going to start hyping D day. One way to do that was to create some so-called news stories."

"Like digging up Sonny Skies and bringing his body to Washington, D.C?"

"Pretty weird, huh? Make a big deal out of a reburial, with honors, at Arlington. Which is why I want you *and* Mr. Richards to go to Normandy. Meet the body coming up out of the grave, as it were. In front of our cameras. Exclusive. No one else knows about this, so keep it to yourself."

"Why Mr. Richards? You know he was fired at the *Flick* because he got them in a big libel suit?" She wanted to help Richards. But she didn't want Charlene getting into trouble if Richards ever screwed up.

Charlene's reaction surprised her. "He's precisely the kind of guy Mr. Kane likes. To him, libel suits are proof that a good news operation is doing its job."

Elle was shocked—and thrilled. Libel suits! She had a feeling her life was going to get very interesting—and maybe a little dangerous. "Okay, when do you want us to leave?"

"When *can* you go? Can you leave Gremmie? The little unburial ceremony will take place in Normandy on, let's see —" She consulted a note on her desk calendar. "July fourteenth. That's a Tuesday."

Elle said, "Gremmie's no problem. She's out of school. She was already planning to spend some of her summer with her grandparents in the Valley. Her dad's also planning a trip for the two of them to Alaska."

Charlene Burr nodded. "Good!" She explained to Elle that she wanted her to arrange for a camera crew from London to go shoot the footage in Normandy. "When I hit Mr. Kane's New York office tomorrow morning, I want to be able to tell him I already have three or four things in the works, things that anticipate his yen to have his media entities deeply involved in 'what's really happening.' That's what he likes to say: 'what's really happening.' I also want to tell him we're already staffing the exhumation of Sonny Skies."

Charlene Burr zipped up her briefcase and looked directly at Elle. "If you hadn't informed me that people in

France were going to make D day into a big deal in 1994, I would have been lagging yesterday. Instead, I could tell Mr. Kane's lieutenant we were on the same page with Sonny Skies, and maybe a page or two ahead of him."

Charlene paused. "I just wanted to thank you and say, 'Good going.'" She smiled and raised her hand, and Elle slapped her palm with hers. It was a congratulatory gesture, one Elle had learned from watching the Dodgers on TV. Elle had told Charlene she didn't know a thing about American baseball, so Charlene, a mentor of Elle's in more ways than one, had taken her to a couple of Dodger games. Elle was still trying to puzzle out the game by watching it on TV.

Charlene picked up her purse and a carry-on bag and asked Elle to walk her to the exit, where a limo was picking her up. "You can help me with my briefcase, huh?"

On the way to the limo, Charlene Burr told Elle that she wanted HMO to do a Ken Burns kind of treatment on D day. "I want you to stay in touch with me. I may want you—and Richards—to help us out in Normandy with some other interviews. Before you come home."

Elle's head was whirling. Working on a second documentary on D day while she was trying to put together *The Search for Sonny Skies* might be taking on too much. But she didn't feel it was a good idea to show anything but complete understanding—and a willingness to work. She asked her boss how much autonomy she was going to get.

Charlene Burr said, "I'll probably be talking to you on the phone from New York. But you just go ahead and do what you have to do. Don't worry how much anything costs. Get all the extra footage you can that might help us tell the story of Sonny Skies at Ste.-Mère-Église. And anywhere else around there. There's a place called Omaha Beach. Funny name for a beach in France, isn't it? Maybe I got it wrong. And tell Richards I will phone him from New York tomorrow."

☆ ☆ ☆

A little over a week later, on a Friday afternoon, Jay Richards and Elle McBrien jetted from LAX to London non-stop, first-class, taking Virgin Airways (and HMO) for all they had. For comfort, they were wearing jogging suits and Nikes. Elle's was a stylish white, emblazoned with a rainbow of green arcs, all different shades of green. Richards's suit was gray with a red stripe. So were his new Nike shoes, gray with a red stripe. They weren't shoes-shoes, but he told himself he hadn't purchased them in defiance of Elle. He just wanted to travel in comfort. So, it turned out, did she. She had new Nikes, too.

His head was still reeling. Charlotte Burr had phoned him, not to give him a job at HMO, which is what he'd been hoping for, but something better: a $1,000-a-day consultancy. His mandate: to help Elle get the story of Sonny Skies, the full story, no holds barred. If HMO had to expose a bunch of dead white males for sending Sonny Skies to his death on D day, well, that was what she—and Foster Kane—wanted. He had agreed with her on that aspect of the story. It was a piece of investigative reporting that had loads of promise. But Richards wondered out loud about the exhumation of the body of Sonny Skies. Wasn't it slightly dotty to dig it up in France and move it to the United States?

She had laughed. "Get with it, Richards. 'All the world's a stage, and all the men and women merely players.'"

"I can handle that," he told her. "I just didn't think I was going to have a supporting role in such a dumb show."

She met his piece of insolence with silence. Maybe, thought Richards, Charlene Burr wanted to say and do all the funny things on this stage. But damn it, he wasn't at all sure he liked the idea that his taking the *Flick* down with a libel action was exactly the qualification Charlene Burr needed to put him on the payroll. He liked to think he was—

usually—better than the Verdugo incident might have indicated. But what the hell? If Foster Kane wanted yellow journalism, he knew he could certainly provide it. The main thing: He wasn't on poverty row any longer. And, most important, he was with Elle.

☆ ☆ ☆

Elle and Richards checked into separate but adjoining rooms at the London Hilton. It was Saturday afternoon when they arrived, and they tried to avoid jet lag by fitting into the hurly-burly of London on a balmy night in July. They showered and changed into casual evening clothes, caught supper at an Italian restaurant in SoHo—Elle's choice—and, just before curtain, slipped into some half-price stalls to see the latest Stoppard play. Clever fellow, Stoppard, but neither Elle nor Richards could concentrate closely enough on the play to really enjoy him.

Not this night. They should have been tired from the trip, but each of them held an electrical charge, one that kept jumping back and forth between them whenever they touched. In the darkened cab, after the theater, their lips barely met and gave off sparks. "Whoa!" said Richards. "What's happening?"

Elle said, "We are." She put a gentle hand on his knee.

"Oh." Richards was surprised by her touch. He suspected that their mutual vows of celibacy had ended. Maybe it was the transatlantic trip. Maybe travel, as Michael Jackson once said, *was* an aphrodisiac. He suspected this when he learned that Elle did not phone her parents in London, hoping this meant that she wanted to spend what little time they had here with him. His suspicions were confirmed when they got their room keys from the concierge and, alone on the elevator, held a kiss all the way up to the twentieth floor.

She didn't have to ask him in. He knew. Once inside her room, he kissed her, and she responded again, wetly, warmly. They stood there in the dark, their tongues inter-twined. He stood back. "Can we have a little light?" he said.

"Over here," she said, leading him to her bed. She turned on a lamp on the far side of the room, then came back, put her arms around his shoulders, and pulled him down to the bed, on top of her. They kissed some more. When she started to sigh, he rose and kicked off his shoes. She stood and pulled back the bedclothes, took off her blouse, and lay down. He followed her lead by removing only his shirt. They were shy at first, disrobing bit by bit, until finally they were naked together and glowing.

They walked in Regent's Park, hand in hand the next morning, stopping three times in the first several yards they covered to kiss each other deeply. They returned to the ho-tel, had coffee in the lobby, then took the elevator back up to the twentieth floor. She pulled him into her room and asked him how much time they had.

"None," he said. "We have a meeting in half an hour with our film team."

"Oh," she said. "A pox on them." She giggled.

"You're kidding."

"Yes, I am." She looked at her watch. "We have less than a half hour. And I still have to dress. And you. You might put on some real shoes."

Their film crew consisted of a cameraman and a soundman. The man with the camera was Colin Coyne, a wiry little guy with a lot of hair and a ruddy complexion. The soundman was Stephen Cord, a tall, round fellow with a sandy handlebar mustache. They were young, not too pro-fane in Elle's presence, and eager to get the work. They knew they'd get extra pay for going abroad, even if it was only to France, and double that pay because they were being asked to get their gear together over the weekend. Coyne and Cord agreed to meet them at Heathrow at noon on Monday, where they would catch a twelve-passenger prop plane for Le Havre. From there, Coyne would rent a van for the trip to Ste.-Mère-Église.

"These three Australian ladies?" asked Colin Coyne. "They already in Normandy?"

"That's what we understand," said Elle. "We're to meet them at the Hôtel DeVille in Ste.-Mère-Église."

The plane trip was uneventful. So was the van ride to Ste.-Mère-Église. Neither Coyne nor Cord were very fluent in French, but Elle was. She helped them negotiate a better rate on their van rental, and soon they were zipping along a two-lane road with little traffic, through rolling farmland, where the parcels were broken up by giant hedgerows.

To Richards, Elle McBrien was a glittering diamond. Now another facet of her personality had begun to shine. "Where," he asked fondly, "did you learn French?"

"Hey," she said, "most London kids who go to good schools learn French. We also took holidays in France and practiced like crazy."

Richards shook his head and smiled. He knew all kinds of people were multilingual, many of them of only average I.Q. But he considered anyone who knew how to speak more than one language a genius.

By 4:00 P.M., they were checking into their hotel. It wasn't very big—twenty rooms at best. The sign on the front said, simply: *Hôtel.* It didn't have any other name. It wasn't the "Hôtel DeVille." The citizenry simply called it *"l'hôtel de ville."*

Elle asked about the three Australian ladies. The concierge said they were off doing some sight-seeing but had booked supper and had left a note for Mademoiselle

McBrien. She took it, read it, and told the others, "We're invited to join the Australian ladies for supper. At nine P.M."

It had rained that morning, but now the rain had passed, and the sun was out. Colin Coyne said, "We've got a few hours. I think I'd like to look over the American cemetery. Anyone care to join me?"

Elle said she wanted to get a little rest. Richards could understand why. They'd made love during most of the night before, and Elle had been yawning for the past hour. He decided that she'd rest better without his presence, so he said he'd join Coyne.

"Good," said Coyne. "You won't have to change. Your jogging suit is perfect. It's going to be a bit wet out there." He explained that there were still four hours of light left. The late-afternoon sun, he said, could yield them some spectacular shots of the grave markers. Nice long shots. Then a close-up of the marker of Sonny Skies.

They met the assistant curator of the cemetery, a Monsieur Duval, who said he was excited about the ceremonies the next day. And then they went out and got some very usable footage—some close-ups of the marker of Sonny Skies, some long shots of the entire cemetery at sunset. They returned to the hotel just in time to get out of their wet things and dress for dinner. Richards even put on a pair of shoes.

The three Australian widows were all bleached blondes and a little overweight. Daphne Doyle, Cynthia William, and Stephanie Slater were steadfast friends, and they were wearing fashionable pantsuits that looked as if they might have come from Paris. They were apparently not a bit worried about spending their fortunes before they died. Richards was direct with them. After the introductions, he asked them why they were here.

Stephanie Slater said, "We spend our days—and our nights—looking for adventure. Wherever we can find it." The other two nodded vigorously.

Hey, Richards thought. These gals are in their seventies.

But they've managed to shed two decades somehow, somewhere, along the way.

"And when we can't find it," hooted Daphne Doyle, "we try to create some. Which is why we're here. We wouldn't be here if we hadn't been able to sell Foster Kane." Everyone laughed. Soon the three of them had the whole table fascinated with their tale—how they had gotten Foster Kane to take an interest in the exhumation of Sonny Skies.

"How did you do it?" asked Richards.

"Not a bit difficult," said Daphne Doyle. "The man got his start in tabloid journalism. You know how the tabloids do it."

Richards rolled his eyes. Yes, *he* knew. But Elle's eyes were glowing, and Richards noted with amusement that she was listening to Daphne Doyle's story with evident relish. And she was the one who didn't like tabloid journalism.

Daphne waved her soup spoon like a baton. "Romance. Murder. Death. Celebrity. Money. All the elemental stuff of most good stories."

Richards added, "Cats who eat parrots—and talk. Two-headed men who have chats together. Jackie Kennedy kidnapped by Martians, as foretold by Jeanne Dixon." Everyone screamed.

Everyone except Daphne. She didn't appreciate Richards's spoiling her story. "A Hollywood star who dies for his country," she continued in a serious tone. "I told Foster Kane this is just one of your elemental stories. Kane could see that right away. Isn't that right, chums?" Her chums nodded.

"How do you know Foster Kane?" asked Elle.

"We're stockholders in his company, Media Unlimited," said Daphne.

"Uh-huh. That where you met? At a stockholders' meeting?"

"No," said Cynthia William. "Eons ago we all belonged to the same yacht club—at Perth. That's when our hubbies were quite the most farley dinkum blokes down under."

"They died together," said Daphne Doyle, "in quite the most frightful storm about twelve miles off the coast." She said it proudly.

"Oh!" cried Elle.

The three of them waved off her sympathy. "We've gotten over it," said Stephanie Slater.

"We had to," said Cynthia William.

"No choice," said Daphne Doyle.

★ ★ ★

The U.S. Army had a whole battalion at the cemetery in the morning, and a band besides. Richards asked one of the bustling lieutenants, who had introduced himself as an army public information officer based in Heidelberg, where they'd come from. He said, "Brussels. The band comes from Brussels. The others, they came in from Cologne."

The soldiers must have arrived at dawn; they had set up a little bleachers for the assembled guests and planted a half-dozen American flags around the grave of Sonny Skies. A hundred American tourists were there, and some local French officials. So was a three-man team from French television.

"What the hell are they doing here?" he said to Elle.

"I don't know. Charlene said we'd have an exclusive on this."

"I wonder how she thought it'd be a secret. The world is crawling with reporters."

"That's right," said a burly, bearded man with a decided Australian accent. He turned to Richards and stuck out a friendly paw. "Riley of the *Sunday Telegraph*. That's a Sydney paper in case you Americans didn't know. But I also string for your *Daily News* in New York."

"Pleased to meetcha," said Richards. He shook the man's hand gravely. He wasn't pleased. The fewer newsmen around this story, the better he liked it. So far, there hadn't been a breath of it leaked anywhere in the United States.

But that was a situation that wouldn't last.

When the diggers opened the grave of Sonny Skies, they found nothing, not even an empty coffin.

Elle and Richards were right behind Colin Coyne and Stephen Cord. The two of them hesitated when they saw the looks of stunned surprise on the faces of the diggers, who were assisted by a big piece of machinery called a backhoe. "Come on," Elle said to Coyne and Cord. "Get your asses right in there. Get the hole. Get the hole. Stay with me. I want to talk to the commander here, and I want you to keep the camera running no matter what!"

Richards was amazed. Yes, he was amazed to find no trace of Sonny Skies. But he was even more amazed at the transformation of Elle McBrien. Not too long ago she had told Richards she didn't much like reporters. Now she had suddenly turned into Tabloid Tess.

The commander, a Major Watkins, tried to maintain his composure in face of Elle's insistent questions. Yes, he had the right marker. Yes, he had checked and double-checked his orders. It was DD-114. "But there must be some mistake," he said.

Elle turned to Richards. "Those the numbers you had?" she demanded. "DD-114?"

Richards was looking at his notebook. "Yes, I am ninety-nine percent certain this is the address I got from Morley."

"And Morley got it from the Pentagon?"

"From Suitland."

"And what is Suitland?"

"Record warehouse in Maryland. Pentagon warehouse."

"Maybe," said Elle, "we have the wrong cemetery."

"Is this likely?" asked Richards. "This battalion didn't get the information from me, you know! They got it from the Pentagon."

"Well, maybe they got it from the same place Morley got it. From Suitcase."

"Suitland."

"Suitland, then."

Richards shrugged.

By now the three widows from Australia had climbed down out of the bleachers and were making their way through the crowd. Then they were circling the grave site of Sonny Skies, swooping down on Major Watkins like three vultures, or maybe *Macbeth*'s witches. Richards half-expected to hear them chanting, "Double double, toil and trouble."

Major Watkins tried to walk away from them so he could confer with some of his officers and with a very large and very intelligent looking and very black staff sergeant. The sergeant whispered in the major's ear, and in moments the two of them were sprinting for a nearby Jeep. With the sergeant behind the wheel, the two of them headed for the cemetery's office.

"Come on," said Elle to the camera crew, "let's follow 'em."

"Wait!" cried Daphne Doyle.

"Later!" shouted Elle. The four of them—Richards and Elle and Colin Coyne and Stephen Cord—jumped back into Coyne's rented van and headed over to the offices with the sign outside that read: *Musée.*

There was only one burly man on duty. It was the man Richards and the crew had met the day before, M. Duval. He was talking to Major Watkins and his sergeant when the four of them burst in. Riley of the *Telegraph* was right behind them.

The curator spoke English, but with a decided accent. Yes, this was Ste.-Mère-Église. No, there was no other cemetery here other than what they could see. He waved his hand toward the crowd that was milling around the marker of Sonny Skies.

The major looked angrily over at the film crew, which

was shooting away, but there was nothing he could do about them now. He turned his attention back to the curator, who was now being grilled by Major Watkins's sergeant. "You have some records of the men buried here?"

"But of course," said M. Duval. He'd been a jolly fellow the day before, but he looked very unhappy now, almost as if the snafu was his fault. He led the sergeant (and the trailing major) over to a large, modern file cabinet. "We have our guests cataloged by name, by unit, and by, how you say it, 'hometown?' We have three master lists."

"Try the name first," said the major. "Sonny Skies." He spelled it for M. Duval. Yes, the cemetery's name file had Sonny Skies listed at the same site, DD-114. He also had him listed with the other men in his unit, the 508th, also slotted in DD-114. And in his California file, which had only seven names in it, Sonny Skies was again listed. Also at DD-114.

Elle was angry, and she paced back and forth while the curator and the sergeant and the major dithered. Finally, she stopped her pacing, stomped over to the group, and suggested they look under another name. "Maybe he was buried under another name," she said. "Try Homer Brownlee."

Richards intervened. "That's probably it. His legal name. That's probably how the army knew him."

The major snarled at them. But then, exasperated, he told M. Duval to look under the name of Homer Brownlee. Maybe that was the answer. But there was no Brownlee in this cemetery, either. Now everyone was seething. Elle wondered if there were any other American cemeteries in this area.

"In France?" said M. Duval. "Hundreds!"

"No, here in the Normandy area," said the major. "Our man—I hear he was a great movie star—died on June 6 at or near Omaha Beach. He was a paratrooper. And some eighty percent of his unit were either killed or wounded."

M. Duval said, "Ahh, that is easier, then. There are two other cemeteries near here. I can tell you where they are. Do not fear. This happens all the time. Americans come here to pay honor to their fathers, or their grandfathers, who died parachuting into France. At first, they do not find. Then, after a little searching, they find."

But they searched, and they did not find. A whole caravan, American tourists, the Australian ladies, the Seventy-seventh Infantry Battalion from Cologne, and the U.S. Army band from Brussels, HMO's camera crew, the film crew from French television, and Riley of the *Telegraph* made their winding way to two other cemeteries—one to the east and one to the south of Ste.-Mère-Église—and they found no trace of Sonny Skies. Or of Homer Brownlee either.

The U.S. Army gave up and set out for Cologne, away from the setting sun. The army band packed up and got into their bus for Brussels. The French TV people disappeared. Riley of the *Telegraph* went looking for—what else?—a telegraph. Elle and Richards and their camera crew returned to their hotel and repaired to the bar. They were wet and tired and, not having eaten since breakfast, very hungry. Members of the camera crew were philosophical. "Just one of those things," said Colin Coyne.

"What the hell do you mean?" demanded Richards.

"I just meant—"

"I don't give a damn what you meant," said Richards. "Don't you see—"

The soundman, Stephen Cord, said, "I think I'll have a whiskey."

Richards said, "I think I'll have one, too. I feel like getting drunk."

Elle gave him a sidelong glance and told the waiter, "*Le tonic,*" and held up two fingers, indicating that the tonic water was for her and her angry gentleman friend. "Drink all the tonic you want," she whispered into his ear, "We've got to get to an AA meeting. We've gone too long without a meeting."

He growled softly, "I don't give a damn about the goddamned AA. How could we have come so far for so little? How stupid! The people at HMO will be furious."

Elle agreed. But then the Australian ladies arrived. "Isn't it too delicious?" gushed Daphne Doyle. "Now you've got yourself a real story! Imagine! Somebody snatched the body of Sonny Skies!"

Elle and Richards both blinked. Yes, that was the logical conclusion, wasn't it? They had to learn to think more like tabloid reporters. Richards could just see the headline in the *Daily News* over Riley's dispatch from Normandy: "France Swallows Half-Pint."

Now everyone in the bar joined in the game—for a game it was. It was called Sleuth, and the Australian ladies were past masters at developing all possible scenarios. They had a riotous time of it, including Coyne and Cord, normally taciturn fellows until they started on the whiskey. Coyne had a logical answer to the whole thing. The Jerrys found Sonny Skies's dead body dangling from his parachute in a treetop, and they just spirited him away. The others loved that idea.

"But why on earth would Herr Hitler want the body of Sonny Skies?" said Stephanie Salter.

"It would be a trump card at the peace talks!" said Daphne Doyle.

"He'd trade the body of Sonny Skies for a letter of transit to Lisbon," said Cynthia William.

"Or Brazil," said Stephanie Salter.

Neither Elle nor Richards joined in the fun. The others put them down for not drinking, and Cord made a nasty remark about reformed drunks—which prompted Elle and Richards to excuse themselves, as they wanted to get some supper before the dining room closed.

Over a delicious *paillarde de veaux,* they tried to put the situation in perspective. As far as HMO was concerned, Elle said, they now had a much better story on their hands.

"Yes," said Richards. "But our friends in there"—he waved in the direction of the bar—"are all barking up the wrong tree. The Germans didn't grab the body of Sonny Skies."

"Because?"

"Because Sonny Skies was never a part of the Normandy invasion."

Elle shook her head.

"You disagree?"

"I don't know, Rich. It's pretty far-fetched."

"What? That the U.S. Army was lying?"

"Yes. I just don't think the army would lie about a celebrity like Sonny Skies—say he was killed in action when he wasn't. I mean, what if some newspaperman wanted to check out the story?"

"Newsmen didn't check official stories in those days," said Richards. "Particularly in the middle of the war. And those were the days when the government told the truth."

"What about Hollywood newsmen?"

"That's an oxymoron."

A contradiction in terms?"

"Right! I oughta know. Hollywood news is news by handout. In this case, whatever the army handed out on Sonny Skies was the first word and the last word."

"And no one ever bothered to interview members of his parachute battalion?"

Richards shrugged. "Apparently not."

They were both silent for more than a minute, pondering the implications. Finally, Elle said, "But this is too incredible. If Sonny Skies isn't here, then where is he? How did he die? And when?"

"And where," said Richards. "We have to ask where he died."

"Yes," she said.

"Fort Huachuca?" said Richards. "I wonder if he died at Fort Huachuca."

9

Elle McBrien and Jay Richards were both ready for collapse when they returned from London to Los Angeles. They had left London at noon and arrived at LAX at five—a very long afternoon that left the two of them exhausted. "I want nothing so much as sleep," said Elle. "Alone, in my own bed."

"Me, too," said Richards. He didn't really feel that way. For five days in Europe, he'd gotten used to sleeping with Elle. Why stop now? But he was too tired to push it. He told the cab to wait for him, helped Elle get her things into her apartment, and then headed to his own place.

He found six messages on his answering machine. None of them seemed as important as the one he had from his friend at the *Washington Post*. "Rich, this is Dan. I saw some cockamamy story in the *Daily News* about the empty grave of Sonny Skies. But nobody else seems to be working on it. The AP had a twenty-second item on it on their radio wire, and the story died. I think the *Times* is too busy with something called the election of a president. Looks like Clinton might pull an upset. But I'm sure you don't give a damn about that. I've got some intriguing news for you. Your man never got back to Fort Huachuca after his mother's funeral. Interesting? Call me."

"All right!" said Richards. He phoned Elle immediately. The phone rang four times before she answered.

"Elle!"

Her voice was full of sleep. "Rich?" she said. "Couldn't it wait?"

He was still miffed that she hadn't wanted to sleep with him. And now he was pained by this rebuff. "Oh, sure," he said. "Sorry. Call me when you get up." Then he hung up before she had a chance to respond.

She phoned him right back. "Now *I'm* sorry," she said. "You wouldn't have called if you didn't have something good."

"It's all right," he said. "Go back to sleep."

"Not now." She paused, waiting for him to tell her the news. When he didn't, she said, "Come on. Don't pout. Tell me."

He hesitated; then he told her about Dan Morley's message.

"Did you call him back?"

"I'll call him tomorrow. But I wanted you to know."

"Okay, okay," she said. "This will help. Now it makes our course clear. If Sonny never got back to Fort Huachuca, then we have to retrace his steps in L.A."

"In a way, we already have. Elle, we have to take another look at your tape of Billy Dwyre. I think Dwyre may be the man who can help us."

"But will he tell us anything?" she said. "That's the question."

"Ve haff vays to make him talk."

"Torture, huh?"

"Maybe something close to that. How about we threaten to take him to the D.A. for molesting a minor?"

Elle said, "You've got to be kidding."

"Okay," said Richards. "Let's just pay Dwyre a call. Tomorrow?"

"Okay," she said. "Good night."

Hell, Richards told himself, if I can wake up Elle, I can wake up Morley. He looked at his watch. It was nine o'clock. Midnight in D.C. He phoned Morley and apologized.

"No, it's all right," said Morley.

Richards told him—quickly—about their chaotic time in Normandy. "I'm just worried that we're going to have a lot of competition on our story, on our search for Sonny Skies."

"By the time the *New York Times* and the *L.A. Times* wakes up," said Morley, "we'll have the case solved. We still have a deal, don't we?"

Richards said, "Absolutely."

Morley said, "You were right about this all along. You figured Sonny Skies was never with the guys of the Twenty-ninth Infantry Division. I have to agree. There was never enough time for Sonny Skies to transfer from the cavalry to the infantry—to the paratroopers at that—and get shipped off to England in time for the invasion of Normandy. That's why I had my friend at Suitland go back and check on Fort Huachuca. And as I said on my message, Sonny Skies never reported back to Fort Huachuca."

"Could he have gone directly from his furlough in L.A. to the 508 in England?"

"Could have. But not likely."

"Can you have your friend at Suitland do some cross-checking? Find out for sure?"

"I've already asked."

"And she will do it?"

"Do bears poop in the woods?"

"That good a friend, huh?"

"Uh-huh. I was with her tonight."

"All right!" Richards was thinking out loud. "You know, Danny boy, this story could win you a prize."

"Hey," he said, "I already won a prize."

Richards had forgotten. Five years ago, Morley had been part of an investigative team that won a Pulitzer. "Well, another prize."

"We'll see," said Morley. "Keep me posted."

Richards's telephone told him he had another call waiting. "Okay," he said to Morley. "We'll stay in touch."

The other caller was Elle. "I can't sleep. I'm a jumble of thoughts. I think Billy Dwyre is more central to this thing than we ever thought. I want to go over his tape again with you."

"Talking about Dwyre isn't going to put you to sleep. Just get your mind spinning faster."

"Yes," she said. "That's why I called. I want to sleep with you. Correction. I want you to come sleep with me."

He laughed and said, "I'll be right over." Elle had never said she was in love with him. But now it was apparent she was in lust, at least. As tired as they were, they kissed, caressed, and made love, and the name of Sonny Skies was never mentioned. Their spent passion was the soporific that Elle had been looking for. They slept a solid eight hours, and both of them awoke looking at each other, smiling.

"Yes, it is a good morning," he said.

"Let's watch that Dwyre tape again," she said.

"No coffee first?"

"I'm out of coffee. I have tea."

"Yuck. Let's watch the tape, then go over to Maisie's."

Elle found the tape and fast-forwarded to Billy Dwyre.

So the two of them watched Billy Dwyre in action again the same Billy Dwyre who tipped his every lying word.

Here was Richards on the videotape: "You saw him at the funeral?"

"Yes. I was with him the whole time. Met him at the church. Went to the cemetery with him. Forest Lawn."

"Interesting," noted Elle. She stopped the tape, rewound it for a few moments, then let it run again. "I was with him the whole time."

"No heel lift here," she interjected.

"Met him at the church."

"That's a definite heel lift. He didn't meet Sonny at the church. In all probability, he drove Sonny to the church."

"Went to the cemetery with him. Forest Lawn."

Elle said, "No heel lift there."

"Was Frances Farnsworth there?"

No.

"Who was there?"

"Just Sonny and me and the preacher and a couple guys worked for Forest Lawn."

"No heel lift in any of that," said Elle.

Back on the tape, Richards was asking, "And then what happened after the ceremony?"

And Dwyre was responding, "And then Sonny took off."

"How did he take off?"

"Now here it comes," said Elle. "The big lie."

And that's what the videotape demonstrated. "Let's see. I, uh. I think he was driving a rental car. Planned to leave it at the Santa Monica Airport and take a charter to Fort Huachuca. That's the last I saw him."

"See the heel come up?" said Elle.

"Way up. No doubt."

"So it's not likely," said Elle, "that Sonny had a rental car. He had three cars at that time. It is highly probable that he was using one of his own cars on that L.A. furlough. He had a Lincoln Continental, didn't he? Car given to him by Henry Ford himself? His favorite set of wheels?"

"Yes," said Richards. "So why would he rent an ordinary car?"

"And that moment at the airport?" said Elle. "I don't think it was the last time Billy Dwyre saw Sonny Skies. I think he was there when Sonny met his untimely end."

"Where?"

"I don't know. But it had to be somewhere in L.A."

It was the same scene with Dwyre in Oxnard. Same upscale trailer court. Same pool. Same chairs and table. Same nymphet sunning herself nearby. Only this time it would be different.

Elle McBrien was there with a still camera so they could get copies of the pictures in Dwyre's photo album. That was no ruse. They really wanted those pictures. Elle also had her minicam so they could have Dwyre tell them about his own work in the two Sonny Skies musicals with Noelle Sparks. That was the ruse. At this point, Richards didn't give a rat's ass about the budding musical-comedy career of Billy Dwyre. He wanted Dwyre to tell them how Sonny Skies met his demise one smoggy day fifty years ago in L.A.

But they feigned fascination with Dwyre's account of his career in musical comedy—of how chances like this didn't come along every day in Hollywood, of how he studied for the musical parts with a voice coach and two dance coaches, of how he—well, he never got any other roles in a musical, but he came close a couple times. Got an audition with Steve Ross, who was one of Busby Berkeley's protégés, and he might have had a role in *Dolly's Follies* if only he had agreed to sleep with Steve Ross; that was the trouble with Hollywood, wasn't it? Even a guy who liked girls had to sleep with a director every now and then if he wanted to get ahead.

Finally, Elle made a show for Dwyre's benefit. Her minicam had jammed. She wasn't sure why. When she started to fiddle with it, Richards made a little show of his own. He removed the Lavalier mike from Dwyre's shirtfront, put down his notebook, and plunged into a line of questioning that might, just might, be a moment of truth in the search for Sonny Skies.

"Billy," he said, "we've done some checking with the Pentagon about Sonny Skies."

"The Pentagon?"

"The U.S. Army's records center at Suitland, Maryland, actually. According to those records, Sonny Skies was given a furlough on May 25, 1944—to come home for his mom's funeral on the twenty-ninth. But he never made it back to Fort Huachuca."

"He didn't?"

"No, Billy, he didn't. He just disappeared. *Phttttt!* Like that, he was gone, as far as the army's concerned." Richards glanced over at Elle. She was still fiddling with her minicam. But if she was able to do what he knew she intended, she was taping a wide shot of this colloquy and recording it on a small shotgun mike, with a subject, Dwyre, who was unaware he was speaking on the record.

"Well, hell," said Dwyre, "he was a war hero. Killed in Normandy."

"That's bullshit, Billy, and you know it." Richards was surprised at his own vehemence.

Dwyre shook his head. He was speechless. Finally, he said, "How can you say that?"

"Easy. Elle and I jetted to Normandy last week to get some shots at Sonny's grave marker in the U.S. cemetery at Ste.-Mère-Église. We found a grave marker. But no grave. And no Sonny."

"But he got a Bronze Star. Posthumous, it was. Citations from the army, along with a lot of other brave boys who lost their lives parachuting behind the Nazi lines."

"All a charade, Billy. The *Washington Post* has some investigative reporters looking into the whole mess as we speak."

"Well, that's what they told me. Why would the army lie about it?"

"I don't know. Maybe the same reason as you, Billy?"

"Hey, I wasn't lying to you!"

Richards glanced down at Dwyre's boot. His right heel had risen three inches. "Yes, Billy, you were. But now you're gonna tell us the truth."

"I am?"

"Yes, Billy, yes, you are. Otherwise, we're gonna file charges against you."

"Charges? For something that happened fifty years ago?"

"We weren't thinking about fifty years ago, Billy. We were thinking of right now. How'd you like to face charges of statutory rape?"

Dwyre's head swiveled to the voluptuous young body of Timmi Tyler, sunning herself ten yards away. "You mean my daughter?"

"No. Not your daughter. We've checked on your so-called adoption. You and your wife had the county's foster care division declare Timmi a ward of the juvenile court. And you had her put in your care—at some cost to the county—and that was the end of any overview by the county. You're in deep shit on this, Billy."

"You wouldn't turn me in!" he said. "Timmi's not here against her will, you know. She likes being with me. You've seen that."

Richards lowered his voice so Elle couldn't hear. "*I* might not turn you in," he said, "if you help us on this other matter—a fifty-year-old matter that may, in fact, be far beyond any statute of limitation."

"You mean Sonny?"

"Yes, I mean Sonny. You—and maybe only you, Billy—can tell us about Sonny's last day on this earth."

" 'Last day on this earth'?"

Dwyre laughed. "You think that?"

"Isn't that what happened, Billy? Didn't Sonny meet with some foul play here in L.A.? Isn't that why he was never seen back at Fort Huachuca?"

Dwyre sighed. Then he smiled. "You dumb shit. You're just guessing. How do you know Sonny Skies isn't still alive? Anything I can't stand is a know-it-all. And you don't know shit!" Dwyre got up from his chair. "I gotta go take a pee."

"Whew!" said Richards to Elle as he watched Dwyre go off to his trailer. "You get all that?"

"I got it," said Elle. "Some of the video's going to be a

little wild." She pointed to her small shotgun mike. "I got all the audio with this. But I don't know how usable it'll be."

"How come?"

"Most of the last part is you threatening Billy Dwyre. We can't use that."

"Well, we got him telling us Sonny Skies may be alive!"

"That's true. But we have to see what more Billy can tell us. He may be just blowing smoke. Personally, I think Sonny Skies has been dead for forty-eight years."

Richards shrugged, glanced impatiently over toward Dwyre's trailer, and then saw Timmi Tyler. She was walking toward them.

"You get your minicam fixed?" asked the fifteen-year-old blond apparition in a white bikini.

Elle looked up. "I think so," she said.

"I've been watching," Timmi said. "You were having trouble with your minicam. But you got it working. You were shooting all the time, weren't you. Without telling Billy he was on the record?"

Before Elle could answer, Billy Dwyre returned to the pool area, very full of himself. He said he had just talked to his lawyer, who advised him to speak no more. "And he says you can't use any of my stuff on a documentary without getting a release. All I can say is, good thing your minicam hasn't been working."

"Well," said Richards, trying to look disappointed, you gave us some fine memories of your career in musical comedy."

"Yes," he said, "but even on that, on me and Sonny and Noelle Sparks, you're gonna have to get a release. From me. And I ain't gonna give you one 'less I get paid. Good."

"A release?" As a journalist, Richards had never gotten a release in his life. People told him things. He printed them. But this documentary for HMO wasn't exactly journalism. Maybe Billy Dwyre was right. "Your lawyer," he said. Is he a criminal lawyer?"

"Entertainment. He specializes in entertainment law."

"Well, Billy, I think you better ask him to refer you to a criminal lawyer." He nodded toward Timmi Taylor. " 'Cause you're gonna need one."

"Come on, Rich," said Elle. She had her camera slung over her shoulder, and she handed Richards her tripod and her tote bag; she was moving toward her Volvo. "Let's get out of here."

They stowed their gear in Elle's Volvo, with Billy Dwyre and Timmi Tyler looking on silently from fifty paces away. Elle got behind the wheel and turned on the engine before Richards got in the car. "Come on," she said, and her voice had steel in it. "The kid is on to me. You heard her. She knows I was shooting Billy when he thought my camera wasn't working. Let's get out of here before she tells him."

Richards got in the car. But he had one more thing he wanted to ask Billy Dwyre. He turned and saw Timmi Tyler whispering something in Dwyre's ear. And suddenly Billy was striding toward them with an ax that had appeared magically in his upraised hand.

Elle gunned the Volvo and squealed out of there, spraying sand and gravel behind her.

★ ★ ★

"Why'd you peel out like that?" asked Richards once they were on the main road headed south.

Elle slowed down. "You see that ax he had? You want to go back and find out what he was planning to do with it?"

He laughed. "Well, we got a lot today. We didn't get everything. But we got a lot."

Elle said, "You're pretty sure we're not looking for a dead man, aren't you? You think Sonny Skies is still alive."

"Billy Dwyre would like me to think so."

"But if he's alive, where is he?"

Richards said, "I can't help but think Howard Kenelly was involved in this. And may still be involved."

"But Kenelly's dead."

"I think his reach extends beyond the grave."

"Meaning?"

"Meaning I think there was some kind of collusion between Howard Kenelly and the U.S. Army. Old Howard wanted Sonny put out of the way. I think he got the army to help him do it. He was very close to the highest army brass. He even had a lot of them on the pad. After the war, all sorts of high-ranking officers went to work for Howard Kenelly, for God's sake. So would they finagle around with the service record of Sonny Skies? Hell, yes, they would, if ol' Howard asked them to. Who'd ever know?"

"They wouldn't be taking a chance by billing him as a war hero?"

"Big lies are always easier to float than little ones," Richards said, and noticed that Elle had been stepping on the gas, fearful, perhaps, that Dwyre was in hot pursuit.

"I suppose so," she said. "But that was then. What about now?"

"Cover-ups are harder today, after Watergate. But I think the Kenelly cover-up goes on. I'll bet my membership in the Backstabbers that Billy Dwyre knows more than he's telling. And that he won't remember anything as long as he's being paid off to keep quiet."

Elle had been speeding along the coast highway south of Oxnard, and as Richards paused to collect his thoughts, she glanced in the rearview mirror. When she saw a Ventura County sheriff's car coming up behind them, she slowed down.

Richards didn't see the cop car. "Yeah," he said. "You don't have to go eighty miles an hour. Nobody's chasing you." That's when the red light went on in the cruiser behind them. "Whoops!" said Richards. "I was wrong."

Elle pulled over to the shoulder. Two officers, one man

and one woman, got out of the sheriff's car. The woman officer spoke first—to Elle. "May I see your license, please?"

Elle handed it over.

The officer was very polite. "My partner is going to stand by while I get on the radio. Please excuse me."

Elle began to tremble. Looking stiffly ahead, she whispered to Richards, "What's going on?"

"Maybe Dwyre called one of his old buddies in the sheriff's office. Maybe they're checking us out."

"For what? Can they arrest us?"

"I guess they can do anything they want to do."

But Richards was wrong. The woman officer—the name over her pocket said she was Sergeant O'Shaughnessy—returned and said, "Ms. McBrien? Doesn't seem we have any reason to hold you. Maybe it was a mistake."

"Maybe what was a mistake?"

"We had a bulletin on a car that matches yours, but it's been withdrawn. Take it easy on your drive back to Hollywood." She smiled and gave Elle a little salute.

Elle nodded, still afraid to smile. She eased out onto the freeway and stepped on the gas. Only after she got up to 55 mph did she exhale. "What," she said, "do you suppose that was all about?"

"Maybe our friend Dwyre only wanted your name and address," suggested Richards.

"Oh, ducky! What a relief! He *only* wanted my name and address! So he had a sheriff's cruiser come and get it. Well, he's got it now, hasn't he?"

Richards nodded. "First thing to do is get any relevant notes on the Sonny Skies project out of your apartment. Don't leave your tapes there, either."

"You think Dwyre might break in?"

"Wouldn't put it past him. Or he may hire some goon."

"Great!"

"Maybe you'd better stay with me."

She thought for a moment. "Yes," she said finally.

"I'm sorry," said Richards. He knew she wasn't ready to move in with him permanently or even semipermanently.

"Hey, don't be sorry," she said. "Now we got people chasing us. Our story just keeps getting better and better. If we live through it." She smiled. But her smile was a little forced.

10

Richards got a phone call from Tom Greenberg the next morning. "Hey," said Greenberg, "welcome back. How'd we do in Normandy?"

"It's 'we,' is it?" asked Richards.

"We did agree to be partners, didn't we, Rich?"

"Partners?"

"Come on, Rich. You got amnesia?"

"I don't have any power to make you a partner, Tom."

"At Chasen's? You don't remember the deal we made at Chasen's?"

"No, no, I don't." They hadn't made a deal at Chasen's. But they had agreed on a fifty-fifty split of the proceeds from Sonny Skies's screen test, way back when Richards had found it during a meeting of the Backstabbers Poker Club.

"You got a short memory, pal. You agreed to give me half of whatever you get out of the Sonny Skies project."

Richards tried to sneer. "We agreed to nothing of the sort. That night at Chasen's, we agreed to disagree. We talked about your lawyer. And we talked about my lawyer. But we didn't agree to become partners."

"I remember your telling me you'd split your share with me."

"My share of what? You want half my plane fare, half my hotel bill in Europe? So far, that's all I've gotten."

"You're not getting a healthy consultant's fee? A nice day rate?"

That surprised Richards. How the hell did Greenberg

know the terms of his sudden deal with HMO? But it was clear he did know. Better, then, not to lie about it. "Yes, I am." He said it defiantly. Better to let Greenberg think he hadn't been trying to hide it. "You want half of that?"

"A deal's a deal," said Greenberg.

"Son of a bitch! You want that? Was my consultant's fee ever a part of any agreement we had?"

"We have nothing on paper," said Greenberg. "You know that. But I've already told you I could make a lot of legal trouble for you—and Elle—at HMO. And you had me back off. My quid pro quo was going halfsies with you on the Sonny Skies deal."

"But I told you, this isn't my independent production. I'm not selling a property to HMO. I'm just trying to help a nice lady get started in the business." Elle had been in the shower. Now she was standing in front of Richards, toweling herself off, listening to his end of the conversation, and making no attempt to hide her beautiful curves. "Or do you want half of *her*, too?"

Greenberg laughed. "Look. I'm not the bastard you think I am."

"I don't think you're a—"

"No?" interrupted Greenberg. How come you didn't phone me when you got back from Europe? How long you been home?"

"Little over forty-eight hours."

"There! See?"

Richards softened. "Tom, if you really want to help me— and Elle—let's talk it over. Face-to-face."

★ ★ ★

The two of them did have a heart-to-heart talk, in Tom and Tillie's kitchen off Laurel Canyon. After swearing Greenberg to secrecy, with only the Greenbergs' calico cat as a witness, Richards told him damn near everything—about finding Sonny Skies's empty grave in Normandy. And about Billy Dwyre's tipping them off to something mysterious that happened to Sonny Skies forty-eight years ago, something that may have sent him into either into an early grave or some kind of exile at the hands of one Howard Kenelly.

"We're on the verge of getting one of the great scoops in the history of Hollywood, Tom."

"Just one more break and you'll have the whole story, huh?"

"Well, maybe not the whole truth. Whoever gets the whole truth of anything? But we could take a giant step if we could get inside the Kenelly industrial empire."

"So how I can help? I'm not the CIA. I'm a record producer. Was a record producer."

"Neither Elle nor I are very good at espionage. Presuming we knew where to look. Which we don't. But if Billy Dwyre was ever getting a payoff from the Kenelly people, it's possible he's still getting a payoff."

"And I have access to the Kenelly payroll?" Greenberg smiled, more of a curious smile than a smart-ass one.

"You don't. But I wonder if Dave Benton—"

Greenberg exploded in laughter. "Fat Ben? You believe his bullshit about being a hacker. You believe the FBI's after him?"

"Look," said Richards, "I never have much truck with Ben's stories. But I know he's had some fairly interesting tales to tell about his meanderings on the Internet. Last conversation I overheard, he was bragging about getting inside MCI. Electronically, that is. If he can do that, get inside MCI, there's no telling what he can do at the Kenelly Corporation."

Greenberg shook his head with bemusement. "Rich, I think you're giving Ben too much credit."

"Well, I just wish you'd ask him."

"Whyn't you ask him yourself? You know Fat Ben as well as I do."

"I just thought if you told him this was going to be a Backstabbers' project—"

"That how you see it now?" Greenberg gave Richards a look of wonder. "A Backstabbers' project?"

"Why not? At least as far I'm concerned. That won't mean you've got a piece of Elle, mind you. Just me. I will go beyond our previous agreement. You seem so interested in getting a piece of my earnings. I *will* give you a piece of my earnings, whatever they are. I'm doing this for Elle, anyway. I'm not really interested in the money."

Greenberg grinned. "Are you in *love?*"

Richards didn't answer. But the look on his face said it.

"Old fart like you? Well, tell you what I'm gonna do." Greenberg reached over and picked up the phone and punched one number—automatic dialing to Dave Benton. "Ben? Tom. Rich is here with me right now. He wants the help of the Backstabbers. Yes, Richards. On the Sonny Skies thing, that's right. He's got the damnedest thing going. Might provide us all with a little excitement in our old age. Uh-huh. Uh-huh." Greenberg looked up at Richards and covered his phone's mouthpiece. "Ben says he wants to come over and talk. Says he's got an idea or two."

★ ★ ★

Dave Benton wasn't pleasant; it was not in his nature to be. But he did have a strong desire to be loved, or, if not loved, at least feared. So after Richards and Greenberg talked at him for an hour, he did allow that he might, just might, be able to help them.

"But if I can help you guys," he whined, "I want a little respect." He looked pained. "I've been the target of your jokes for too long." He gave his best, whiny interpretation of Peter Lorre on the "for too long." He added: "Now I want a little respect. That's all I want. A little respect."

"If you can help us find out what happened to Sonny Skies," said Richards, "you'll have a lotta respect."

"Give me some time," said Benton. "This will take days."

"How will you do it?"

"Heavens to Betsy Ross," said Benton, rolling his eyes, "that would be telling."

☆ ☆ ☆

However he did it, he did it. Three days later, Ben was on the phone to Richards. "After some thirty-six hours on my computer, Mr. Richards, I have some very interesting news for you."

Richards tried to butter him up, in advance. "I have no doubt. If you've been working on this for thirty-six hours, it's going to be very interesting."

"There's an account number out of a slush fund in the office of the chairman at Kenelly Aircraft that gives us a key. I'm not sure what it all means."

"How do you know the account number is significant at all?"

"Because there's very little activity in this account. In fact, only a couple of names: One of them's William J. Dwyre. Sound familiar?"

"Billy Dwyre!"

"Yes, it seems that your friend Billy Dwyre has been getting a nice little monthly stipend here."

"Nice little stipend?"

"Three thousand a month."

"That tells us something," he said. "Who's the other one?"

"Somebody named Ellen Daugherty. Same account number. Name mean anything to you?"

"No. How much she get?"

"Ten thousand a month."

Richards whistled. "Nice piece of change. I wonder what she did for Howard Kenelly?"

Ben shrugged. "Other than ball him, you mean? I don't know. You're the deep thinker. What more do you want from me?"

"Where does the money come from? Can you tell that?"

"Regular transfer from an account at the Howard Medical Foundation. On the computer you can see it come in, and you can see it go out. Compared to all the other ins and outs, though, it's really just chicken feed."

"Have you seen the accounts of the Howard Medical Foundation?"

"No."

Richards asked Ben if he could tap into the records at the foundation.

"Like maybe get some more information about the source account that goes to pay Dwyre. And see what more I can find on this Ellen Daugherty?"

"Yes," said Richards. "Or allied accounts. And Ben?"

"Uh-huh?"

"You might be on the lookout for the name of Homer Brownlee, too. Okay?"

"Who's he?"

"Another guy who might fit in the scenario. Tell you about him later."

Benton said he would see.

☆ ☆ ☆

Richards thought Elle would be ecstatic over this breakthrough—or, to be more exact, break-in. He couldn't wait to tell her when she got to his place that evening after her stint at HMO. But she was not ecstatic. "What you're telling me is that now we're breaking and entering?"

Richards said he didn't think now was the time to get legalistic on him.

"Legalistic? Is that the term you use when you want to ding someone who objects to breaking the law?"

"You got any better ideas?"

She admitted she didn't. "But hiring this Dave Benton character!"

Richards said he hadn't hired him. "What Dave Benton does, he does for kicks."

"You think that someday he isn't going to ask for his pound of flesh?" She tossed him a copy of the day's *New York Times.* "They just happened to have a piece on Benton today. Seems he's a fugitive from justice. The FBI is after him, even though I understand all they have is his hacker's handle. They don't know his real name."

Richards hadn't seen the day's *New York Times.* He scanned the article. "The Fugitive Hacker. Hunt Continues for Man Accused of Raising Havoc With Computers." Elle pretended to be busy in Rich's kitchen, but she was watching to see Richards's reaction to the article. He was obviously amused, for he kept laughing throughout the piece. Some years ago, Ben had apparently gotten involved with a group of hackers, mischievous types who entered the computers at the U.S. Air Force's Air Defense Command at Colorado Springs without ever setting foot in Colorado. They did it all by telephone.

The feds had rounded up the group and given them all probation—on the condition that they never enter another computer system illegally. But the feds had no way of enforcing that. And these guys were addicts of a particular type.

Like many a hacker, according to the article in the *Times,* Benton was a compulsive guy who couldn't help himself. For kicks, he had disconnected people's phones. He had even had huge funds transferred into their checking accounts— funds so huge (one transfer from the U.S. Treasury Department amounted to $7 million) that they'd drawn the immediate attention of bank auditors and the FBI. From there Dave Benton had gone on to other pranks. He had once put an instruction into the computers at Merrill Lynch that would have automatically transferred $1 million every month from the account of a pornographer in the Valley to the account of Mother Teresa. After a month, the move was discovered by an alert trader, and the pornographer was now suing Merrill Lynch *and* Mother Teresa—and having a helluva time getting his million back from the good nun. He had appealed to a federal judge in L.A., guy named Dunne, who happened to be a member of the Knights of Malta, and the judge was stalling the pornographer. And now the FBI was after Benton for intercepting voice mail in the computer system of Pacific Telephone.

"Jeez," said Richards. "Our own Peter Lorre, one of the Backstabbers!"

"Yes, and now he's working for *us!*"

"I don't know whether to laugh or cry," said Richards. But he did know. He was smiling broadly. "All I can hope is that Ben will get us the information we want before they catch him."

Elle laughed. "You're a real piece of work. This is a friend of yours?"

"Hell, no. I can't stand the guy. I won't care if they put him away for life."

"Wouldn't it be funny if you both ended up in prison? Together?"

Richards waved off the thought. "Yeah. That'd be a real stitch."

"Seriously. You think this is all worth it?"

"It is if Ben can tell us anything more about Sonny Skies." Richards shook his head. "I know. You think he's dead. But we still have no proof that he is. I haven't been able to find any death certificate in the records of L.A. County."

"Not for Sonny Skies, not for Homer Brownlee, either?"

"Right!"

Elle said, "They could have buried him under an assumed name."

"If they did, we'd have no way of knowing—not by simply looking at the records."

"He could have died anywhere."

"Also true. In Denver or Detroit or Rio de Janeiro."

"So what are you saying? Where does that leave us?"

"Don't you see? Looking for a death certificate is working at the wrong end. We're only on track when we pick up the trail of Sonny Skies in L.A. back in May 1944."

Elle said, "I'd agree with that. You feel like going for a walk?"

11

When they got home, Richards found two messages on his answering machine. One was from Tom Greenberg, wanting him to play tennis at noon. He had a private court lined up in Laurel Canyon. He left the address. The other message was from Dave Benton, saying, "I've got *news!*" Now Ben was trying to do an imitation of Paul Harvey. Richards wondered what happened to Peter Lorre. Ben's voice said, "I'll see you at the tennis court, *at noon!*"

He looked at his watch. Eleven o'clock. He dialed Greenberg and told him he'd be there. "You heard from Dave Benton?"

"Oh, yes. He's coming today." Greenberg said, "Bring your asshole pills. Bob Jones will be the fourth man." Jones played to win.

When Richards showed up, the other three were already hitting balls. He was dying to know what Dave Benton had learned, but he did not want to hold up the game. He pulled off his sweats and joined the group to warm up. The four of them were evenly matched, and they played a very competitive game of doubles, round robin, each player playing one set with each of the other three. A lot of good rallies, and some good sallies, too—if you didn't mind Benton and Jones chipping their teeth at each other, amiably and not so amiably, during the entire three sets, even during the set they played together as partners.

When the match was over, Benton turned his wit on Richards. "Okay, cretin," he said to Richards. "Better sit down for this one."

Since Richards was already sitting down, wiping his face with a towel, he stood up.

Benton only laughed at his own jokes, but this time he laughed at Richards. "Okay, okay. Now get this," said Benton. Richards sat down. So did Tom Greenberg, who had lugged a pitcher of lemonade and four glasses to a courtside picnic table, and so did Bob Jones.

Greenberg stopped Benton and turned to Richards, "Okay with you if Jonesy hears this?"

Richards looked at Jones. "Hell, yes. This is becoming a Backstabbers' project, anyway."

"What?" asked Jones. "What project?"

Greenberg made a patting motion in the air with his right hand. "Patience, Jonesy. You'll see. You'll see."

"Okay," said Richards. "I'm all ears."

"So am I," said Bob Jones.

Benton said, "You know that account number I found at Kenelly Industries? The one paying out a monthly stipend to William Dwyre? And to an Ellen Daugherty? Well, there's an almost identical account number on the Howard Foundation payroll. Same first seven digits are the same. The foundation has been sending checks to thirteen women on that same account number. Including Frances Farnsworth."

"Bingo!" Richards slammed his hand down on the table so hard that he spilled his lemonade.

"Hey," said Benton, "you're ruining my printout here." He snatched it up from the table and started putting it in his sports bag.

Richards tried to calm himself. He was excited about this news. It was the confirmation he'd been looking for—that Frances Farnsworth was getting a payoff from the Howard

Foundation. Along with twelve other women. From a mysterious account. "Uh, Ben, he said, "mind if I see that printout?"

"What printout?"

Richards tried to laugh, but he wasn't enjoying Ben's tease, and his laugh sounded more like a death rattle. He nodded in the direction of Ben's bag. "You know," he said.

Ben pulled it out, leaned back in his chair, and held it up in the air so he could study it again. Richards could only see the reverse side of the sheet. But it seemed to him that it was list of roughly thirteen names. Damn! He had to see that list. But if he knew Benton, the more eager he, Jay Richards, was to get it, the less likely Ben was to hand it over.

At this point, Tom Greenberg said, "Ben, mind if I see it?"

Benton gave it to Greenberg. Without looking at it, Greenberg took it, then handed it over to Richards.

"Thanks, Tom," said Richards, glaring at Benton. He scanned each of the names, but he learned nothing from the list. "All women," he said.

"Hey," said Benton, "Howard Kenelly was a real coxman. These gotta be old girlfriends of Howard Kenelly. Maybe ladies he knocked up. But what the hell? He could afford to pay off whole chorus lines. And probably did. He was always generous."

Richards shrugged. He read through the list again. Finally, one of them jumped out at him. Lee Brown. "You know anything about this Lee Brown," he said to Benton.

"Can't tell. All I got's her record for the year. She gets as much as Frances Farnsworth. Ten thousand a month. It's sent directly to a bank. Goes directly to her account at a local bank in Arcadia, California."

"Ben," he said, "any chance this Lee Brown isn't a she?"

"Yeah," said Benton. "I thought a that."

Richards stood up and began to pace back and forth.

"Whatsa matter?" said Greenberg.

"Maybe we've found Sonny Skies."

"How d'ya figure?" said Greenberg.

Richards paid him no attention. He turned to Benton. "We don't know a damn thing about this Lee Brown character except that she—or he—has a bank in Arcadia."

"What's in Arcadia?" asked Greenberg.

Richards said he didn't know. "Arcadia is one of those affluent bedroom communities along the San Gabriel foothills, just east of Pasadena. Maybe fifty thousand people live there. Mostly white."

Bob Jones said, "Santa Anita Racetrack's in Arcadia." He knew it was too early in this conversation to demand to know what was going on. But he knew the racetrack was there because he worked at the track.

Richards said, "Maybe we reach Lee Brown through the bank. Do we stake out the bank?"

Benton said, "You don't have to do a stakeout at the bank, Rich. I took the liberty of checking Brown out with the Sacramento computer of the Department of Motor Vehicles. Lee Brown is a white male, five feet five inches tall, brown hair, blue eyes, sixty-seven years old, owns a Chevy Blazer, and he lives in Altadena."

"You said they were all women on this list."

"Take it easy," said Benton. "I was just playing a little game. To see how smart you are."

"I pass?"

"Yeah. As a matter of fact, it took you less time to figure it out than it took me. I looked at that list a long time before I figured Lee Brown was an alias for Brownlee."

"So you actually checked him out with the DMV?"

"Yeah. All all the others, too."

"They all women?"

Benton nodded. "And they're all in their sixties."

You mean you checked their driver's licenses, too?"

"I was already in the DMV computer. I figured it would save me some time."

"You have a chance to check out Ellen Daugherty? She isn't one of the thirteen. But she was on another account."

Benton shook his head. "Forgot about her."

"But you have the dope from Lee Brown's driver's license?"

"He doesn't have a driver's license. He doesn't drive. Does have an ID with the DMV, though."

"Then you also have his date of birth."

Benton consulted a slip of paper he'd been carrying in the pocket of his sweatpants. "Yes. April 23, 1924. That'd make him, uh, sixty-eight."

"April twenty-third?" said Richards. Well, that's gotta be Sonny Skies, then. That's Sonny's birthday."

"Hey," said Bob Jones, "whenever you guys feel like it, would somebody tell me what's going on?"

Greenberg took Jones aside and explained what was happening while Richards grilled Benton. "Any way of tapping Brown's phone?"

"Maybe, but it'd be a lotta trouble, and I wonder whether it's worth it."

"Why?"

"It's easier to get a line on a guy by just listening to his answering machine. You can learn a lot about a guy—or a gal —by checking their answering machines for a few days running."

Richards got a sudden chill. Had Benton been listening to his own answering machine? It would be an easy matter once you cracked the simple two digit remote code on his machine. Of course! Not only had Benton been monitoring his calls; he'd been telling people like Greenberg what he'd heard. That's how Greenberg knew he was working as a consultant for HMO at $1,000 a day. Because Benton told him! "You've been listening to my answering machine, haven't you, Ben?"

Benton ignored the question. "Or you can learn a lot by

calling a guy and talking to him," he said. "Like, for instance, Lee Brown."

"You already phoned Brown? He have a listed number?"

Benton shook his head. "Unpublished number."

"Then how—"

"I can get into the phone company, too. I get you any unpublished number you want. You want Heidi Fleiss's number?"

Richards felt the blood rise. "You phone this guy? Just out of the blue? Why that is absolutely—"

"Sure I phoned him. His answering machine said he's out of town. Real cute voice. Says he'll be working the races down at Del Mar till early September."

"Jeez! Why did you call him?"

"Why not? I wanted to ask him if he was Sonny Skies."

"Hey! You coulda screwed up our whole thing!"

"Kiss my ass."

"What?"

"You heard me."

Greenberg intervened. "Okay, Ben, what's the problem?"

"No problem. I just don't like people telling me what to do."

Richards counterattacked. "I guess you are going to experience a lot of people telling you what to do when you go to prison."

"Whaddya mean?"

"You're not the Dave Benton wanted by the FBI?"

Benton laughed and said defiantly, "Yes, I am. But that doesn't mean I'm going to prison. They have to find me first, then indict me, then convict me. And they don't have proof of one damn illegal thing. They can't lay a glove on me."

"Okay, okay, boys," said Tom Greenberg. "Simmer down."

"Well," complained Richards to Greenberg, "he just

went ahead and phoned Sonny Skies. He could have queered the whole deal."

"What whole deal?" said Dave Benton.

"I thought you understood. Elle McBrien and I are trying to do a documentary called *The Search for Sonny Skies*. One of the big payoffs for us—and our viewers—is going to be the moment of truth. When we first walk in on him with our minicam going and say, 'Sonny Skies, this is your life.' Or something like that." He hadn't thought of that moment until right this minute. But now that he knew Sonny Skies was alive, it *was* going to be a big moment. Some called it kamikaze journalism. But that's the way you had to do it.

Benton said, "You're playing a game called 'This Is Your Life'? What bullshit!"

"Ben, is *everything* bullshit?" Richards looked pained.

"Yeah. Or chickenshit. Or elephant shit. It's all shit. Everything." He waved expansively—a gesture that could encompass the whole universe.

"Jeez!" Richards grabbed for his tennis racket and his sweatpants. "I'm outa here."

"Aw, I've hurt his feelings," said Benton. "Where you goin' now, candy ass? You going to your beautiful little Irish doll?"

Richards stopped. "How do you know she's Irish? I never said she's Irish. I never told you she's Irish. You've never seen her or spoken to her."

Benton grinned.

Now the anger really rose in Richards. Of course, the son of a bitch had not only been checking on his answering machine. He had probably been listening to Elle's as well. He headed for his car.

Bob Jones followed him. "Hey, Rich!"

Richards said over his shoulder, "Yeah?"

"Don't let Ben get your goat. He got your goat pretty good there."

"Hell with him! And I don't even have a goat."

Jones followed him out to the curb and said, "Look, I got a little tip for you. If this Lee Brown is working the races at Del Mar, as Ben says he says on his answering machine, then what do you suppose he does up here in L.A.? In Altadena? In Arcadia?"

"I don't know!" said Richards. He said he was angry with Benton, and he wasn't thinking very clearly.

"Hey, come on," said Jones. "He lives in Altadena, and he has a bank account in Arcadia. And he works the horses. There's one place you gotta look first, and that's Santa Anita."

Richards smiled. "Jeez, of course. Jonesy, you're a genius."

"I ain't no genius. But I do get a good idea every now and then. I got one more. You know I work the clubhouse at Santa Anita? Well, if you want a line on this Brown guy, you might call a friend of mine at the track. Martha Goode. In personnel. Tell her you know me and I said you're okay. If Brown works at the track, she may be able to tell you more about him."

"What's the difference? He isn't at Santa Anita right now, anyway."

"I know. But if you're going to go down to Del Mar, which I think you are, you gotta know where to start looking for the guy. Is he a track steward? Or a trainer? Or does he work the totes? Or what? You capture my drift?"

Richards shook his head as if to clear his brain of confusion. Of course! Jonesy was giving him the kind of shortcut he and Elle needed if they were going to get to Sonny Skies before Dave Benton did. He didn't know why he feared Benton. He just had a feeling that he should.

Elle was bitchy when she arrived at Richards's apartment that evening. She was working too hard. Not only was she involved in trying to put together her own documentary, *The Search for Sonny Skies,* she had also been called in to help edit HMO's documentary on D day. As a consequence, she was putting in long days and a good deal of work in the evening while she was under the added stress of living out of a suitcase at Richards's apartment. Still fearing a drop-in by Billy Dwyre or one of his goons, she hadn't been home in days.

Richards tried to greet her with a hug and a kiss. She pushed him away and turned her head. "Not now," she snapped. "I'm tired. And I need more of my things."

"Things?"

"Clothes." She did not expatiate on her needs. And Richards didn't ask her to. When she started getting mono-syllabic, Richards was learning not to toy with her. She had an Irish temper—the other side of the coin of her Irish pas-sion—and he didn't want to test it. So he went with her, back to her apartment, without question. They went in her Volvo, which Elle parked at the front curb, and entered the apart-ment through the front door.

It was clear to Ellen that someone had been there. Sev-eral dozen videotapes had been removed from a cabinet un-der her TV. The tapes were sitting there in three piles on the living-room carpet. "They take some?" he asked.

"Can't tell." Elle went to her bedroom and looked in her walk-in closet.

Richards followed her. "Something missing here?" he asked.

"Give me a few minutes," she said. "I just can't figure out what it is," she said.

"Maybe just your imagination," said Richards.

She gave him a pitying look. "Don't do this to me," she said. "I don't mind us playing Mattie and David. But don't bullshit me in the process, okay?"

He nodded wordlessly, contrite. She moved off to the

kitchen, then to the laundry room at the back of her apartment, where she uttered a sharp cry.

"What? What?" asked Richards as he came rushing to her side.

"This back door? It was ajar, just like this."

"You didn't open it yourself?"

"No. I didn't even come back here until just now. Whoever was here, they went right out this back door."

Richards pushed the door wide open with his elbow—he didn't want to smudge any fingerprints that might be on the doorknob—and stepped out onto an asphalt driveway. He saw nothing except some storage units spaced on the far side of the drive. "What's back this way?" he asked.

"In the back? Carports."

"Stay here," he said. He ran to the back of the building, saw about half the ports occupied—with cars, but no people in sight—then returned quickly to Elle.

"See anything?"

"*Nada.*"

"Rich, I'm sure whoever was here when we arrived."

"Well, if they were, they're long gone by now." He made a clucking sound with his tongue. "On the other hand, if we surprised 'em, maybe they didn't get what they wanted. Maybe they're coming back."

"Coming back for what?"

He shrugged.

Elle said, "I think we oughta call the police so they can stake out the place."

Richards nodded. "You want to call? Or should I?"

Elle said, "It's my place. I'll call." She called 911, but because she wasn't reporting a crime in progress, she was handed on to someone from the Hollywood P.D.'s burglary division. He didn't seem very excited about her story about a break-in, especially since she could report nothing missing. He said he'd notify the patrol division. A police cruiser would "keep an eye on the place." And that was that.

"What does 'keep an eye on the place' mean?" she asked Richards when she hung up.

"Beats me," said Richards. "They ask you if you were going to spend the night here?"

"No."

"They tell you how long they were going to keep an eye on the place?"

"No."

"Then how in the hell will a passing police car know what to look for? If they see a light on, will they stop? Or not? This is dumb."

"Rich," she said, "I just figured out what's missing." Elle had been roaming the apartment, still casing the place, and Richards was following her, room to room. Now, in the living room, Elle told him, "There was a picture on this end table— of Gremmie. It's gone."

Richards had a sudden sinking feeling. Up to now things had been fun. "Why," he said, "why would anyone want a picture of Gremmie?"

"So they could have her snatched?"

That was the first thought he had had. But he didn't like hearing her confirm his fear. "Oh, jeez!" He reached over and touched her gently on the shoulder. "Elle," he said, "let's get out of here."

She nodded. "Let me get some things, though." She went to her room, gathered up some clothes, and put them in a hanging bag. She took a small sports bag into her bathroom and stuffed it with some cosmetics. "Okay," she said, "let's go."

When they got into her car, she said she felt like going to an AA meeting. "There's a late nine o'clock meeting at the Hollywood Y," she said.

"You sure?" he said. "You sure that's what you need?"

"Yes." She said it with such finality that Richards didn't argue.

Richards asked Elle as she drove west on Franklin

toward Highland if she felt at all like the character played by Cybill Shepherd in *Moonlighting*."

"Mattie?" Elle laughed. "The fantasy has crossed my mind. But this is no fun. This isn't like a TV show. This is scary. How about you? You feel like the Bruce Willis character, David?"

"No. Other than the fact that he had a little drinking problem."

"Yeah," she said. "But you don't."

"Well, let's just say I didn't—today. So far. One day at a time, remember? As they say at AA, pride goeth before a fall."

Elle nodded, chastened by the thought that Richards, sober today, could go over the edge tomorrow. A lot of people in AA never got to their first full year of sobriety. Their life was a series of jumping on—and falling off—the wagon. But she felt vaguely encouraged by Richards's own assessment of the ongoing danger that he might fall back. That in itself was a kind of insurance.

★ ★ ★

The AA meeting at the Hollywood Y was not very inspiring. A blond actress named Nancy Z, who hadn't worked in a good long while, gave her pitch, a story of her own trip to Drugville—and back. God bless her for trying, but it was rambling and incoherent and spiked with too many "you knows." But Elle and Rich didn't go to AA to be entertained, just to be reminded of the steps they needed to take on a continuing basis if they were going to remain sober.

As they were leaving the Y's parking lot in Elle's Volvo, he asked Elle if she was worried about Gremmie.

She shook her head. "She's in no danger now. She's with her father, and they'll be in Alaska for a month. I won't have to worry until she comes back. But there's something that worries me more."

"Which is?"

"What kind of people are we dealing with here? That's what bothers me. Steal a picture of my daughter? That's going over the line."

"Whose line? Yours or theirs? You're old enough to know the world is full of all kinds of people. They don't all share the same moral boundaries."

She shuddered. "I got into the sleuth business. Now I'm not so so sure I like it."

"You like the adventure. You just don't like the notion that your own daughter may be on someone's kidnap list. But, hey, it's normal to be frightened. Not to be afraid? In L.A.? Who isn't afraid in L.A. these days?"

"I'm not frightened," she said. "I'm mad. Going into my home is a violation. Taking Gremmie's picture is a violation. Now that I think of it, I want to go back home and finish looking around. Then I want to call the cops again and make out a report. Do you realize how much I left things hanging? Couldn't even tell the police what was missing?"

"You want to go back to your apartment now? Why? And why now?"

"I don't know. I just have a feeling. I want to go back."

12

Never underestimate the power of a woman's intuition, thought Richards as he preceded Elle through her front door and found Billy Dwyre and Timmi Tyler, his so-called foster daughter, kneeling in front of her TV cabinet, pawing through her videotape collection.

"Find what you're looking for?" said Elle very coolly.

Dwyre was still on his knees when Richards got to him, hitting him in the shoulder and shoving him over sideways into a stack of videotapes. But Timmi had already bolted. Elle went after her, but Timmi was too quick for her. She escaped out the back door and ran off into the night. When Elle got back to the living room, she found Richards there with a knee on Dwyre's throat. "Keep him like that for a minute," she said. She went off to Gremmie's room and returned with an aluminum softball bat. "I think," she said, "that Mr. Dwyre is now going to answer some more of our questions. Honestly this time."

She handed Richards the bat. Richards took it, released his knee from the man's throat, and said, "Just slide over into the corner there."

Billy Dwyre did so, but very slowly. "Ya hurt me," he said hoarsely. "My throat."

"I'll do more than that," said Richards, waving the bat.

Dwyre raised an elbow as if to ward off a blow from the bat.

"Don't hit him," said Elle. "Not yet." She asked Dwyre if it was he who broke into her place earlier that evening. He nodded. "Timmi with you?" He nodded again. "You know where she went?" He shook his head. "She take your car?" He shook his head again and dug into the pocket of his denim shirt and produced a set of car keys.

"All right, then," said Richards. "How about you answer some questions?"

He whined and held his throat. "I can't talk."

"Get him a glass of water, Elle."

Richards waited until she came back with the water. As Dwyre started to down it, Elle said, "I think we can make a little deal with Mr. Dwyre here. He talks, we don't call the cops. We call the cops, he and his little Lolita are in trouble. Jail for him. Juvenile hall for Timmi. When the cops catch her."

Dwyre shook his head. "No. I'll talk. Whaddya want from me?"

"On-camera?" said Elle. "You'll talk on-camera?"

Dwyre said, "No camera. Maybe later. Not now."

Richards said to Elle, "Should we proceed?"

She said, "I don't know."

"We need to get some things clear. Billy can help us a little. Maybe he can help us a lot if we can protect him." Dwyre nodded at that.

Elle gave it some thought. "All right. Let's see what Mr. Dwyre can remember now. Let's go back to square one, Billy. Let's go back to that day you last saw Sonny Skies. Our guess is that Howard Kenelly was there that day."

"Howard Kenelly? There? Where is 'there'?"

"We don't know," she said. "We think you do. Tell us, did you see Howard Kenelly—anywhere—on the day that Sonny Skies was supposed to be returning to Fort Hua-chuca?"

"I might have."

"Where did you see him?"

"Well, I'm not sure." He wasn't going to offer anything. They would have to pull it all out of him, piece by piece.

"Okay," said Richards. "Let's go back to Forest Lawn. Did you see Sonny drive off in a rental car."

"Truthfully, no."

"Truthfully, what happened?"

"I was driving Sonny around during this visit. In his blue Lincoln Continental. After the ceremony was over at Forest Lawn, Sonny was pretty upset. He'd hoped that Frances would show up at the church, at least. She didn't. So Sonny wanted to see her. We drove."

"Who was driving?"

"I was. I drove over to her place in Westwood. When we got there, a guy with a mustache was just getting out of his car, an old beat-up Chevy. He wasn't dressed all that well. Kinda shabby. He had another guy with him, better dressed, but he had a kind of look about him."

"What kind of look?" asked Elle.

Dwyre smiled. "Well, I seen a lotta plainclothes cops in my time. This guy, he looked like an off-duty cop."

"What made him look like an off-duty cop?"

"I don't know. There's a kind of a look. Like an unmarked car, you know? Kind of Brand X, no chrome."

Elle smiled. "This guy wasn't wearing any chrome?"

Dwyre laughed. "No, no chrome. Kind of a nothing tie. A shiny, nothing suit. He looked kinda Irish. Lotta cops were Irish then."

"Something wrong with being Irish, Billy?" asked Elle.

"Hell, no. I'm Irish. I think you're Irish, too, Miss McBrien."

"Okay, okay. Anything else about him?"

"He had a big bulge in his back pocket."

"To you, that meant 'cop,' huh?' "

"Yeah. Bulge was probably a gun."

"Okay," said Richards. "What else you see?"

"Well, the two of them went up to the front door."

"The shabby guy and the guy who looked like a cop?"

"Right. Understand, we see all this very quick like. So I

park our car, right behind the old Chevy, and Sonny gets out, just in time to see Frances open her front door, and her arms, too, kinda like she's happy to see this shabby-dressed guy with the mustache."

"And Sonny sees all of this unfolding right in front of him?"

"Yeah! He sees it, and he's outta the car and running up the walk. She doesn't see him at first. When she finally does and recognizes it is him, in his army uniform—"

"Where are you?" asked Richards.

"I'm watching from my seat behind the wheel of the Continental. Don't interrupt me, okay? Well, then she wipes the smile from her face, and she looks really pissed off. She talks right past the other guy like he isn't even there, and she shouts at Sonny. And that's all I see. This guy with the mustache, he skips inside, and his maybe-cop friend goes right in with him, and Sonny follows them in, chipping his teeth at them. Frances follows the three of them in and slams the door. And I just sit there and wait. And I wait. Maybe a half hour passes. Then comes an ambulance. It pulls up right in the driveway. Two guys in white coats get out and go up to the door. They're not in there more than a minute, and then they're back out, setting up a stretcher and wheeling it into the house. In a few minutes they come back out again with a body on the stretcher and Frances Farnsworth trailing behind the stretcher and the guy with the mustache behind her."

"You didn't get out of the car?"

"No."

"Why not?"

"I was scared. I didn't know what was happening."

"You know that was Sonny on the stretcher?"

"Not at the time I didn't."

"It could have been the guy who looked like a cop?"

"Yeah. It could have. But it wasn't. It was Sonny."

"How do you know?"

"I'm getting to that."

Richards paused. He couldn't figure out why Dwyre stayed in the car. His man is in that house. And then somebody's wheeled out in a stretcher. And he's frozen behind the wheel of the car. "Okay," he said. "So then what happened?"

"The ambulance drove off. No sirens. It just drove off."

"And Frances and her friend, the one with the mustache?"

"They went back into the house. She was waving her arms. He was trying to calm her down."

"You still didn't get out of the car?"

"Not until later."

"You stayed there?"

Dwyre shrugged. "I had no place else to go. I wanted to talk to Frances. But I wanted to wait until this guy left."

"And his maybe-cop friend, right?"

"Right."

"When did they leave?"

"Maybe a couple hours later."

"Couple hours! What do you suppose they were doing in there for two hours?"

"I don't know."

"Okay. So, two hours later these two guys come out?"

"Well, no. Just one guy. The guy with the mustache."

"And you still don't get out of the car?"

"No. I didn't have to. This guy comes right over to me, to the driver's side of the vehicle, and he asks me what I'm doing there. I tell him I'm with Sonny. He asks me my name. I tell him. He asks me does Frances Farnsworth know who I am and how to find me. I say yes. And that's all. Doesn't say another word. Then he turns and goes to his old Chevy, and he is off."

"You didn't ask him where Sonny was?"

He laughed nervously. "No."

Elle said, "Then you went in and talked to Frances Farnsworth?"

"Yes. Well, I didn't exactly go in."

"Where'd you talk to her?"

"Right there in her driveway. She was leaving the house, backing out the driveway in her Buick convertible. But when she saw me walking up the driveway, she recognized me, and she stopped and rolled down the window on the driver's side. She left the motor running, so I knew she didn't want to talk. She just wanted to know what I wanted."

"You ask her what happened to Sonny?"

"Sure! Whaddya think? But she was very upset. She was almost hysterical. She said Sonny and her friend had a helluva row, kicking over furniture and all. And when Sonny knocked him down and then started to choke him, that's when her friend reached up and grabbed a heavy glass ashtray and hit Sonny in the head with it. Sonny crumpled like a dead deer. That's what she said. 'Like a dead deer.' Only Frances said Sonny wasn't dead."

"Then what?"

"I asked her what she was going to do, was she gonna call the police or anything? She said her friend couldn't afford to have the police in on this. He was going to take care of Sonny and take care of her and take care of me, too. Yeah, me, Billy Dwyre."

"You ask her who the man with the mustache was?"

"No."

"You ask her who the other man was, the man in the shiny suit?"

Dwyre shook his head.

"Why not?"

"Because it was clear from the way she talked about both of them. They were mystery men as far as I was concerned. And always would be. That I shouldn't be concerned. Ever."

"You take that as a threat?"

Dwyre hesitated. "Maybe."

"You see the man in the shiny suit? Was he in the Buick with Miss Farnsworth?"

"No. She was alone in the car."

"Would you be able to identify the man with the mustache if I showed you his picture?" asked Elle.

"His picture?"

Elle went into her bedroom and came out with a picture of Howard Kenelly taken by a *Life* photographer in 1944. Handsome in a rugged Clark Gable sort of way, with a mustache like Gable's. "Was this the man with Frances Farnsworth?" she asked, looking directly into the eyes of Billy Dwyre. "His name, if you don't know it already, is Howard Kenelly."

"No," Dwyre said, "that's not the man." Elle and Richards looked at each other and nodded. They were in silent agreement—that Dwyre had responded far too quickly. After fifty years, you'd think Dwyre would have wanted to study the picture. But he had his mind made up in advance.

In her soft, charming Irish voice, Elle said, "Are you trying to shield Howard Kenelly, Billy?"

"Hell," said Billy, "he's been dead a long, long time. I don't have to shield him."

"Did Howard Kenelly pay you to keep your mouth shut about Sonny Skies?" demanded Richards.

"No."

"Is he still paying you?"

"Hey, he's dead."

"Yes, that's right," said Elle. "But his company's still going strong. Very big player in aerospace."

Richards said, "And his medical foundation is the biggest foundation in the world. Assets of maybe forty billion dollars."

At that, Billy Dwyre's jaw dropped. And then, suddenly realizing he had given himself away, Dwyre tried to compose himself and make the best out of a bad situation that was turning worse. "Hey, I've been giving you my story for free! But now you're selling it to HMO and the *Washington Post*. I should go sell it myself, right now, to tabloid TV. I can get good money for my story, maybe a half million."

Elle stepped in. "Right now, Billy, there is no story. *Inside Edition* is offering to pay one million dollars to Rodney King, who was beaten up by the LAPD. But it isn't paying a farthing to Rodney Taligalop, who was beaten up by bums in the Los Angeles Mission's flophouse last night."

"Who's Rodney Tally-glop? I never heard a him."

"Exactly my point, Billy. You may, indeed, be a part of a story that Mr. Richards and I are trying to develop. But after our story appears, you will certainly not be a hero. You didn't lift a finger to help Sonny at the very time in his life when he needed you most."

"And besides that, Billy," Richards said, "you're in no position to bargain with us."

"Well," said Elle. "Billy can bargain a little bit. We have the budget to pay for Billy's help on this story, and we can help Billy with his story—if he'll go on-camera." She turned to Dwyre. "Sort of like a talent fee, Billy."

"How much?" he said.

Elle shrugged.

"You have to make it worth my while. It'd have to be more—" He caught himself and stopped.

"More than the Howard Foundation is paying you now?" asked Richards.

"You know about that?" Dwyre said.

"Never mind. The thing is, Billy, the Howard Foundation will soon find it doesn't have to pay you hush money any longer. We're going to tell the whole story about the shenanigans of Howard Kenelly, and there won't be any further need for your silence. So if it's money you want, you might as well look to HMO."

Dwyre pondered this. Finally, Elle said, "Look, I might get HMO to come up with as much as a hundred thousand for you."

The ringing of the front doorbell startled all three of

them. Elle answered the door. Timmi Tyler stood there, but she was not alone. A policeman was holding her left arm. And another policeman stood behind the two of them. "Miss McBrien? I'm Officer Ramirez. This is Officer Cheatham. We had a call to keep an eye on your place tonight."

"Yes. That's right. We had a break-in earlier today."

"Well, we just made a pass and observed this young lady looking in your side window over here. She looked suspicious to us, so we stopped and grabbed her. But she says you know her."

"Uhhh," Elle stammered, "yes, I do, Officer. She's okay." To Timmi, she trilled, "Come on in! Where have you been? We were worried." She shouted over her shoulder to Dwyre, who was still sitting on the floor in a corner of the living room, out of the line of sight. "Billy, it's Timmi. She's back! She's all right."

"Any problem, ma'am?" said the second officer.

"No," said Elle. "No problem. Come on, Timmi. No one's going to punish you." The youngster hesitated, then strode into the living room, sized up the scene, and took a seat on the couch while Elle got rid of the officers. "No," she said. "I still haven't discovered anything missing from the break-in. Yes. I'll let you know. Yes. Okay. I will. Thanks."

When Elle walked back into the living room, Billy Dwyre said, "Let's do that interview on-camera right now. Get it over with."

"What will you tell us?" asked Elle.

"The whole story. Basically, what I just got done telling you. How Sonny Skies got conked on the head and who conked him. It was Howard Kenelly. I can tell you that. That what you want to hear?"

"You going to tell us what happened to that guy with the shiny suit, maybe an off-duty cop, who was with Howard Kenelly?"

Billy Dwyre was on his feet now, trying to ease the cramped muscles in his leg. He said, "I don't know. I *swear* I don't know." Then Dwyre looked over at Timmi. "You might as well hear this, honey." He turned to Richards. "You can put down that baseball bat."

"It's a *softball* bat," said Timmi, blinking back her tears.

13

On the drive down to Del Mar with Elle, Richards wondered what was so important to Billy that it made him say something that seemed out of character.

"Huh?"

"He said, 'I *swear* I don't know.' That's the first time I ever heard him swear to anything."

"Didn't know what?"

"What happened to the man in the shiny suit."

"Isn't it just a manner of speaking?"

"If it were, we'd have heard it before. We haven't heard it before."

But Elle's mind was leaping ahead to Del Mar and their upcoming meeting with Lee Brown.

Richards had had good luck with Martha Goode, Bob Jones's friend in the office at Santa Anita. Lee Brown was registered with track security at Santa Anita, fingerprints and photographs and everything. Ms. Goode said Lee Brown was a groom and had worked for the same trainer for the last twenty years, a man with a solid reputation in California racing circles named Bill Osgood. Like many of the top trainers, Osgood took his best colts to Del Mar every season, and his top workers went along. Martha Goode assured Richards he'd find Lee Brown on the backside at Del Mar. All he had to do was find Osgood's assigned stables. Thoughtfully, she provided Richards with Brown's official color picture, the one on his Santa Anita pass. And his fingerprints, too.

Richards had brought the picture home and shown it to Elle. "You think this is Sonny Skies?"

She studied the picture and said, "Well, it could be. He's obviously changed since I saw him in *Pearly Grave.*

"Of course. A lot thicker in the middle and a lot thinner on top. But look at the smile. Is that Sonny's smile, or isn't it?" From his bookshelf, he pulled down an old history of M-G-M, opened it to a full-page picture of Sonny Skies, from his Oscar-winning performance in *The Master of Ballantrae.* They put their heads together over that picture and compared it to Lee Brown's Santa Anita ID.

"Uh-huh," said Elle. "It sure looks like the same person. But, gee, this picture, it's fifty years old! How can we be sure?"

"We'll only be certain when we get the report back from our fingerprint expert."

"Tell me again. Who is that?"

"An officer from the LAPD's criminalists' division. Name of Al Mangino. Guys from the LAPD moonlight all the time. As private security guards, mostly. But there's no rule against hiring a criminalist of our own. Yet." He laughed.

"Don't do that to me," she said. "I used to be a law-abiding citizen. Now I can't even sleep in my own bed at night."

"You're loving it," he said. "Before we became Mattie and David, we were bored out of our gourds."

"True," she said. "Bored and unloved. Now I have almost more excitement—and love—than I can stand."

"You can't stand the love?" He touched her lightly on the arm.

"It's part of my dependency pattern," she said. "I'm beginning to understand myself. I didn't get the love I needed as a kid. Now, when I do get it, I feel like I don't deserve it. Then I get scared and pull away." She reached over and touched him. "It's okay, Rich. Stay with me."

Elle had heard a good deal about Del Mar. It was a

traditional, old-fashioned track. For decades in California racetrack aficionados loved to attend the summer meet there, side by side with the likes of Bing Crosby, Jimmy Durante, and Desi Arnaz, three of the stars who used to camp there and help bring in other show-business celebrities, and the celebrity-conscious public as well. And that fun couple, J. Edgar Hoover and Clyde Tolson.

Crosby had recorded a song for Del Mar, "Where the Turf Meets the Surf"—which was, in fact, a favorite tag line for the track in most of its advertising. Richards wasn't sure which came first, the song or the motto. But the song was, by now, part of tradition, and the management still played the crooner's recording at one o'clock every afternoon. "That's Crosby's voice now," explained Richards to Elle McBrien as they were entering the pass gate just before the first race. Yes, that was unmistakably the old crooner. His voice even sounded old, on the antiquated public address system that Richards felt should have been buried with Bing.

Where the turf meets the surf down in Old Del Mar
Take a plane, take a train, take a car.
There's a smile on every face.
And a winner in each race,
Where the turf meets the surf at Del Mar.

"A winner in each race, huh?" said Elle.

"Yeah. Only trouble is, figuring out which one—ahead of time."

When they got their press passes, one of the track's PR representatives had them come up to the office so he could tag Elle's minicam, a move that would allow her to take it anywhere she wished. "Just one thing," he said. "You can't shoot any of the races. Anything but the races."

"I understand," she said, although she really didn't.

After they left the office, Richards explained why. "The

track has its own official videotape record of each race. The track doesn't want to contend with other video records—say, in case of a dispute over the placement of horses in a close finish. Other videos could lead to lawsuits."

"I see."

"Racing's a multi-billion-dollar business in California. Brings in lots of tax revenue to the state, too. So the authorities don't want to do anything that could hurt the credibility of racing. This is serious business."

"Uh-huh. And so is ours."

He said he couldn't agree more. He was lugging her minicam, and her bag of sound equipment, as usual, and they were headed toward the paddock, where the PR man told them they could pick up a courtesy car to take them to the barns.

They found a uniformed guard at the paddock. "We're going to the backside," Richards told him confidently. He showed him their passes.

"You got permission for the minicam, too?" he asked.

Richards pointed to the tag they got in the PR office.

"Okay, I see it. Right this way." He took them to a line of golf carts and introduced them to an usher type with a nametag that said Jim. He was wearing black pants, a white shirt, and a red bow tie. The guard told him, "Take these people to the Osgood stable area on the backside," he said. "Section twenty-three."

The backside was a kaleidoscope of new sights and sounds for Elle. The voice of the PA announcer had become muddy and indistinct, and his harsh accents were now replaced by the soft Spanish of exercise boys and hot-walkers all around them. Elle noted that the stalls were all freshly painted in dark green, stall after stall, hundreds of them in neat rows and most of them adorned with bright-colored stable plaques hanging from each stall door. The trainers (or, perhaps, their wives) had hung colored awnings over some of the stalls—those with a sunny southern exposure. And they had stacked bales of hay and straw in neat piles alongside each stall. An occasional pickup truck was parked here and there alongside the wide lanes that separated the stalls, and a lot of empty horse vans were parked there, too. The sound of neighs and whinnies rose all around them, and a donkey kept braying somewhere close by.

"Jackass?" said Elle.

Deadpan, Richards said, "I don't call *you* names!"

She punched him playfully. "No. I meant, what's the donkey doing here?"

"Sometimes"—he chuckled—"a stable will have other animals around. Not sure if they're here for the entertainment of the trainers and the grooms or for the benefit of the horses. Some say horses like to have a jackass around. Calms 'em down."

"They need calming?"

"Some of 'em do. Stud colts, for example. They're the bad boys at any stable. Full of mischief. They bite the grooms, try to get into the saddle with their lead ponies, chew on their leads, kick their owners." Elle laughed at that. Richards said, "What's the matter. You think that's what owners deserve?"

She said, "Throwback to my Labor party background, I guess." The golf cart slowed down at the entrance to Section 23 and finally stopped in front of two Hispanic teenagers wearing Levi's and white T-shirts. They were playing hackysack, a beanbag game played with the feet. The kids were as skilled at controlling the bag as good soccer players. "Señor Osgood?" said the driver to the boys. They halted their game and pointed to one of the stables down the line. "*Aquí.*"

Bill Osgood was lean and very blond, a sober Nordic type with cool blue eyes. He was not friendly. On the other hand, he wasn't unfriendly, either. He said he didn't have a horse running until the seventh race, a six-furlong sprint on the turf course, and he allowed that, yes, he had a few minutes to talk to them about Lee Brown.

Osgood turned out to be a decent, careful man who

ended up thanking them for bothering to do a feature on the little people who made racing possible. Which was the story Richards had given him when he phoned from L.A. asking for permission to visit the backside and talk to his groom.

Nor did he refuse to talk to Elle's camera about Lee Brown.

"I don't really like being on TV," he said, "but I'll do it because it's good for racing. Be good for Lee, too. He's the nicest little fella. As reliable as God ever made anybody. Came to me twenty years ago, he did, when another trainer-friend of mine retired. Lee's never wanted to be anything but a groom, and he's only worked for two trainers his whole life in racing."

"Who was the first trainer?" asked Richards.

"Steve Parker. A real old-timer. Passed away a few years ago. I'd known him for years. Used to train for Howard Kenelly."

Richards said, "I didn't know Howard Kenelly had horses."

"Well, he flirted with horse racing for a while. He ran a string of ponies in the fifties. Did pretty well, but he soon lost interest. Had too many other things going, I guess."

"And Steve Parker was his trainer?"

"Right. Nice guy. He helped show me a thing or two when I was on my way up. When he retired, he came to me and said he had a couple good people he thought I could use. Lee Brown was one of 'em. I took him on. Never been sorry."

Elle asked, "How does Lee Brown live?"

Osgood said he paid him well over union scale.

Elle said, "No, I mean, does he have a family or anything?"

"Not that I know of. He has a kind of a housekeeper, I think. What I do know is he loves horses. He talks to 'em. What's more, they talk to him, too. You'll see."

Elle looked up from her camera. It was a look aimed at

Richards. It was a mixed kind of look, part delight and part alarm.

"Uh," said Richards, "just where is Lee Brown right now?"

"He's about five stalls down thataway, giving a rubdown to Skiin' Jill. That's the five-year-old mare I have running for C. C. Carter in the feature race tomorrow." Osgood looked at his watch. "But he'll be finished in about five or ten minutes."

"He know we're coming to see him?"

"I told him you were coming. He said he's never talked to any TV reporters before. But he said he'd do his best to tell you about how it is, being a groom. He's a very simple fellow, so don't go too fast with him. Just let him talk. He'll do fine if you don't rush him. Go from A to B to C."

Elle said, "Can you excuse us for a moment, Mr. Osgood? Mr. Richards and I have to go over a few things first."

Richards nodded. "Yes," he said. "Miss McBrien and I have to have a private little talk." They retreated to the shady side of one of the barns. He half-sat on a stack of hay bales. She straddled him and put a hand on each side of his shoulders and looked him straight in the eye. "What are we doing here?" she said.

He had to avert his eyes from her direct gaze for a moment. Then he said, "I know. You're worried about what we're going to do to this little fella?"

"You're damned right I am," she said.

"We have to play it by ear," he said.

"If he is what Bill Osgood says he is, he's happy here working as a groom. Can we just charge in and unmask him?" Richards didn't answer. She answered her own question. "We can't go charging in and say, 'Hey, we know who you really are?' We'd ruin his life. Do we have any right to do that?"

"It's a dilemma, isn't it?"

"No! Not a dilemma. Our course is absolutely clear."

"What about our story?"

"I don't know about our story," she said. "But if he is what Osgood says he is, we can't destroy him."

"With the truth?"

"Whose truth?" she said. "Yours? Mine? His? HMO's?"

"*The* truth."

She shook her head. "We can't do this."

"Can't even go ahead with the interview?"

"I don't think so."

"Oh, Elle." Richards shook his head. "Look, what if we play it absolutely straight? Just do what we told Osgood we were going to do: ask Lee Brown about his life with the horses. If he wants to tell us where he came from or how he lives when he isn't at the stables, he can tell us."

"We won't try tell him we know who he really is?"

"How can we? We don't know for sure ourselves. Let's just ask him what he knows. *We* are not the story. He is. Later, maybe, we'll figure out something, some way of telling the whole story of our search for Sonny Skies."

She shook her head. She was almost in tears.

"We don't have to decide today," said Richards. "But if we lose this chance today . . ."

Elle took her hands off Rich's shoulders and slipped them down around his waist and pulled him closer to her. She kissed him. Her eyes were a little wet. "Promise me you won't hurt him, okay?"

"I promise. This won't be kamikaze journalism."

"Okay," she said, "let's go."

14

They saw Skiin' Jill before they saw Lee Brown. Jill was a magnificent chestnut mare, with four white forelegs and a white star between her eyes, which were half-closed when Elle and Richards appeared in the breezeway outside the stall. Lee Brown was down on his knees, working on the horse's left leg, applying what might have been liniment in long, even strokes with a dark, damp rag.

"Don't call him," said Elle. "I want to get this shot." She turned on her minicam and had it on for a full minute before the groom noticed them. "Hey," he said without getting up and without missing a stroke, "you must be the people from the TV? Come on in here."

They weren't ready for his voice. It was the voice of an eight-year-old. "Jill won't hurt you," he said. "She's just had a nap, and she's real content right now. You can watch this. We call it rubbin'. This is what makes a good racehorse." He looked up at Elle and smiled. "Lots and lots of rubbin'—the most expensive medicine there is."

"What is that stuff you're putting on there?" asked Elle.

"It's called Billy Hills number four, but I call it Six Points. I picked it up once at a tack shop over at Six Points on old Garvey Boulevard, but then they started putting it together in these big plastic jugs under the name Billy Hills number four. Same stuff. Nothin' will tighten down a leg better than this stuff. Got everything in the world mixed into it. Tan bark, witch hazel, Epsom salts, vinegar, benzoin, you name it. Darn good stuff. Been using it for twenty years."

Richards noted that one foreleg was already done up in a kind of legging. Now, when Lee Brown had finished rubbing the other leg, he proceeded to put a cotton roll around it and then wrap it with a cotton bandage, around and around and around, then secure it neatly with two safety pins. "Notice how I put the safety pins on the outside of her leg," he said without looking up at the camera.

"Why on the outside?" asked Elle.

"So when Jill lies down, she can't rub the pins loose. Then the bandages would come undone, and we'd just have a mess here. There. That's it." He inspected both bandages. Satisfied, he stood and arched his back and smiled at them. He had a nice smile. Richards thought you might call it a sunny smile.

Lee Brown was a round little man with wisps of white hair on a mostly bald, very tanned head, and he wore faded Levi's and boots and an old maroon-colored T-shirt that said Dance Ten, Looks Three. Richards recognized the line from a song in a musical called *A Chorus Line*. What it meant to Lee Brown, he couldn't imagine. "Now, then." Brown looked up brightly and smiled again.

"Take your time, take your time," Richards told him. "You got something more to do?"

"No, no. I'm finished." He patted the mare on the neck. "She likes it. Don't you, Jill?" The mare nodded vigorously, as if in reply. He turned to Elle and her minicam, as naturally as if he'd been in front of a camera all his life. "This stuff kinda smells like a locker room." He moved back toward the camera and held up one of his rags so his visitors could smell it. "But it's pretty good stuff."

"What does it do?" asked Elle.

"It takes out soreness."

"Soreness?"

"Oh, yeah," he said. "You see, when these horses race, their legs take a terrific pounding. Especially the front legs. Jill here weighs 2,119 pounds, and when she's sailin' down the stretch, she's really pounding. Most of that 2,119 pounds comes down on those front legs. After a race, my little girl's hurtin'—pretty bad." He walked back to the mare, who'd had her eyes on him. The mare whinnied softly when he approached her again. He reached up and stroked her neck and talked to the horse.

"But you feel better now, don't you, my little girl?"

Skiin' Jill nodded, as if in reply, and gave a little sound that resembled a whimper.

Lee lifted the jug and turned it around so that Elle could catch the label with her minicam, Billy Hills no. 4. "Here. You can get a shot of this stuff. Sometimes, we use Bigle Oil, too. We got lots of other stuff."

"How do you know which stuff to use?" Elle seemed very interested.

Lee Brown smiled at her. "Oh, the horses, they let us know what they like." He smiled again and turned to Skiin' Jill. "This sweet little girl lets me know. Don't you?" The mare bared her teeth and whinnied.

Elle turned and gave Richards a look that was filled with meaning. He shrugged.

Lee Brown dropped the jug and dug in the pocket of his Levi's and withdrew several white rectangles that said Domino on their white paper wrappings. They were lumps of sugar. He unwrapped them, put them in his left palm, and offered them to the mare. The mare lapped them up, then nudged him on the neck with her nose. "Yeah, you like sugar, don't you?" he said to the mare.

The mare snorted.

He nuzzled her back. "Oh, yes, you do, you do."

The mare answered with another snort.

"And you know what? You're gonna get another lump of sugar in the morning."

The mare licked her lips and whinnied.

Lee turned to the camera again. "She's racin' tomorrow, but I don't ever tell her when she's gonna race. I don't want her to get butterflies or anything like that, get so excited she doesn't run her race. But I think she kinda has a notion she's gonna race, 'cause on race days she doesn't do an early-morning work. Of course, when we groom her extra good in the morning, she has a pretty good idea she'll be running.

"Then what happens?"

Lee Brown looked directly at Elle. She noted his deep blue eyes. "Well," he said, "we take her to the paddock area about a half hour before the race. They weigh her saddle there and generally put some weights in it; then they take her out on the track with the other horses in the race, and she hears the trumpet. You know, the fanfare? And she hears the voice of ol' Alvey Sellars." He lowered his voice several octaves and imitated the throaty voice of the track announcer. "'And the horses are—on the track!' That's when the adrenaline really starts to run for Skiin' Jill."

"That's when she knows she's running for real money?" asked Richards.

"Oh, my, yes. She does. She does. She starts trottin' real perky like and struttin' and showin' off and eyeballing the other horses."

"Kind of like sizing them up?"

"Oh, yes. If that's one thing horses know, it's class. They can tell class. And when the others are up against a class horse like Skiin' Jill, they know there's nothin' they can do against her."

"What do you mean?"

"Well, for example. Last year, a five-year-old colt named Skip Tracy came over here from Phoenix. He'd been racing at Turf against a lotta cheap horses, and he set the world's record at seven furlongs over there. Yeah, Turf Paradise in Phoenix. You could look it up. And so Skip Tracy went off here at two to one, but when that colt saw Jill, he could tell he was goin' against class, and he just ran out."

"Ran out?" asked Elle.

"Out of the money. Didn't run anything like his last race in Phoenix.

"Jill beat him?"

"Oh, my, yes. She won the race. But she ran it three seconds off the world record Skip Tracy set in Phoenix." Now Jill seemed to be calling to Lee Brown. He glanced over his shoulder at her and said to the camera, "Just a minute, huh? I gotta see what she wants."

He walked back to the mare and whispered in her ear at some length. The mare nodded, almost imperceptibly, and when Lee Brown was finished whispering in her ear, she seemed a bit calmer.

"I think she overheard me talking about the race and started getting too excited. I had to talk her down a bit."

"You don't want her to get excited?"

"Well, yes, yes, we do. But not too soon. She gets too excited too soon and she'll leave her race right here in the stable. So we better finish this talkin' somewheres else so she can't hear us." He motioned to a shady area under a shedrow a few stables down. "Down here, okay?"

Richards grabbed Elle's tripod, and Elle took the minicam, and they followed where Lee Brown led them. Richards noted his walk. It was a strut that was not unfamiliar to Richards. Millions of Sonny Skies's fans would have recognized it.

For a half hour or so Lee Brown chatted easily about his life in the stables. It was clear he loved horses. "Horses aren't the smartest people in the world," he said. "But they're loyal. They stick with me no matter what."

"How long you been with horses, Lee?"

"All my life," he said. "Far back as I can remember."

"You raised on a farm?"

Lee Brown gave Elle a quizzical look. "You know, I don't really remember where I was raised."

"You don't remember?"

"I asked Bethany once, and she said, 'Hey, kiddo'—she calls me 'kiddo' sometimes—'if you don't remember, how you 'spect me to remember?' That's the way she talks. I kid her about it sometimes. Maybe that's why she calls me 'kiddo.' I say. 'You talk like an Okie.' And she says, 'Whadda you know about Okies?' And I just laugh, because I don't know much about Okies at all. Only I know she talks like an Okie."

Elle said, "Who's Bethany?"

"She's my housekeeper in Altadena. She's been with me forever."

Elle turned and looked at Richards but kept her mini-cam focused on Lee Brown.

"She here with you now in Del Mar?"

"Well," he said, "we have this little furnished cottage by the beach. We rent it from a schoolteacher for the summer. Maybe you know him, Miss McBrien. His name's O'Brien. Maybe you're cousins, heh-heh. It costs a lot, but Bethany says it gets the sea breezes, and it sure beats the foothills in the summertime. You ever been to Pasadena in the summertime?"

Elle shook her head no. But Richards nodded and smiled.

Lee Brown said, "Kinda smoggy, isn't it?"

Richards nodded again, preoccupied in his own mind with thoughts of this Bethany woman. He didn't know how far they should probe into Lee Brown's relationship with her. Who was she? What was she doing with Lee Brown? How long had she been in the picture?

Elle was obviously thinking the same thoughts. She asked a very general, open question. "Tell us more about Bethany," she said.

"Oh, she's a very nice lady. She drives me wherever I have to go. She gets up at five o'clock in the morning, and she makes me a nice breakfast, and she drives me to the track in our van. She'll pick me up here at five-thirty. By the time we get home, dinner's all ready for me. She has a nice dinner for me every night at six o'clock. Sharp."

"I see. Bethany has your dinner all planned?"

"Yes. She's a very nice lady. She washes my clothes for me, too. And she handles all the money, you know. I'm not much good at that."

"What money, Lee?" Elle was being very gentle in her probe, and Richards admired her technique.

"Oh, Mr. Osgood pays me real good, and Bethany tells me the bank pays real good interest on my trust."

"Your trust?"

"They call it a trust because I trust the bank and the bank trusts me."

Elle looked puzzled. "You mean a trust fund?"

Now Lee Brown looked puzzled. "Fund?"

"Dollars?"

"Oh, yes, I guess it's in dollars. I don't think it's in marks or francs or yen." He giggled, pleased at his little joke.

"And it's a trust fund?"

"Well, the bank trusts me not to spend it foolishly. Banks don't like you to throw your money away, you know."

Elle hesitated before she asked the next question. She wondered how to phrase it, then quickly decided to keep it simple. "Okay. You have this money. Where did the money come from?"

"Well, I work for it. Mr. Osgood pays me real good."

"No, I mean the money in your trust fund."

"Oh, that? The money in my trust fund? Oh, the medical people at UCLA put it there a long time ago. And the bank pays me interest on it besides. 'Interest' means the bank can loan some of my money to other people who need it and pay me a little extra something to keep me interested. I think that's why they call it 'interest.' "

"You find it interesting, do you?" asked Richards.

"Bethany thinks it's interesting, 'cause she can write checks on it for the household. We don't need much. Mortgage was paid long ago. I saw the piece of paper that said Mortgage. So all Bethany has to pay is the water bill and the electricity and the groceries. We had to spend a lot of money gettin' a new TV in April, though. Our old one gave up."

"You watch a lot of TV?"

"Oh, yes!"

"You watch the news? Documentaries?"

"No. The news is too violent. Too scary. We have our own little world. We're happy in it. So we watch things like *Jeopardy* and *Wheel of Fortune*. Bethany and I like those the best. Old movies, too. Bethany likes the old movies on cable."

"Which movies does Bethany like?"

"She's a big fan of all those old black-and-white movies."

"Oh," said Elle. "Movies like *Casablanca?*"

"No, these movies—Bethany calls them M-G-M movies —they aren't in color, but they're good stories, and they have these old stars in 'em, like Clark Gable and Spencer Tracy and Mickey Rooney and Judy Garland."

Elle said, "And Sonny Skies?"

Lee Brown got excited at this. "Oh, my, yes. Bethany loves Sonny Skies."

"How 'bout you?" asked Richards. "You like Sonny Skies's movies, too?"

"Oh, my, yes."

"Which ones? You remember which ones?"

Elle looked up from her minicam to give Richards a be-mused look and a nod. From that, Richards understood that it was okay with Elle to ask open, innocent questions like this. But that he'd better not start asking hard or accusatory questions.

Lee Brown gave the question a few seconds of thought. "I guess those musicals he did with Noelle Sparks. We saw one the night before we drove down here. I think it was called *Springtime in the Minarets*. There was even one about a racetrack we saw last night on AMC. We have cable TV in our beach cottage, you know. It was a musical, too, so you can imagine how much I liked that one. Sonny Skies and Noelle Sparks in *Two Kids at Ruidoso*.

"Oh, yes," said Elle, *Two Kids at Ruidoso*. I don't remember that one." Richards was sure she remembered it. He figured she was just trying to keep Lee Brown talking.

"That one," the groom replied, "was made at a track in New Mexico where they only run quarter horses. Some people think quarter horses are only one-fourth as big as regular thoroughbreds, but they call them quarter horses because they always run one-quarter of a mile."

"You ever been to Ruidoso?"

"No. Mr. Osgood says we'll never take any of our horses there. Our horses run longer than that. Anywhere from six furlongs to a mile and a half."

"A mile and a half!" said Elle.

"Yes. That's a pretty long race for a speed horse like Skiin' Jill. She likes six furlongs, nothing longer than seven. And she likes those furlongs best if they're on grass. I can understand that. If I were a mare—well, I couldn't be a mare 'cause I'm a boy—but if I were a horse, I'd rather run on grass, too. Wouldn't you?"

It was a long monologue, but Richards just let Lee Brown run on. It seemed clear that if Lee Brown was Sonny Skies, he had completely forgotten it.

An alarm went off on Lee Brown's wristwatch. "What's that?" he said. He knew what it was. He meant, "What's that mean?" Because he ticked off several of the possible reminders signaled by his wrist alarm: pill time, lunchtime, nap time. "Oh, yes," he said. "I'm supposed to take a nap every afternoon at three. Doctor's orders."

"Who's your doctor?" asked Elle.

"Oh, I have a nice doctor at UCLA."

"You remember his name?"

"Lee Brown. Dr. Brown says I have to have my nap. Every day. At three."

Elle looked at Richards. Lee Brown wasn't the doctor's name. He'd given them his own name. "Where do you nap?" she asked. "You don't go back to your cottage?"

"Oh, goodness, no. I have a little cot back here. You want to see it?"

He took Richard and Elle by the hand—one on each side of him—and led them to a little wooden annex behind the stall of Skiin' Jill. He had a tiny room there with just enough space for a narrow bed, a chair, and a floor lamp and a 1955 calendar on the wall featuring a brilliant painting of a bluebird by Tamayo, the Mexican artist. "This is where I take my naps," he said as he ducked into the room and bid Richards and Elle to come in.

Richards let Elle in first so she could get a shot of the room's interior, which admitted enough light for her purposes through an unshuttered window high above the bed. "Nice smell in here," she whispered to Richards.

"Uh-huh," he whispered back. "Smells like horseshit."

"Pretty warm in here," said Lee Brown. "But all I have to do is open this window a little bit. We get the sea breezes here every afternoon." He proceeded to stand up on the bed so he could unlatch, and then open, the window.

"We'll let you take your nap, Mr. Brown," said Elle.

"It's okay. Soon as I close my eyes I go to sleep."

Richards noted the 1955 calendar. "This calendar?" he said. "This calendar here when you got here?"

"Oh, no," said Lee Brown. "I brought that with me. That's my favorite piece of art. There's a song goes with it."

"Oh?" said Richards.

"I'm sure we'd like to hear it sometime," said Elle. "But we'd better let you get your nap."

"You want to hear my bluebird song?"

Elle said no at the same time that Richards said yes.

"Okay," he said. "Won't be a minute." He sang in the beautiful soprano voice of an eight-year-old:

Every little bluebird flies by,
I say what's your name?

Every little bluebird flies by,
Lands on my windowpane.
You're a naughty little bluebird
You better learn to do what I do . . .
Mr. Bluebird, bluebird fly, and bye-bye.

When he was finished, he had a far-off look in his eye.

15

Elle gave Richards a glance that said Let's get out of here.

Richards said to Lee Brown, "Look, you've been great to give us this time—part of your nap time, really."

"It's okay, Mr.—uh—Richards." He turned to Elle and said, "It was very nice meeting you, my dear. Did anyone ever tell you you are very pretty?" He waited for her answer. When Elle nodded, he smiled. "I thought so. Well, thank you for coming. If you ever get to Santa Anita, please stop and say hello. But that won't be till next winter."

Elle nodded, hesitated, then set her camera down abruptly and hugged this dear little man—who talked like a little boy. He looked away shyly when she embraced him.

"Only one more thing," said Richards. This time it was not a Colombo type question. "Do you think Skiin' Jill has a good chance tomorrow afternoon?"

"She has a very good chance," said Brown. "All of our horses have a good chance. Mr. Osgood doesn't enter them unless he thinks they have a good chance. Otherwise, it wouldn't be fair to the people who support racing in this state." Richards grinned. This guy was too good to be true. But Brown wanted a more positive sign of agreement from Richards. *"Would it?"* he insisted.

Richards said no, it wouldn't be fair. Not at all. "But what I was thinking, maybe I'd make a little wager on Skiin' Jill tomorrow—if you thought it was a good bet, that is."

Brown said it was a good bet.

"How much of a good bet?"

"Sir?"

"I mean how much would you bet on Skiin' Jill? If you were me?"

"Oh," he said. "I'd bet two dollars—across the board."

"That good a bet, huh?" Richards shook his head.

Elle chided him. "Come on, Rich."

Brown picked up her words exactly, same intonation. "Come on, Rich."

"Okay," said Richards. He shook Brown's hand and went looking for some wheels to get back to the clubhouse. He heard an announcer's voice over the PA system saying, "The horses are on the track for the seventh race. Post time in fifteen minutes."

Bill Osgood came up to them. "Get what you want?"

"Almost everything. But Elle and I were wondering. Could we come back after the race tomorrow? See how Lee Brown handles the horse after the race?"

Osgood seemed pleased at the thoroughness of their interest. "Well, I don't see why not. Just stay out of his way. He'll give Jill a bath, scrape her off, put a cooler on her—a cooler's a light blanket—give her a drink, and hand her to the hot-walker. We got some kids—hot-walkers, we call 'em— who take over." He jerked his thumb back over his shoulder at the two Mexican kids who were sitting in the shade, playing cards. "They cool the horse down. Walk it for forty minutes. Later, they'll feed her, not too much, some oats and some barley, and water her. Then she'll settle down for the night. But Lee—he'll talk to the horse first, make sure she's okay, before he hands her over to the boys. You might wanta get a shot of Lee's conversation with Skiin' Jill."

"That'd be great," said Richards.

"Oh," said Osgood. "There's a chance this mare'll win tomorrow. If she does, they won't be bringing her back here right away. Then she'd go to the test barn, where the state steward will give her urine and saliva tests. You know about that?"

Richards nodded.

"So if she goes to the test barn," said Osgood, "Lee'll be there to greet her, give her a bath, turn her over to the hot-walkers, and so forth."

★ ★ ★

As soon as they were alone, Elle said, "Thanks, Rich." They stood under a shedrow on the backside, waiting for an usher to come with a cart.

He nodded. He knew what she meant. He hadn't tried to pull a corny "This Is Your Life, Sonny Skies" routine with Lee Brown. "It's okay," he said. "It's obvious Lee Brown doesn't know he's Sonny Skies. Anyway, it would have been a lousy scene. 'Hey, you're Sonny Skies!' 'No, I'm not.' 'Yes, you are.' 'No, I'm not. I oughta know my own name.' 'Okay, if you say so.' " Richards laughed. Stupid scene. It wouldn't have made good television. Not at all.

"Besides which," said Elle, "it would have been cruel and heartless. Imagine! He likes watching old Sonny Skies movies!"

The cart came, and they hopped aboard. Elle whispered into Richards's ear, "But are we really sure this is Sonny Skies?"

Richards smiled at her and nodded. "Very little doubt, now. The Howard Kenelly connection. The trust fund. And, of course, the bluebird song. I guess that did it for me."

"Yeah, me, too!"

"I kinda got chills when he sang it. It sounded just the same as it did when he sang it in that screen test more than fifty years ago. I can hear it now."

"And I guess you made some mental notes on this. We picked up some more clues."

"UCLA?"

"Yes," she said. "Maybe that's where Sonny Skies ended up when he got conked on the head?"

"You mean at the university's brain clinic? I'm not even sure UCLA had a brain clinic there in 1944. We'll have to see."

"But the biggest lead we got was Bethany."

"Yeah, I was thinking about that. You remember where we heard that name before?"

"Billy Dwyre told us. There was a Bethany at the wedding of Sonny Skies. The sister of Frances Farnsworth, from Oklahoma. But you don't think—"

"Well, Lee said his Bethany talked like an Okie. Right now, I don't know what to think. But we gotta see this gal. If we're lucky, we may get a peek at her. Did he say she comes at five-thirty to pick him up every day?"

"We'll be looking for a horse-faced gal?"

"That's the way Billy Dwyre described her."

"But if this is Frances Farnsworth's sister, then there's still some kind of tie between Frances Farnsworth and Sonny Skies."

Richards smiled. "The story just keeps getting curiouser and curiouser. Why don't we go see a horse race?"

Elle laughed. "And make a small wager?"

"Another old addiction, me and the races. But a couple small bets aren't going to kill me."

"Uh-huh!" she said skeptically.

"Well, stop me if I go over the line, okay?"

They got back to the grandstand in time to watch the horses coming out for the eighth race. They'd have time to get a bet down. Richards skimmed a copy of that day's *Form* and started making quick notes in its margins. Elle had her own method. She thought she'd pick out a cute jockey. "Excuse me," she said to a woman in a nearby seat, "may I borrow your binoculars for a moment?" The woman handed them over with a smile, and Elle focused on the boys who were up on the contending horses in this race. Richards spent ten minutes on the form and came up with three horses and linked them in an exacta, the two and the four and the six.

Elle dug into her purse. "Put two dollars on the two horse for me. That's two for Pat Day. He's cute. And I like his colors here, red and gray. Red and gray become him."

Richards laughed. "Two whole dollars? You're as conservative as our little Lee Brown."

All three of his horses finished out of the money. But then, so did hers. "So much for our 'methods,' " said Elle. "Now what?"

"Now we wait for the ninth race." Richards put his nose back in the *Daily Racing Form*.

"Why do that?" said Elle. "Your method doesn't work."

He rolled his eyes. "Didn't give me a winner last race. But you don't throw out your method after one race."

She was smiling.

Richards said, "Well, laugh if you will. Who laughs, laughs last. Laugh after your jockey method works and my handicapping doesn't."

"I smelled popcorn back there," she said, inclining her head to an area they'd passed through to get to their seats. "I have a yen for some popcorn."

Richards was deep into his form. "Uh-huh, go ahead. Bring me a Coke, okay?"

Elle was back in ten minutes, and ten minutes later, the horses were on the track for the ninth race. "There's my horse," she said. "Number one A, with the red-and-gray silks."

"Why is he your horse?"

" 'Cause Pat Day's on him. I found out Pat Day's the leading jock here. And he hasn't won yet today. He's due."

Uh-huh," said Richards. He noted that horse number 1 was a seven-year-old son of a famous old Derby winner named Spectacular Bid and this horse, David Crook, was trained by the Cooper Stables. It was listed on the morning line at 5 to 1 odds. He checked out David Crook in his *Form* and shook his head. "I'm going to bet an exacta—baseball the two, and the four and the six."

"Baseball?"

"Link all three so no matter how they finish, I win."

She didn't understand.

"Well, exacta means you have to pick the first two horses in the exact order of their finish. If you pick 'one-two' and the race ends up 'two-one,' you lose. You've got to pick 'em in order. So when I baseball the two, the four, and the six, I get six tickets: a two-four and a two-six, a four-two, and a four-six, a six-two, and a six-four. But instead of saying all that when I get to the window, I just say, 'Baseball the two, four, six.' "

Elle dug into her purse. "Put two dollars on David Crook for me."

Richards laughed. "Can you afford the two?" he asked.

They watched the tote boards with some interest after Richards returned from the windows with his six exacta tickets and her $2 ticket on David Crook. David Crook won by three lengths and paid $18. Richards threw his losing tickets down and handed Elle her winner.

"Gosh," said Elle, "I guess these are worth something, too." She dug into her purse and flashed five $100 win tickets on the one horse.

"You imp!" said Richards.

She shrugged. "I guess Pat Day was due."

"If I'm not mistaken," he said, "you just won $12,500."

She held up the other $2 ticket. "Correction $12,518. Not a bad method, huh?"

"Yeah," he said. "You shoulda bet five thousand. Then you'd be going home with—$125,000. And eighteen."

"You're mad at me!"

"Mad? Why would I be mad?" In fact, he was not so much angry as upset. This was a new, more independent Elle

McBrien, and he wasn't sure how to deal with her. Maybe the change in her meant a change in their relationship.

She smiled and thought of a favorite expression of her dad's: "If you're so tootin' smart, why ain't you rich?" Now her Rich was smart. But he wasn't rich with a small r.

★ ★ ★

Jay Richards had better luck the next day at Del Mar. He found adequate justification in the *Form* for betting Skiin' Jill in the seventh race and did so. He took Lee Brown's advice (and the cue given him by Bill Osgood) and bet $60 on her across the board.

Skiin' Jill won the seven-furlong race by a neck, and Elle threw her arms around Richards and gave him a big, wet kiss.

"What does that mean, Rich? How much did you win?"

"We have to wait and see. They'll post the prices in a minute or two." When the tote board flashed again, they could see that tickets on Skiin' Jill paid $12.80, $4.60, and $3.00. "Let's see," said Richards. "I bet sixty—across the board. That gives me a return of exactly two hundred and four bucks. That oughta pay for a nice dinner tonight at Remington's." He turned to her. "I suppose you made a quiet little bet, too?"

Elle dug into her purse and produced one ticket.

Richards goggled at the amount printed on the ticket. "You bet—you bet—six thousand dollars? To win? Why, Elle, this is incredible."

"I bet about half of what I won yesterday." Almost apologetically, she added, "It wasn't like I bet the grocery money. I was playing with the track's money."

"Uh-huh." Richards's look was one of admiration and awe.

"How much do I win?" she said.

"I'll have to figure this out. Let's see, $12.80 for a two-dollar bet means $6.40 for one dollar. So six thousand times $6.40 will give you a little more than"—he made a calculation in the margin of his *Form*—"$38,000."

"Whee!"

"Yes, Elle. I should say. Whee! Give it several whees." He pretended to be miffed, but it was a cover for his joy—for her. She had had a good deal of bad luck in her life. She was overdue for some prosperity time. And that time had come. He shook his head. Maybe there was a God, after all. "Same method? You pick the jockey?"

"No. But Joe Badilla was up." Richards smiled. She picked up the racetrack lingo pretty fast. "And he hadn't won all day. He was due."

He hugged her again. "Well, any method that works is a good method, I guess. Of course, it isn't as good as talking to the horse."

"Well," said Elle, "I talked to a guy who talked to the horse. And speaking of Sonny Skies, alias Lee Brown—don't we have to be somewhere?"

"Oh, my god, yes!" he said. "We want to get down to the stables—no, the test barn, right now." He looked down at the track and saw a small crowd in the winner's circle—the owners, Mr. and Mrs. C. C. Carter, and Bill Osgood, the trainer, were getting their picture taken with Skiin' Jill and a dozen other friends and well-wishers. Elle picked up her tripod and her bag, Richards snatched her minicam, and they dashed to a waiting golf cart—at least, they'd had the foresight to have an usher waiting for them—and sped off toward the barns.

Lee Brown was talking to the mare when they pulled up at the test barn. What's more, the mare was talking to him, making little whinnying sounds in response to his affectionate congratulations. Richards handed off the minicam to Elle, and she focused in on the two of them, the groom and the winning mare, Skiin' Jill.

"Yes, little girl," he said in his boyish soprano, "you ran well today. Wasn't it nice out there on the turf course? Nice and easy on those beautiful legs of yours?" The mare was still breathing very hard, from exhaustion and from the exhilaration of winning the race, nostrils distended, flanks heaving in and out. But she whinnied and nuzzled him on the neck. "I told you you'd love it. Yes, I did! And you believed me. And you went out there and ran your best. And that was enough to win! You don't have to win all the time. All you have to do is run your best. That's all you need to do. That's all we want you to do." The mare raised her head and bared her teeth and made a sound that sounded to Richards like nothing so much as a laugh.

Richards said to Elle, "You get that. You get that on tape?"

She nodded and panned over to the trainer, Bill Osgood, and a coterie of well-dressed folks about forty feet away. She surmised that this was Mr. and Mrs. C. C. Carter, the mare's owner, and a group of their friends who had come over to the backside to hang around and congratulate themselves if they bet Jill or kick themselves if they didn't.

"Back here," said Richards. "Get this scene now."

She stopped shooting the owners' party, swiveled around, and saw Lee Brown, wearing a cowboy hat today, going to work on Skiin' Jill. He had taken off the mare's bridle and was slipping a halter around her neck. He drew a bucket of hot water from a nearby spigot, poured antiseptic and liquid soap into it, and bathed the mare with it, using a large brown sponge. Then he scraped off the suds with a kind of squeegee and wiped her head and eyes with the sponge. Still talking softly to her, he slathered her all over with alcohol, threw a colorful cooler marked CCC on her, tied it, and only then allowed the mare a drink of water from a red bucket, also marked CCC. "Here," he said to the two Mexican boys, his hot-walkers. "Forty minutes, huh?" He pointed to his watch. *"Cuarenta."*

Elle got the entire thing on tape and moved in tight on Lee Brown when he handed the mare off to the boys. Only then did he notice her, and when he did, he smiled. "Well, I told her she could do it. And she did it."

☆ ☆ ☆

Richards and Elle walked Lee Brown back to the Osgood row of stables. Elle couldn't help telling the groom about her incredibly good luck.

"Thirty-eight thousand dollars?" he said. "My my. That *was* lucky. But, my dear, I guess you had to bet a lot to win that much. At least a hundred dollars, huh?"

"Uh, yes," she said. "Even a little more than that. But I wouldn't have done that if you hadn't told me Jill was a good bet today."

He reached out and squeezed her hand. She hugged him back. And then she asked him if he and his Bethany would like to help her and Mr. Richards celebrate with a dinner tonight at Remington's. He didn't know Remington's. "Mr. Richards says it's the best place to eat."

"Oh," Lee Brown said, "I'll bet it's a nice place, a place where the big owners eat."

"Well," she said, "a groom will eat there tonight."

Lee Brown said he would ask Bethany. "We never eat out. But a lotta people eat out. Maybe she'd like to eat out tonight."

Shortly, his Bethany was pulling up to the stable in a blue-and-white Chevy Blazer, short gray hair poking out from under a bright red fedora. The hat gave her a jaunty air, and she hailed the groom with a raucous shout. "C'mon, honey," she said, "the roast is in the oven, and we've gotta move our ass."

Lee Brown hustled over to the car door, spoke to her quietly, than turned and waved at Elle and Richards to come over. As they approached the Blazer, Elle flipped on her minicam. But when the woman behind the wheel saw the camera, she bawled, "Hey, I said I'd say hello. I didn't say I wanted 'em to take my picture."

The little groom looked embarrassed. "Hey, nice people," he said, turning back. "No pictures, okay?" Elle and Richards kept walking toward the Blazer, and Elle aimed her minicam at the ground. Lee Brown turned to the woman behind the wheel and spoke gently to her. "Bethany, these are my friends Elle and Rich. They work for the TV. Elle and Rich, this is my friend Bethany."

To Richards, up close, she was not an attractive woman. Her mouth was too big. So was her nose. And so was her jaw. On a horse her face would have looked just fine. On Bethany Whatever-her-name, it must have been a burdensome piece of baggage through the years. Bethany had not turned off the engine and did not get out of the Blazer. Instead, she motioned for Lee Brown to climb in on the other side. While he was doing so, she mumbled a hello to Richards and to Elle and said, "You didn't take my picture, did you?"

"No," lied Elle. "I couldn't do that without your permission." In fact, she had gotten a shot of Bethany behind the wheel in profile. But it was from a distance—certainly not what she wanted.

Lee Brown said, "Bethany, Elle and Rich want to take us out to dinner tonight. She won big today with a nice bet on Skiin' Jill."

She shook her head. "No, not tonight."

"But—"

"I said, 'Not tonight.' Got a roast in the oven right now. Gotta get back. Sorry." She made an effort to smile at Elle, but it was a tight smile that said she wasn't a bit happy.

Elle said, "Well, we would like to talk to you, Bethany. Maybe tomorrow?"

"Uh-uh. You don't need me. I'm just the housekeeper for this little guy. That's all. Just the housekeeper."

"But a housekeeper with a very interesting background," said Richards. "I think we need you more than you know."

Bethany's jaw dropped. She turned and said something to her companion, then, her face suddenly grim, stepped on the gas. She made a tight U-turn and was soon out of sight in a cloud of dust.

"That's what you get," Elle said.

Richards shrugged. "This isn't the end. I promised we wouldn't do any kamikaze journalism on Sonny Skies. I never promised I wouldn't go after the sister of Frances Farnsworth."

"You think this *is* her sister?"

"I'd bet on it." He paused. For God's sake, she even lives in Altadena. That's where Nigel Parrish said she was living.

"I thought that was Pasadena?"

"Same thing. Altadena. Pasadena. Twin cities. I'd bet six thousand dollars this is the sister of Frances Farnsworth."

"That much, huh?" said Elle with a smile.

"This is something we've got to do, Elle."

Elle looked slightly pained. "Do we? Can we talk about it?"

Her pain caused him some pain. "Hey," he said, "are you losing heart for this?"

"I didn't know it would be such a dirty business."

"Dirty?"

"We're going to hurt people."

"We have to talk about this."

"Okay," she said. "Let's talk."

Richards shook his head. "Let's give ourselves a break first? A nice dinner, maybe?"

Elle nodded. She plucked at the silk shirt she was wearing. "I feel sticky. How about a shower first? Then dinner?"

They had booked a room at the Inn at Rancho Santa Fe, a small, ancient hotel with white adobe walls half-covered with purple bougainvillea. Once they were inside, Elle disappeared into the bathroom. "I'll be a human being," she said, "in five minutes."

He found out how human she was in less than five. He joined her in the shower, a luxurious Swedish contraption with jets coming at them from all directions. After they soaped each other and rinsed and kissed each other all over, they staggered out of the stall, toweled off, and threw themselves on the middle of the king-sized bed and made love for an hour. They were, as a result, all sweaty again. "Nothing to do"—she laughed—"but have another Swedish shower."

"Okay, okay," he said. "But let this one be G-rated, huh?" He touched his back. "I am not," he said, "as young as I used to be."

"Ohhh, honey," she said, "did you hurt yourself?"

He grimaced. "I think it happened when we were hanging upside down from the overhead spigot."

★ ★ ★

They didn't go all the way back to Remington's; instead, they had dinner in the hotel at a fine French restaurant called Mille Fleurs and were lucky enough to get a corner table with enough privacy to talk freely.

Richards said, "This started out as a simple piece of Hollywood history. Now it's a full-blown mystery story that's leading us into the heart of one America's great companies, into the Pentagon, and into some hanky-panky that would enkindle the imaginations of America's great tabloids."

"Tabloids. Oh, that's one of the things that bothers me."

"We can't help it if the tabloids jump on the story. We still get to tell it our way first."

"What makes us so sure we'll do it first?"

"What do you mean?"

"I think I saw Tom Greenberg in line at the mutuels today."

"Greenberg?"

"Uh-huh. He was with a very large, very ugly man, dressed like a tout. Big checked red-and-white sport coat, baggy white pants."

Richards groaned. "You've just described Dave Benton."

"I wonder what he and Greenberg are doing down here?"

"I don't have to wonder. I know. They're on the trail of Sonny Skies."

"You think Dave Benton would sell this story to the *National Enquirer*? Or *Hard Copy*? Or both?"

"I wouldn't put anything past Fat Ben."

"But we don't know that he really wants to do that, do we?"

"No, we don't. In fact, he's helped us. If he hadn't accessed the Howard Foundation's computer system, we'd still be looking for Sonny Skies."

16

Richards phoned his own Hollywood number after dinner that night and was surprised to hear a message on his machine from one of the Australian ladies. "Daphne Doyle here, Rich. The girls and I are in town. We've been booked on the *Frances Farnsworth Show*. Call us. Four Seasons Hotel in Beverly Hills. Ta ta!"

Elle said, "Rich, we've got to get back up to L.A." And the debate began. Richards wanted to stay close to Sonny and Bethany. No telling what Fat Ben and Tom Greenberg were up to. Elle figured that Sonny and his Bethany would keep. They weren't going anywhere. "But our friends are booked on the *Frances Farnsworth Show!*"

"Yes," Richards finally said. "Frances Farnsworth's our Maltese Falcon. Let's go on up."

For a week running Richards had been watching the *Frances Farnsworth Show* at 4:00 P.M. on L.A.'s Channel 4. He found her to be the pseudoessence of class, the kind of lady, indeed, who wouldn't say shit if she had a mouthful. Nevertheless, she specialized in presenting a lineup of almost nothing but sex freaks with weight problems, for whom she pretended the most obvious maternal concern. He once told Elle, "You won't believe the lineup Miss Farnsworth had on today. Men who can't get off unless they're being choked to death by men dressed up as cops."

"Huh?"

"Do I have to say everything twice?"

"Listen, Buster," Elle had retorted, using her term of

nonendearment. "Can you please explain to me how, if a guy knows he can't have an orgasm unless he's being choked to death, he will ever live to tell about it on the *Frances Farnsworth Show?*"

"You have to see the show. These fat boys are real fantasists."

"Well, then," she said, "you should have no trouble getting on the show."

But now he didn't have to wangle his way onto the show. The girls from Australia had beaten him to it.

It was 10:30 P.M., but he put in a call immediately to the Four Seasons and talked to Daphne Doyle. "The girls" had trumped up the most delicious plan, she said. They'd found the show's booker quite interested in doing something along the lines of "Lesbians Who Eat Too Much." Once he'd spoken with talkative Daphne, he was almost sold. He loved her story about Red Riding Hood scolding the wolf who leaped out of the bushes crying that he was going to eat her. "Eat, eat, eat!" she said. "Damn it! Doesn't anybody fook anymore?"

"You know any others like you?" asked the booker. When Daphne told him about Cynthia and Stephanie, he was three-quarters sold. "The others have your cute Australian accent?" he asked. When she assured him they did, he said, "You're on."

"So," said Richards. "When *are* you on?"

"Saturday. NBC in Burbank. And we've got tickets for you and Elle. You can be part of the studio audience."

"Saturday," said Richards. "You mean tomorrow night?"

When he hung up, he went to the open door of the hotel bathroom where Elle was brushing her teeth. "Well, Elle," he said, "we're closing in."

When they got to Richards's apartment the next day at noon, Richards had a letter waiting for him. It was from Al Mangino, the moonlighting cop, with a make on Lee Brown's prints. They were the same as Sonny Skies's. The documentation was accompanied by an invoice—for $1,000. Across the invoice was printed: "No Extra Charge for the Info on Mick Daugherty."

Richards looked inside the envelope and found another sheet of paper. It looked like a Xerox copy of an official report. "MISSING PERSONS," it said. And it presented the details on one Mick Daugherty, white male, forty-five; sergeant, LAPD; married to an Ellen Daugherty. He was listed missing on May 29, 1944. Down at the bottom of the form, under "REMARKS," was the handwritten notation "Worked as guard, off-hours, part-time, for H. Kenelly."

"Elle," he shouted. "Look at this! Now we're looking at a murder."

She examined the two reports. "Yes," she said, "and we're looking at a cover-up for murder, too."

"Pretty darn effective cover-up, too, I'd say. Howard Kenelly takes care of the widow, and nobody says a thing about Mick Daugherty."

"Not even his buddies at the LAPD?"

Richards shook his head. "We don't know, Elle. We'd have to check the newspaper files. They had five major papers in L.A. then. If there had been an official inquiry, the papers oughta have some reports on it.

★ ★ ★

The late-afternoon taping of the *Frances Farnsworth Show* was notable, not so much by the appearance of the overweight trio of self-described lesbians from Perth as by the scene that took place in the parking lot outside NBC's Burbank studios. Elle and Richards had foregone the pleasure of being part of the studio audience. Instead, they had climbed into the limo with their Australian friends for the trip from Beverly Hills to Burbank, and then they stayed in the limo during the taping so they could spring upon Miss Farnsworth according to plan.

According to that plan, Daphne, Cynthia, and Stephanie would hit it off with Frances Farnsworth, as they had managed to hit it off with almost everyone on their worldwide adventures, simply by making Miss Farnsworth laugh. "I haven't laughed as hard as this," she had told them during the actual taping of the show, "in a long, long time."

That tape would later be part of the coroner's inquest and a key piece of evidence to demonstrate (according to HMO's expert witness) that Elle and Richards were not the cause of Miss Farnsworth's coronary but that her collapse was brought on by more than a half hour of excessive laughter.

After that laff riot, when the taping was over for the day, the four of them—Daphne, Cynthia, Stephanie, and Miss Frances Farnsworth—had become bosom buddies. They joined her in her dressing room, told her more jokes, and finally persuaded her to join them for dinner that night at Chasen's. "You can come with us in our limo," said Daphne.

"No, let's take mine," said Miss Farnsworth.

"Well, why don't you just come with us and have your driver follow our driver?" said Cynthia.

Done and done. That's the way they'd go, together. So the girls stuck with Miss Farnsworth until she was ready to leave NBC, laughing and gabbing all the way out into the parking lot to their respective limos, which were parked side by side in the spaces always reserved for limo parking at the Burbank Studios. They pranced along, the four of them, right up between the limos, Miss Farnsworth's white limo on the right and the girls' black limo on the left. And at that moment Richards and Elle crossed over the line into kamikaze journalism.

Richards burst out of the backseat of the black limo and barked, "Miss Farnsworth!" He was not more than three feet from her, and Elle was right behind him with her mini-cam up and running. "Do you know we've found Sonny Skies?"

She seemed momentarily stunned. She looked around for her security guard, and he was nowhere to be seen. He was busy, twenty paces back, trying to help Stephanie capture her pearls, which were bouncing all over the parking lot. "Who?" she said. "Sonny Skies? Why, you damned fool, who are you? Sonny Skies was a war hero. Lost his life on D day almost fifty years ago."

"Is that why you've been collecting his pension all these years?"

"Of course, you idiot! Why shouldn't I?"

"Because he's alive. Because you know he's alive. Because your own sister has been his keeper all these years just so you'd know when—and if—the poor little fella got his memory back."

"Bethany?" she said. "You've found Bethany?"

Richards nodded. He knew he'd never get another chance like this again, so he charged ahead. "Miss Farnsworth! Are you aware that you've robbed American taxpayers to the tune of a half million dollars?"

"That's a lie!" she cried. "Not nearly so much as that!"

"Then you admit it? You've defrauded the government all these years. And covered up the murder of Mick Daugherty besides?"

Now her limo driver and her bodyguard were trying to get to her side, but Daphne, Cynthia, and Stephanie surrounded them and, with their arms joined, got them into a huddle, or as they later described it, "a rugby scrum"—effectively blocking them out of the action for a full minute.

That was long enough for Frances Farnsworth to cry out a guilt that had been building up inside her for almost fifty years. "I didn't mean to kill him," she said. "When he knocked out Sonny with that heavy hunk of glass and started to go after him again, I had to stop him. So I grabbed my gun. It was right there in a drawer in my coffee table. And I fired over his head to scare him off. But he raised up just as I fired—and took the bullet right in his ear. But I didn't mean to kill him. *I didn't mean to kill him!"*

"Lucky for you," said Richards, "that Howard Kenelly was right there to fix things for you."

"Yes," she said. "Yes, I was lucky. And so was Sonny. It would have been a grim life for him—and for me—if Howard hadn't been the generous guy he was. He was a prince. He was the best. He was—"

At this point, Miss Frances Farnsworth clutched her heart and crumpled to the ground.

"Get the hell outta the way," screeched Elle to Richards. "I wanta get that look on her face."

"You get all that?" demanded Richards. "You get her whole confession?"

"Shut up," Elle whispered huskily. She came in close on the twisted features of a woman who had once been dubbed as the most beautiful woman in the world. When she was finished, she panned across the scene in front of her: her security guard down on his knees, his head to Frances Farnsworth's ample chest; her limo driver, jumping up and down; Daphne, Cynthia, and Stephanie, their heads together, all abuzz; and twenty yards away, a trio of NBC security guards running toward the two limos. Within two minutes, the black-and-white squad cars of the Burbank P.D. squealed into the lot at NBC, their sirens screaming.

☆ ☆ ☆

Elle and Richards, Daphne, Cynthia, and Stephanie were booked for reckless endangerment, fingerprinted, and bailed out late Saturday night at the city jail in Burbank. Daphne Doyle put up the bail, $50,000 for each of them, and they repaired to the Four Seasons for a glass of champagne. Elle and Richards had Cokes but celebrated in other ways when they returned to Richards's apartment in Hollywood.

The next morning, Daphne managed to locate her friend Foster Kane. He was sailing off the Southern California coast, not far from Catalina—close enough to make a meeting bright and early Monday morning at the offices of HMO.

Charlene Burr had already viewed the confession of Frances Farnsworth in her office, with Elle and Rich at her side. "What I can't understand," said Charlene, "is how the police ever let this tape out of their sight."

"They never had it in their sight," said Elle. "Before the police ever got there, with all the confusion, people shouting, Daphne in the throes of her false hysterics and all, I removed the tape from my camera and slipped it to Cynthia, who, in turn, slipped it to her driver, who hid it under the carpet of his limo."

"And the police couldn't find it?"

"They didn't know enough at the time to realize what they were looking for. I mean, they confiscated my camera, but I had a new tape in it by then. They searched the limo and all, but they were totally confused, and they let the driver go. In fact, they *ordered* him to go—after he insisted that if the ladies had to go to jail, he wanted to drive them. 'They'll goddamn well go in our squad cars,' said the sergeant in charge. And we did." Elle giggled. "But our driver was there, waiting for us outside the Burbank jail after we made bail, all smiles. He gave Cynthia the tape when he dropped us at the Four Seasons. And Cynthia gave him a nice tip. And then she gave me the tape. 'Good luck with it, ducks.' That's what she said. 'Good luck with it, ducks.' "

Foster Kane entered the room to catch the end of Elle's account. Elle saw him standing there, a bit sunburned from his recent sailing weekend but still as handsome in the flesh as he was in the news photos she had seen of him. Beaming, she said, "Our driver deserves a tip from us, too, Mr. Kane. But not money. He's really an actor, Mr. Kane, moonlighting as a limo driver. And I think we have to help him get a break. He needs work. We can find him work, can't we?"

"Let me see that tape," he said. "If it shows what Daphne says is on it, I think we're going to have to help him a lot."

"Yes," said Richards exuberantly. "Even if he has no talent!"

Foster Kane frowned and walked over to Richards. He was six feet six if he was an inch, and in his Western cowboy boots and Stetson hat, he towered over Richards. "Talent has nothing to do with anything, my friend. All you have to have in this world is balls. If you've got balls, Mr. Uh—"

"Richards."

"Oh, you're Richards, are you?" He smiled. "If you've got balls, Mr. Richards, you can go wherever you want to go. And from what I've heard, you've got balls." He turned to Elle. "You've got an Irish accent. You must be Miss McBrien."

Elle smiled and almost curtsied.

"From what I've heard, Miss McBrien, no offense intended, you've got balls, too. Now let me see that tape."

★ ★ ★

Foster Kane was not disappointed by Elle's footage. The picture got very herky-jerky when Frances Farnsworth went down to the asphalt, but he liked that. Gave the scene precisely the feeling it needed. A feeling of chaos. And they could delete the sound track where Elle was telling Richards to get the hell out of the way. "You did the right thing, young woman," said Kane. "Story first, story second, story third. There's nothing but the story."

Kane wanted to know when Charlene Burr's unit could have the documentary finished. He believed *The Search for Sonny Skies* would win every award there was. And that it would get a helluvan audience. It would also be a confirmation of his vision for HMO. "These murder stories. They bring the human condition to a focus."

Charlene, Elle, and Richards were agape. Is that what they were doing? Bringing the human condition to a focus?

"Can you have the thing ready in a week?" asked Kane.

"Well," said Charlene, "what do you guys think?"

Elle and Richards had a story conference then and there. "We've got a few more interviews to do," said Elle. "Then we can go to edit."

"A few more?" said Kane.

"One, with Sonny Skies," said Richards. "That'll be the big payoff scene. *The Search for Sonny Skies?* This'll be the end of the search. Two, with his housekeeper. You know, the faithful sister of Frances Farnsworth who kept a watch on Sonny all these years? That'll pull on the heartstrings of every woman in the world. Three, with the widow of Mick Daugherty. He was the off-duty cop that Frances plugged fifty years ago. Lord knows what she'll say on-camera. And four, with the head of the Howard Foundation, George Tjitcomb."

"Well," said Kane. "One and two, I would agree with. In fact, the interview with Bethany is so important that I will authorize you to pay her for her story. She may not talk without a handsome payment."

"How much," said Richards, "is handsome?"

Kane didn't even pause to reckon. "Half a million," he said.

Richards whistled.

Kane gave an impatient wave of his hand. "We'll get that back, ducks, on newsstand sales from my three international tabloids. *If* we get her story exclusive. I'll leave that up to you. And I'll count on you to turn her taped interviews into our tab features. Three of 'em. You get ten thousand a piece for writing 'em, Richards."

Richards smiled. He remembered that he'd have to split his fee with the Backstabbers. But $5,000 a piece for a three-thousand-word story was the best rate he'd ever seen, and he'd settle for that. And a deal was a deal.

"But you can pass on Mrs. Daugherty and George Tjitcomb," said Foster Kane. "George is a friend of mine. I ski with him in Chile. And I am fairly sure that neither he nor any of his people would know anything about Sonny Skies, or Mick Daugherty, either, for that matter."

"Well," said Richards. "There was a big cover-up here. Howard Kenelly—"

"No. No," said Foster Kane very evenly. "You didn't hear me. I said forget Mrs. Daugherty and George Tjitcomb. I want this documentary ready to go within the week."

"But—"

"Look," he said. "I don't want the world's other tabloids scooping my tabloids—or HMO—on this story. And neither do you. Do you, Mr. Richards?"

Richards looked at Elle. She rolled her eyes and made the kind of signal she'd seen umpires make at Dodger Stadium when they called a runner safe at home. "Uh, no," he said. "I don't, sir." He knew in his heart that no matter how big his balls were, Foster Kane's were much bigger.

Still and all, Richards was in a stew as he and Elle headed over the Cahuenga Pass toward Hollywood. "Imagine the gall of that guy! Telling us to stay away from his friend George Tjitcomb! That's not journalism. Going easy on one of your skiing buddies. Tjitcomb's part of the story, too. So's the goddamn Howard Foundation. I still think it was someone hired by the foundation got in your apartment and took your portrait of Gremmie. 'Story first, story second, story third,' my ass!"

Elle was driving through a good deal of late Monday morning freeway traffic. She kept her eyes on the road. She clucked her tongue.

"What?" demanded Richards. "What does that mean?"

"It means, 'Let it go.' A month ago I was a novice producer at HMO. You were almost unemployed. Working the dregs of the L.A. beat for that T and A tabloid in London. I'll bet you even had to scout up some nude pix for 'em here in Hollywood, didn't you?"

"Well—"

"Don't answer that. The point is that our stock is very high with the biggest media mogul in the world. We can keep it that way, or we can blow it."

"But this isn't the way—"

"Don't give me any of your middle-class morality, Rich. You can't afford it. Neither can I."

Richards was silent. He recalled the endearing words of Alfred P. Doolittle in Shaw's *Pygmalion*. Doolittle was of a mind to sell Liza to Henry Higgins because he couldn't afford middle-class morality. He said, "All right, Miss Pragmatism. That's fine. But I hope you don't have any qualms about destroying the life of an old gent named Sonny Skies, happy in his eight-year-old innocence."

"I don't if you don't," she said. "He's the heart of the story. We can't win awards with *The Search for Sonny Skies* if we don't have that last great scene with Sonny Skies."

Richards was silent. Then he pointed out that not too long ago she had been full of fears about hurting the guy. "Now you don't care?"

"I care," she said. "I just don't think it will matter what we tell him. As far as he's concerned, he's the good and faithful groom who talks to horses. Lee Brown. We can tell him he's really Homer Brownlee. Homer Brownlee who became Sonny Skies. But it isn't going to matter."

"We'll see. If that's the way he reacts, it won't be good television."

Elle contradicted him. "When we catch his incomprehension on tape," she said, "that'll be all the payoff we need. In fact, we already have caught that naive eight-year-old in this old man's body. Talking about how much he enjoyed those Sonny Skies movies with Noelle Sparks. Don't you see? We can cut to him talking to his horses—nice little colloquy with Skiin' Jill—and the audience will understand. Innocence will always triumph over tragedy. People will love it."

Richards nodded, impressed with Elle's sense of story. "Okay," he said, "I like it. And the best part of this plan is that we never have to even hint to him that he's really Sonny Skies. His ignorance will be his bliss."

"Yes," said Elle. "And ours, too."

17

When they finally found the beach cottage that Bethany Farnsworth had rented for the summer down near the Del Mar Racetrack, it was 6:00 p.m. on Wednesday. It had taken them the better part of two days checking out the local markets and the little real estate offices in Del Mar, asking about the whereabouts of the schoolteacher named O'Brien who rented out his cottage in the summertime.

They finally found a chatty real estate woman who had brokered the rental, and she directed them to the place. "They got a real bargain, they really did," she said. "Ten thousand for the season. That's way below market here." Some market, thought Richards. The summer rental was a small, fairly run down frame cottage with a big, shedding eucalyptus tree in the front yard. And it wasn't on the beach. It was two blocks from the beach, hard by the railroad track.

When they knocked on the screen door, they were stunned to find it was Tom Greenberg who came to the door. "Oh," he said casually, "it's you. We were wondering when you'd show up. Come on in," he said. "Bethany! It's Elle McBrien and Jay Richards, our partners! We can find another coupla plates for dinner, can't we?"

"What the hell you doin' here," whispered Richards.

"We've come to help," said Greenberg.

"Heavens to Betsy Ross!" said Benton. "I was just telling Lee here about our Sunday morning tennis games."

Lee Brown had a white bib around his neck and a broad smile on his face. "Oh, I like company," he said. "This is fun." He had his knife in one hand and his fork in the other, and he was ready for his supper. And Bethany Farnsworth was serving it to him when he invited Elle and Richards to join them. "You set up two more places, okay, Bethany?"

Elle gave Richards a puzzled glance. He motioned for her to take a seat. In fact, he held the chair for her and whispered, "We just play it by ear, huh?"

Bethany had prepared a large meat loaf with mashed potatoes and gravy, backed with a big lettuce and tomato salad bowl and three kinds of dressing, sitting right there in their original jars in the middle of the table. "Help yourselves," she said. She had a look of confusion on her horsy face. But Richards didn't have a clue about how much she knew. Frances Farnsworth's death by heart attack at NBC had only drawn the standard obits in the nation's press. Nothing yet about the strange circumstances that led to her death. But since this weird twosome didn't watch the news on TV, Richards hoped that Bethany Farnsworth knew nothing about her sister's death. If she was confused, he hoped it was because these two men had found Lee Brown at the Osgood stables, befriended him just as Elle and Richards had, and showed up for dinner at Lee's invitation. His hopes were confirmed when he learned that he and Elle had arrived not ten minutes before they did.

"We wanted to get you on-camera again," Elle said, looking to the head of the table where the subject of their long search was working heartily on his meat loaf.

"Yes," he said, "I expect so. My friends here, Tom and Ben, they've been telling me I could become a star."

Richards gave Benton and Greenberg a wild look. "Uh, Lee, what kind, uh, what kind of star?"

"Well, I sang for 'em, same as I did you? The bluebird song? They think I could become a big recording star."

Jeez, thought Richards. What next? He turned to Greenberg. "You want Lee Brown to cut a record?"

Greenberg smiled broadly. He was enjoying every moment of this; he knew what was happening, and Richards didn't. Knowledge is power. And for the moment he had knowledge. "Not just one record," he said. "Lee has a number of favorites. You oughta hear him sing 'Turkey in the Straw.' Plays it on his harmonica, too. And 'Tiptoe Through the Tulips.' He'll bring that hit back again, just like Tiny Tim did."

"I don't know Tiny Tim," said Lee Brown. "But Mr. Greenberg tells me he made a million dollars singing 'Tiptoe Through the Tulips.' "

"Who did?" said Richards. "Tiny Tim or Mr. Greenberg?"

"Rich, Rich!" said Greenberg. "Let's not descend to mere monetary matters."

"Mere monetary matters? Hey, I think if you're gonna do this, you oughta make sure our friend here has an agent."

"Rich, Rich," said Benton. "What agent he gonna get? You know the only good agent is a dead agent. Anyway, the only agent Mr. Brown could get would be one a the old-timers—somebody, maybe, who booked General Custer into Little Big Horn." He grinned, but no one else at the table did. He had to explain his little joke. "You all heard a the agent who boasted he'd booked General Custer? Somebody challenged him. Said, 'General Custer? You booked General Custer at Little Big Horn?' And he said, 'Hey, I only book 'em, I don't tell 'em how to wear their hair.' "

"Very funny, Ben," said Richards.

Tom Greenberg broke in. His voice was very soothing. "Look, Rich, Mr. Brown here—" He looked at Lee Brown and smiled unctuously. "Mr. Brown here doesn't care about filthy lucre. Do you, Mr. Brown?"

"Well," he said, "I don't know what lucre is, but if it's filthy, I don't wanta have anything to do with it!"

"Right! Right!" said Greenberg. "Mr. Brown feels as Ben and I do. He just wants to entertain people. Lord knows, they have lives that are bleak enough. They want to smile."

Lee Brown said energetically, "And if I can help 'em smile, well, then, that's what I wanta do!" Greenberg and Benton cheered, Bethany cheered right along with them, and Lee clapped with delight.

In the hubbub, Richards leaned over to Elle and said into her ear, "What's their game?"

Elle whispered, "I think I get it. Our friends are opportunists. When we come out with *The Search for Sonny Skies,* they'll follow right up with their LPs and cassettes and CDs."

Richards said, "You don't think he knows yet—that he's Sonny Skies?"

She shook her head. "He'll never know."

"But they're gonna exploit him."

"And we aren't?" Richards sat up straighter and looked at her with some surprise. She was right.

"So let it go," she said quietly. "Let it go."

At the head of the table, Lee Brown burped. He had already finished his dinner. "That was a good meat loaf. You guys want some more?" He passed the platter on to Benton, sitting on his right, who took some and passed it on. "Bethany, did you say you made some peach cobbler for tonight? I'll have some cobbler. With ice cream on top, okay?" He turned to his left. "You want some peach cobbler, Mr. Richards?"

Richards knew he was being weak. But he couldn't resist peach cobbler. "Sure."

Lee said, "Give Mr. Richards some cobbler, Bethany."

Elle kicked Richards under the table.

Richards said, "No ice cream on it, though." He patted his stomach. "Gotta watch the ol' ice cream."

After dinner, Elle told Richards to keep Lee occupied. She wanted to talk some business with Tom Greenberg and Dave Benton. And then she wanted to speak privately with Bethany Farnsworth, who was now clearing the dishes off the table and getting ready to wash them.

Elle took Tom and Ben out on the porch, but Richards

found that he didn't have to keep Lee Brown occupied. Lee said to Richards, "Hey, you wanta help with the dishes? I help Bethany every night. You take a towel here. You can dry, too."

Whatever Elle said to the two Backstabbers, it didn't take long. The three of them came back into the cottage just as he was drying the last dish and putting the jars of salad dressing back into the refrigerator.

"What happened out there?" Richards whispered to Elle.

"Hush," she said, "I'll tell you later. Now I need to talk to Bethany. Alone."

She turned to Bethany. "Is there a place where we girls can talk?"

Bethany said, "In my room. Back here."

★ ★ ★

A half hour later, the two women emerged from their private chat. Bethany was smiling. She came up to Richards and said, "I want to say I'm sorry for bolting like that the other day. I didn't know what was happening, and I was scared. You understand?"

"Absolutely," said Richards.

"We're going to have our interview anytime you say. We can have it tonight if you want, right here, while Lee's watching AMC."

Richards said, "Uh-huh."

"You'll be ghosting some stories for me, too, won't you?"

Richards nodded at that, too. "Yes," he said, "I expect I will. I guess you like our offer."

Bethany nodded. "Darn tootin'. About time Bethany Farnsworth had a break."

Richards realized that Elle must have laid everything out for Bethany—her sister's killing of Mick Daugherty, the years of cover-up, and her sister's recent death by heart attack in the parking lot of NBC in Burbank. He was amazed at how amenable Bethany had become. He gave credit to Elle's persuasiveness and to the obvious fact that Bethany didn't intend to mourn a minute for her sister, who had gotten all the breaks in life, and she none—until this sudden visit by the angel of death. And until this visit from some TV people who wanted to give her a lot of money for her story. Payoff time for Bethany Farnsworth! Richards felt happy for her. He wondered whether Elle had promised her the entire half million authorized by Foster Kane.

★ ★ ★

The interview with Bethany Farnsworth didn't proceed that night at the cottage. Bethany wanted to get her hair done so she could look good for Elle's minicam, and so they arranged to do the interview at four the next afternoon in a beach-pool setting against the backdrop of the old Victorian elegance of the Hotel del Coronado. At the same time, Tom Greenberg and Dave Benton had wangled a day off for Lee Brown so they could take him to a recording studio in downtown San Diego.

Richards had complained to Elle about the deal she had struck for Sonny with Greenberg and Benton. "They're just going to exploit him," Richards kept insisting.

"It's tit for tat," she said. "They get Sonny; we get Bethany. We need her now. We don't need him."

Richards frowned. "After we make him famous again, they're going to come out with a Sonny Skies album. They'll make millions."

"Let 'em," she said. "The sun shines on us. It doesn't shine any the less on us because it also happens to shine on them."

Richards shook his head. "So Lee Brown—I keep calling him Lee Brown because he thinks he's Lee Brown—becomes an instant recording star? How long do you think that will last? Will he be happy again working as a groom for the Osgood Stables? I doubt it."

Elle said, "He can't go on working as a groom?"

"He's a simpleton. But even simpletons can go Hollywood."

" 'Hollywood,' " she said. "I think that's your trouble. You really hate Hollywood."

"Sonny Skies is a good example. You helped do the research. You know how shamefully he was exploited by the studio! He was the biggest thing at M-G-M, but L. B. Mayer paid him peanuts—while, for a dozen years, Mayer himself was the highest-paid CEO in America. A lot of his millions really belonged to Sonny Skies."

"What are you," she said, "a Communist or something? Without M-G-M, Sonny Skies would have been singing and dancing on the state-fair circuit."

"Without Sonny Skies, M-G-M—"

"Would have gone on being M-G-M. They would have found some other kid."

"Ah, maybe you're right," said Richards. He shook his head. "But I'm still worried about Lee Brown in the hands of the Backstabbers."

✷ ✷ ✷

The interview with Bethany Farnsworth was pretty special. They did it in three parts, with half-hour breaks in between each session, and Bethany turned out to be a woman with almost total recall. She wasn't the smartest woman in the world. But she had a helluva memory. Richards thought she was a ghostwriter's dream.

She told them about growing up with Frances Farnsworth, about all the sibling jealousies she felt as a youngster —her so ugly and Frances so beautiful, even as a six-year-old. She told them of Frances's going off to Hollywood and about all the money she started sending home as soon as she hit it big. She told them of the thrill she felt at being allowed to attend Frances's wedding to Sonny Skies. And she told them of her own feelings of satisfaction when Frances had flown her out to L.A. from Tulsa in 1944. To think that her rich, glamorous sister needed her, plain ol' Bethany Nobody, when she was in trouble and needed someone she could trust to keep a watch on Sonny Skies. And, finally, she told them about her life with Sonny Skies—Sonny Skies, who'd gotten hit on the head so hard he never remembered being Sonny Skies.

"We were lucky Mr. Kenelly had horses," she said. "That way, he could set Sonny up in something that wasn't beyond him, something he loved. He's had a satisfying life," she said. "I hope it stays that way."

"Will you stay with him?" asked Elle.

Here Bethany paused for a long time. She lowered her head. Then she looked out over the western horizon, far out to sea. The silence was punctuated by the cries of a few seagulls. "I don't really know," she said.

"Is there something you want to do with your life?" said Elle. "Now, you know, you'll be able to do anything you want."

Bethany shook her head. "Not 'anything.' I'm gettin' old. But maybe I'll see the Orient. I've always wanted to go to New Zealand. And, yeah, I wonder what it'd be like to have dinner in Paris, see the stage plays in London, attend the bull fights in Madrid? Maybe I'd get my face fixed first. They've got doctors do that, you know."

"What about Sonny?" asked Richards. "He be able to take care of himself?"

She grimaced. "I doubt it. But maybe we could find somebody. Oh, I don't know. I'm kinda attached to him. He's never spoken a harsh word to me. In his eight-year-old way, I think he—" She started to choke. "I think he—really—loves—me." Her eyes brimmed with tears.

"Okay," said Elle. "I think that's a wrap. Terrific, Bethany. There must be some good acting genes in your family. You were great."

Bethany sniffed. "It wasn't an act."

Richards dug into his pocket and came up with a handkerchief. He thought how much he had changed. A few months ago, he didn't carry a handkerchief. He wore jogging suits. Now he was wearing Ralph Lauren jackets and suits by Brioni. And he carried a handkerchief!

This adventure had changed Elle, too. She let Richards handle the sound and camera equipment and Bethany Farnsworth so she could find a phone and tell Foster Kane and HMO that she had hit a home run with the bases loaded. And that she had gotten the complete cooperation of Bethany Farnsworth for $250,000. "Got her for half price!" she told Foster Kane.

18

$\mathbf{T}$*he Search for Sonny Skies* stunned the world. Foster Kane's ad agencies made sure that the documentary got more hype than any other in history. It didn't need the hype; it was a poignant story, and it told itself. At least that's the way it seemed to the writers who celebrated the documentary with cover stories on Sonny Skies in *Time* and *Newsweek*. *U.S. News & World Report* was a bit more intelligent. It didn't give Sonny cover treatment. But it did do profiles on both Jay Richards and Elle McBrien, and the writer predicted nice new things on the horizon for both of them. He called them "newspeople with a sense of literature" and Elle McBrien as "a woman with a head as well as a heart."

The magazine pieces leaned very heavily on Dan Morley's series on Sonny Skies in the *Washington Post*. It was a four-parter, and it was a sensation in Washington for its revelations about the hanky-panky perpetrated by the War Department back in 1944, falsifying records, making a man a war hero at D day who wasn't even there, all to please a captain of industry who was enriching himself and so few army generals at the taxpayers' expense. Richards had gone back to Washington, to help Morley on the story, after he and Elle had finished their final edit on their documentary. And Elle had taken the break in action to go visit her parents in London.

Congressmen from both parties huffed and puffed about the *Post* story and gave the *Post* their own take on the situation. Sen. Alphonse D'Amato called for hearings by a

Senate subcommittee, and the editors of the *Post* said they would nominate Morley for another Pulitzer Prize.

The first screening on HMO won 173 million viewers, worldwide, setting a record for a documentary film on TV. It played on HMO seven times in September, and then Warner Entertainment picked it up for theater release, which meant that Elle and Richards each got an extra $150,000 for their work on it. Gremmie got back from her vacation with her father, and Elle moved to the West Side. She put Gremmie in a nearby Catholic boarding academy for girls, and then she went off on an extended second visit with her folks in London. Richards bought a BMW convertible and lost forty pounds and started to take tennis lessons.

Tom Greenberg and Dave Benton made $7 million on Sonny Skies's first and only recording, which was released in October. As a soprano, Sonny Skies singing "Tiptoe Through the Tulips" was a novelty, one that brought back campy memories of Mrs. Miller and Tiny Tim. But after the D.J.s had their little howl over it, that was all they wanted. They (and the buying public) were off to the next new thing.

Perversely, Sonny Skies wasn't happy any more as a groom. He quit the Osgood Stables the week that his record hit the charts, firmly believing that he, Lee Brown, had put a good one over on the simple people who thought he was Sonny Skies. He knew he wasn't Sonny Skies, but why go wee-wee on the parade? That's what Dave Benton told him, and it made a lot of sense. People wanted to think he was Sonny Skies brought back to life, let 'em. He, Lee Brown, would cry all the way to the bank. But not the Arcadia Bank.

He switched his trust to the Bank of Singapore's Beverly Hills branch because he made a move—from his place in Altadena to a cottage at the Beverly Hills Hotel, where he paid $1,000 a day. He wouldn't need a housekeeper at this posh hotel, Benton had told him, which took a load off his mind. After Bethany had quit him to take her trip around the world, he had had three housekeepers. None of them stayed more than two weeks.

Now, at the Beverly Hills Hotel, maids came in to make his bed, and bellboys brought him anything on the menu that suited his fancy. He cultivated a taste for Cranshaw melons in the morning, crêpes suzette at noon, and juicy prime steaks at 6:00 P.M. every evening, backed with fine French wines—and banana splits in bed at night, when he watched cable TV. AMC was still his favorite channel. He still loved those old Sonny Skies movies. "Gee," he told the maid in the morning, "that kid Sonny Skies! He sure was good."

Then, one day, he was paid a call by a bright young Asian gentleman in a three-piece suit. He was from the Bank of Singapore. "At the rate you are spending your trust," he was told, "you will be broke in two months."

He put in several phone calls to Tom Greenberg, but no one bothered to return them. He called Dave Benton, his other new friend. Benton didn't return his calls, either. He was too ashamed to call Jay Richards. Richards had tried to give him a quiet warning about doing business with people who called themselves Backstabbers, and he hadn't listened. So Sonny hired a private detective to find Greenberg and/or Benton—to determine what had happened to the millions that he was supposed to share from his one and only record. Seven million dollars? What had happened to that? That's what someone poolside at the Beverly Hills Hotel told him Greenberg and Benton had made on the Sonny Skies album. What happened to his half?

The private eye turned out to be a young woman named Tiffany Bell, a former cheerleader from Beverly Hills High. She showed up at Richards's apartment in Hollywood, a scrumptious dish, a redhead with silicone boobs. "Haven't we met?" asked Richards.

"Yes," she said. "When I graduated from Beverly, I went to work with Gloria Chatham. You and I met one day at lunch on the Sunset Strip."

Aha, Richards said to himself. One of Gloria's hookers. Now she was a P.I.!

"You were with an Irish girl? Where's she now?"

"She's visiting her folks in London," he said. "I think. I haven't heard from her in a while."

Tiffany Bell said, "Gloria told me you'd help me on this case. She says you could be a friend." She explained her assignment: to find out what happened to Lee Brown's royalties.

"I don't know what to tell you," said Richards. "I used to play tennis every Sunday morning with the Backstabbers and take some of their money on our Thursday night poker games. But I haven't seen any of 'em in many a week." He gave her Tom Greenberg's address in Laurel Canyon and asked her to come back and tell him how she fared.

She returned with the sad news that the royalties from the record were, mainly, media hype. She had a notarized audit sheet in her hand. Richards couldn't decipher it, but the bottom line was that there were no funds accruing to Lee Brown. "I don't know if I can believe this," she said, "but there it is. In black and white."

Richards shook his head sadly. "The record business. It's a license to steal. They're past masters at double bookkeeping. Maybe triple bookkeeping. No way to get through the maze."

"What do I do?"

"You gotta tell Sonny," he said.

"Come with me?"

"No," he said. "I don't have the heart."

Tiffany Bell knocked hesitantly at the door of Sonny Skies's cottage at the Beverly Hills Hotel. He was wearing a pair of shorts and his old Dance Ten, Looks Three T-shirt

"Gee," he said when she gave him the bad news, "what am I gonna do now?"

Tiffany Bell said she'd thought he might ask that question. Before her visit to Sonny's cottage, she had gone back to Tom Greenberg and asked him what their man was supposed to do now.

"He isn't 'our man,' " said Greenberg.

"Nevertheless," she said.

"Well," Greenberg told her once he realized she wasn't going to leave his place until she had some kind of satisfaction, "the Backstabbers could have another proposition for Lee Brown. There'd be good money in it for him. For you, too, if you want a piece of the action." He said he'd make her a one-third partner if she could get the cooperation of Lee Brown, a cute little guy who still didn't know he was Sonny Skies.

Tiffany Bell wasn't very bright. She went to Lee Brown and told him all of this, including her chance to make some good money, too, if she could persuade him to go ahead with the plan. She revealed this to Lee Brown in his cottage at the Beverly Hills Hotel, everything right out in the open, no subterfuge.

"What's the proposition?" he asked her.

This was a case of one not very bright person trying to explain to another not very bright person. "They want to cast you in a movie," she said.

"A movie! Is it a musical?" He gave a little jump of joy. "Something like *Springtime in the Minarets?*"

"Well, yeah, sort of. It'll have music in it, that's for sure."

"And I'll make a lot of money?"

"Well," she said, "not a lot. But it's guaranteed. One million dollars up front, cash on the barrel head for you. You get it before they start shooting."

"A million dollars!"

"If you invested it conservatively, it'd bring you seventy, eighty, thousand a year. Maybe more. You could live well on that. Maybe not here in this hotel. But you could live in a nice place. With maid service."

"And room service, too?"

"Well, I don't know about that."

Lee Brown thought about that. "Well, I guess I could go down to the coffee shop and eat, huh?"

She assured him that he could. Long as he lived within walking distance of a coffee shop. "Someplace off Wilshire, maybe, in Santa Monica?"

"Okay," he said. "A movie! Let's do it."

"They'll want to bill you as Sonny Skies. That be okay?"

"Hey, if they want to keep believing that—"

"You haven't asked what you'd have to do in this movie."

"Okay. I will now. What do I have to do in this movie? Besides sing, I mean?"

Tiffany took a deep breath. "You have to make love. To a lotta women. It's a special kind of movie. Doesn't play in theaters. But millions of people buy 'em on videotape."

He didn't have a reaction to that other than deep thought. "You mean kiss and everything?"

Tiffany took a moment to figure out how she could explain. "You know how colts are made?"

"Sure!"

"You've seen mares taken to stud?"

"Oh, yes! It's pretty scary, though."

"Well," she said. She paused.

He said, "Okay, I've seen horses do it. And I guess humans do it, too. But I've never done it. You think I can do it?"

"I don't know," she said. "You wanta give it a try? It's kinda natural. I taught my little brother one summer." She began to unbutton her blouse.

19

Tiffany phoned Richards to tell him what was happening. "Why tell me?" he said.

"Because you asked me to," she said.

"Can he do it?"

"Sort of. Well, he's getting better."

Richards sighed. "He shouldn't be doing this."

She said, "I know. But he doesn't have many options."

"When they gonna shoot this thing?"

"The twenty-second of October. Week from next Thursday."

"Where?"

"Neighbor of the Greenbergs in Laurel Canyon. They're off on a trip somewhere. But they've got a perfect place. An estate called La Paloma. Lotta privacy. Nice pool. It's one of those all-black pools."

"You've seen the place?"

"Uh-huh. Tom Greenberg took me over there yesterday."

"Tennis court, too?"

"Uh-huh."

"I think I know the place," said Richards. "Not far from the Greenbergs' place, right?"

"Yeah."

"Okay, Tiffany. Thanks for letting me know. I hope you —and Sonny—get your money."

"I took care of that. They give me two cashier's checks,

one for me and one for Sonny, and I deposit them before we shoot."

"Okay," said Richards. "And, uh, good luck."

"I'll need it," she said. "So will Sonny Skies."

★ ★ ★

About midnight, still stewing about the fix that Sonny Skies was in, Richards phoned Elle at her parents' home in London. She wasn't there, but her mother said Elle could call him back. She did so, within the hour. "What's up?" she said.

He told her.

She suggested that Sonny needed some professional help. Did Rich remember her friend Dr. Leiter? Yes, the Gestalt therapist that she met at Esalen some years ago. "See if you can get Sonny in to see Dr. Leiter," she said. "He takes people on head trips. Does wonders. As I think I told you once. Sonny should start seeing him. Otherwise, I think he's headed for a crackup."

Elle's voice was very businesslike. Something about the tone made him ask her why she hadn't phoned or written.

"Oh, I don't know," she said.

"You weren't home when I called your folks. It was eight in the morning."

"Yeah?"

Richards felt he didn't want to ask her where she was. But now he was suspicious. What the hell? He might as well tell her he had a certain feeling about their relationship. "Elle," he said, "are you really staying with your folks in London?"

There was a long pause at Elle's end of the line. In the silence, Richards heard other voices bleeding into his connection to Elle McBrien. They were speaking Spanish. "Elle," he said, "are you in Spain?"

"Sort of," he said.

"Sort of?"

"Well, Ibiza. It's a nice little posh island—"

"I know where it is." Richards wanted to ask her who she was there with. Instead, he let his silence do the asking. It was an old reporter's trick. Just wait.

"Rich," she said. "I wanted to write you, but I just didn't know how to say it."

"There's someone else?"

"Uh-huh."

He let his silence put the pressure on Elle. Perhaps a minute passed. "Hello," he said.

"Rich," she said, "it's Foster Kane."

"Oh?" he said. Now he came close to stuttering. "How . . . how long has this been going on?"

"I went skiing with him in Chile right after we finished our documentary. We hit it off. I've been with him for two weeks now here in Ibiza. He's a very exciting guy to be with. He's got a yacht down here. Some interesting friends coming and going. Lot of business action. He says he likes my savvy."

Richards felt like making a smart crack about the shape of her savvy. He restrained himself. He remembered her attacking him one day not long ago. Something about his instability—as symbolized by his not wearing Florsheim or Bally or Bostonians. "I think I understand, Elle."

"You do?"

"Yes," he said. "This is a guy who wears shoes-shoes, right?"

She laughed. "Yes, Rich. I guess that's about the size of it."

He wanted to make another crack—like, about the size of what? Instead, he said, "Okay, Elle. 'Bye. Stay in touch. You might want to know what happens to Sonny Skies. On the other hand, maybe you don't."

"Oh, yes," she said, "I do."

Richards phoned Dr. Leiter the next morning. He had an office not far from Cedars Sinai in West Hollywood. Yes, he remembered Richards. He laughed. He might not have remembered him if he hadn't been a friend of the charming Miss McBrien. And yes, he could find time for Richards. If he could come at noon?

Dr. Alphonse Leiter was a smooth-cheeked fellow who would have been handsome except for his premature baldness. He smiled a good deal, had a soothing voice, and he was easy to talk to. But he didn't know if he had time or space for many more patients, time to see this strange case called Sonny Skies.

"I'll pay for his treatment," said Richards, surprising himself with his own generosity. "Whatever it costs."

"He has no insurance?"

"None."

"All right, then," he said. "We'll see what we can do for Sonny Skies, the man who thinks his name is Lee Brown. *Before* he goes ahead with his piece of performance art."

Richards said, "Huh?" Then, quickly realizing that the expression was Dr. Leiter's euphemism for an orgy scene—in front of some big cameras—he said, "Oh, yes. Before his performance art. That'd be good."

20

As far as Richards could reconstruct the entire episode, it happened like this:

Tiffany Bell picked up Sonny Skies at the Beverly Hills Hotel in her red convertible and delivered him to La Paloma. Three other flashy cars were parked in the courtyard when she wheeled her Mustang in at 10:00 A.M. on October 22. Both she and Sonny came dressed for their roles; both wore Chinese kimonos, as called for by the thin script that had been adapted from an old Chinese folk tale by Tom Greenberg.

The movie, called *The Chinese Pool,* had a simple plot. A Chinese lord would catch one of his daughters in flagrante delicto alongside the pool with one of the palace slaves. For her punishment, he would have his other, loyal slaves tie up her lover, strap him to the diving tower of the swimming pool, and force him to watch while he, the lord and father, ravaged her to a frazzle. Then the father would rape *him.* And cut off the slave's head with the slave's own sword. Exultant in regaining authority over his castle and emboldened by the mighty exercise of his sexual prowess, the lord would then command all six of the maids of the household to his master bedroom suite and have them one by one. Sonny Skies would play the part of the lord, and Tiffany Bell would play the part of his daughter.

Tom Greenberg and Dave Benton explained this all very carefully to Sonny Skies when they met at the swimming pool. With its dark bottom and sides, it provided a nice visual contrast to the pink bodies of the six young women who were already treading water or lounging lazily on the steps of the pool, their faces and their bare breasts turned up to the warm morning sun. Out of shyness, perhaps, or maybe fear, the slave boys were floating around at the other end of the pool. Tom Greenberg was standing at poolside with Dave Benton, each of them with scripts in hand, each of them wearing little berets.

Sonny felt as if he were in some kind of a dream. "Why is there a security guard here?" he said. "And why is he armed with that big machine gun?"

Dave Benton gave an embarrassed smile. "Oh," he said. "You mean that AK-47? For security, of course."

"He needs that big gun for security?"

It did sound a little silly to Benton. He added, "You know, to protect the girls."

"When we start shooting—" Tom Greenberg pointed to three cameramen who were fiddling with their equipment and their lights. "When we start shooting, we don't want interruptions, no unwanted visitors."

"You're not selling tickets, are you?" asked Sonny.

"Now where would you get an idea like that?" said Tom Greenberg. "I mean it's not a bad idea. But we just didn't think of it. And it's too late now to advertise." He laughed.

Sonny kept looking over at the guard. He said the guard didn't make him feel very secure at all. "Why does he have that big machine gun?" Sonny asked again. "And why are you wearing those funny caps?"

Tom and Ben looked at each other and laughed in embarrassment. This was Ben's idea, to wear the berets. "Makes us look more like directors," Ben said.

If they had to take special pains to look like directors, Sonny asked, then maybe they, too, weren't feeling very secure. Greenberg and Benton assured him that they knew what they were doing. They were not only the directors of this opus; they were producers and distributors, too. Already they'd sold $3 million worth of advance orders for the video. "That's how we could afford to give the cashier's check to your friend Tiffany Bell. Check for a million. You get another million when this is in the can." It was a simple statement of fact. But Greenberg made it sound like a threat.

Benton chimed in. "Orders are streaming in from the porn underground." If they were, it was because buyers were titillated by the sell line: Sonny Skies, the sexual naïf, getting it on with the cream of Brentwood's best hookers.

Brentwood's best hookers? What did this mean? As Tom Greenberg explained in a moment of excessive candor to the editor of *Playboy,* who had sent one of his best reporters to cover the shoot, "We got six coeds from UCLA to romp through this thing with Sonny Skies. They're six petite, demure little kids; look like the teenager who lives next door to your Aunt Sara in Brentwood. You know what I mean? Classy kids, buy their clothes at J. Press, use the best shampoos? They're not really hookers, though. Just call 'em liberated. They fool around a lot, for free. If they make a little money on this one morning's work, what the hell."

Tiffany asked whether the *Playboy* writer had arrived yet. "He's in the kitchen getting a cuppa coffee," said Benton. "Hey, here he comes now." The writer walking toward them was extremely handsome, tall, blond, with a nice tan. "Don't waste your time with him, though," said Benton. "He's gay." Tiffany rolled her eyes.

Greenberg said, "We may use him as a double for some a the cum shots. Close-ups, you know, if Sonny can't come. Ben and I may have to double, too, if the slave boys can't get it up. Heh-heh. Right, Ben?"

Tiffany looked nervously over at Sonny Skies. He looked confused. In fact, he seemed to be looking for a way to escape. "Sonny, baby," said Benton. "You look a little tense. You can't be tense here. You got a big morning's workout ahead of you. You gotta relax."

Tiffany went over to Sonny's side. "It'll be okay, Sonny."

She kissed him on the cheek. "Just do it the way I've been showing you. It'll look realistic enough. And then the doubles will fill in for you toward the end of every scene. That's the way these movies are made. In the close-ups, cocks are as interchangeable as, uh, socks. It'll all be over in an hour or two."

Sonny shook his head. He was speechless. Tiffany wondered if he understood anything she was telling him.

"We better get started, Tom." It was Ben. If anyone was tense, it was Benton.

"Okay," said Greenberg. "Tiffany, you're going to be the daughter, right? Well, here's your lover now." He greeted a long-haired giant who might have been a double for the Italian model Fabio. He had emerged from a poolside shower stall wearing nothing but a pair of white knee-high socks. "Kurt! Good. You're ready. Get your socks off."

Kurt shook his head. He didn't want to take his socks off. "I feel better with my socks on," he said. "They're my trademark."

"Oh," said Greenberg. He shook his head. Then he hit his forehead with his palm. "Oh, how stupid of me! Your trademark, of course." He suddenly remembered that he'd auditioned porn stars for this part by watching some of their tapes. Come to think of it, this guy Kurt always wore knee-high socks during his sex scenes. But, even knowing that, Greenberg was still confused. Why did he need a trademark?

Shortly, however, Greenberg composed himself and proceeded to give his directorial instructions. He explained that they wouldn't be shooting the story in strict sequence. "First, we wanta get all the cum shots out of the way. We'll start with Kurt and Tiffany, over here in the shade, on this chaise."

"Quiet everybody," shouted Benton through a silly little megaphone. "Quiet on the set!"

Some of the girls got out of the pool, grabbed towels, and skipped over to the place behind the cameras where

Kurt and Tiffany were getting themselves arranged on the chaise—Kurt in his knee-high socks, Tiffany in her red satin robe. Everyone else on the La Paloma estate gathered around: the security guard; half a dozen slave boys, naked except for their Oriental swords; the three cameramen, standing in three strategic positions; a soundman, the gay writer from *Playboy*, Greenberg, Benton, and Sonny Skies. And the Greenbergs' calico cat.

"Okay, places everyone," said Tom Greenberg. "Kurt! Tiffany! You ready?"

Benton raced around in front of camera one with a clapper that said Scene 7, Take 1. "Okay," said Greenberg, "cameras, and roll 'em and action!"

Kurt came up right away. Tiffany was a lithe little sexual athlete. They fooled around for five minutes of foreplay, no real dialogue, just cries and whispers and little moans. Then Tiffany said, loud enough for everyone to hear, "Fuck me, fuck me now!"

The spectators leaned forward as Kurt arranged his knees between hers.

And suddenly: *"N-o-o-o-o!"*

It was a shrill cry of rage that froze everyone there, and it had come from the throat of Sonny Skies.

Sonny had dropped his stage sword and was leaping on the security guard. He grabbed the guard's AK-47 and proceeded to spray the whole scene with a hail of bullets. Hundreds of bullets. He got the guard first, then Greenberg, then Benton, then Kurt. He got the slave boys and the cute little coeds. And he got the cameramen and the soundman. It was all over in seconds. He spared no one, not even his friend Tiffany Bell. All were dead except the Greenbergs' calico cat and the security guard, who, though mortally wounded, had enough strength to pull his sidearm and shoot Sonny Skies in the back. Sonny could hear the cries of the calico cat in his ear as he lay dying. He felt as if he were in a dream.

* * *

In fact, he was in a dream. Or, to be more precise, in the middle of a fantasy trip under hypnosis, guided by his therapist, Dr. Alphonse Leiter. Later, when Richards told the story, he couldn't give anyone all the theoretical underpinnings for this kind of therapy. It had something to do with "getting out feelings that had been long repressed." Repression, so the theory went, was what made people less than fully functioning human beings. If the therapist could help his patient blow the lid off that repression, then the violent explosion would have a cleansing effect on the psyche of those who had been so twisted by their early histories.

Sometimes the boiler inside a man would explode in real, bloody massacres. Charles Whitman, the mutt who climbed a tower on the campus of the University of Texas and killed twenty-two people with his high-powered rifle, was a good example. So was James Oliver Huberty, the nut who armed himself with a half-dozen weapons and murdered all the men, women, and children who were unlucky enough to be eating a burger one morning at a McDonald's in San Ysidro, California. After Sirhan Sirhan assassinated Sen. Robert Kennedy in a hotel pantry in Los Angeles, eight shots fired off in rapid order from his Iver-Johnson .22, it took a half-dozen men to wrestle him down. A perceptive writer who was there noted that, afterward, Sirhan's eyes were "dark brown and enormously peaceful."

But, if a therapist could have a Whitman, a Huberty, or a Sirhan play out a violent fantastic reenactment, he might be able to relieve the pressure inside the potential assassin. Maybe there'd be no need for real violence. That was the theory.

"But," as Dr. Leiter explained to Richards, "theory shmeory. The best thing I can say about this hypnotic fantasy trip is that it works. It works for a lot of people. It works the very best for people who have long-suppressed, unhappy memories. That's all you need to know."

Richards was in the doctor's anteroom during Sonny's fantasy trip to the poolside orgy. It was the doctor who suggested certain details of the scenario. It was Sonny who expressed his own feelings about each and every story element along the way. And it was Sonny's idea to attack the guard, grab his gun, and kill everyone at the orgy and Sonny's own idea to have the guard shoot him in the back. He had exploded. He had killed everyone in sight. And he didn't want to live anymore.

As Sonny lay dying, in his hypnotic fantasy, on Dr. Leiter's couch, he said in a husky voice, "At last I've found out who—I—am." They were his last words.

The therapeutically satisfying thing about that moment was the tone and the timber of Sonny's chosen last words. He did not speak them in Sonny Skies's normal soprano. They were the words of a mature man. "At last, I've found out who —I—am."

"All right," said Dr. Leiter, "all right." He leaned back in his chair. Sonny was still under hypnosis. In fact, he was more deeply asleep at this moment than at any time during the one-hour session. Leiter rose and went to the door of his waiting room and called for Richards to come in. He said, "There's something I want you to see, Mr. Richards. And, there's something I want you to hear."

Richards slipped in—quietly, according to the doctor's instructions—and took a chair near the feet of Sonny Skies. "I'm putting this all on videotape," said the doctor. "It may come in handy in future negotiations with the Howard Foundation. And I need a witness. You'll be the witness, if you don't mind."

Dr. Leiter went over to a small camcorder mounted on a tripod, checked it to see how much tape he had remaining, turned up the rheostat on his ceiling light, then took his place in an easy chair at the head of the couch. He proceeded to bring Sonny Skies out of his hypnotic trance. "You're going to come out of your nap now," he said. "When you come out of it, you're going to forget everything that happened, forget everything you said while you were on your trip. You're just going to feel very, very good and very, very refreshed. All right, now, you're waking up. You'll wake up completely at the count of one, and you'll feel very refreshed. Five, four, three, two, one. One, that's right. You're awake now, you're awake. You can sit up now."

Sonny Skies shook his head, blinked, looked over at Dr. Leiter, and smiled. He swiveled around so that his feet hit the floor—barely, because he had rather short legs. And then he said, "Hey, I feel very good."

Richards was startled at the sound of his voice. He heard the speech rhythm of Sonny Skies. But it wasn't a soprano voice that he heard. It was a reedy bass.

"Who am I?" asked the doctor.

"Why, you're Dr. Leiter."

"And who are you?"

"Me? I'm—Homer Brownlee."

"Have you always been Homer Brownlee?"

"No. For a dozen years, I was Sonny Skies. I did a lot of movies."

"And then what?"

"And then I married a beautiful woman. And then I lost her. And then I went into the army."

"And then what?"

"And then my mother died, and I came home to bury her, and then I went to see my wife."

"Did you see her?"

"I saw her with another man."

"Who was that other man?"

"It was Howard Kenelly."

"Was he nice to you?"

"We got in a fistfight."

"Then what happened?"

"I don't remember."

"You don't remember?"

"I don't remember."

"You don't remember anything that happened to you since the time you were in that fistfight?"

He shook his head and smiled apologetically. "I'm sorry, Doctor."

"Where are you living these days?"

"The Beverly Hills Hotel."

"You remember some things, then."

He paused. "Yes. People are nice to me there."

"What people?"

"The bellboys. The phone people." He paused.

"Anybody else?"

"Tiffany. Tiffany's nice to me."

"What does she call you?"

"Lee."

"So you do remember some recent things?"

"Yes. They call me Lee Brown at the hotel. But I don't know how I got there or what I'm supposed to be doing there."

"Do you recognize the name Lee Brown as a form of your real name 'Brownlee'?"

He smiled. "I do now."

The doctor pointed at Richards. "Do you know who this is?"

Homer Brownlee, who now remembered that he was once a movie star named Sonny Skies, looked over at Richards, less than two feet away. "No." He shook his head. "No, I don't." He grinned sheepishly. "I'm sorry. I suspect that I should know you. I have a sneaking suspicion that you've helped me recently and that that's why you're here in the doctor's office with me. But I honestly don't remember you."

Dr. Leiter invited Richards to speak.

Richards had a hard time getting started. He was almost speechless with surprise over the change that had taken place in this man. In less than ten days of therapy with Dr. Leiter, Sonny Skies had grown up. He not only had the voice of a mature man. He had the mind of a mature man, too, the presence, in fact, and the quiet confidence of a good trial lawyer.

"Well," said Richards finally, "I'm a kind of reporter. For months I was searching for you. Me and a friend of mine named Elle McBrien, who is a documentary filmmaker. We found you. When we finally did, we saw that you weren't in very good shape. Oh, you were happy enough, but you'd regressed to the age of eight or so—after a severe blow to the back of your head."

"Wait a minute," said Homer Brownlee. "You're going pretty fast for me here. I mean, I'm not an eight-year-old anymore. But I'm no genius, either. A little slower, please?"

Richards said, "Doctor, what if we played our documentary for him?" He dug into his soft nylon briefcase and came up with a videotape cassette.

The doctor said to his patient, "Do you want to see this documentary?"

"Sure! What's in it? Will it help me?"

"It's sort of, well, it's the story of our search for you. It's kind of—well, it's a story of your life. We called it *The Search for Sonny Skies.*"

The three of them rose and regrouped at the other end of the doctor's office, in a kind of conversation pit. The doctor invited Homer to take a seat in a nice rocking chair, right in front of a large TV. He inserted Richards's tape into a cassette player atop the TV. Then he took a seat on the couch, next to Richards, and the three of them sat back to watch Homer Brownlee's life—all of it—unfold before them.

Needless to say, Homer Brownlee was the most interested viewer. He laughed at certain points in the documentary, most of all at some of the best comedy moments in his own films. He cried at other points, most of all when the aging Frances Farnsworth keeled over and died in front of

Elle McBrien's intrusive minicam. And he seemed especially bemused when he saw himself as the earnest groom who talked to horses—as he said, "with the voice of Jeanette MacDonald."

"So," he said, "I was a very good actor for a dozen years or so. And then I went into the racing business for forty or more?"

"That's about right," said Richards.

"Was I happy in either business?"

Richards paused for a moment. "You were abused in show business," said Richards. "People exploited you way back when. They tried to do it again, very recently, by trying to make you a recording freak. And when that petered out, they were ready to put you in a pornographic film."

"I see," he said gravely. "I see. And in the racing business? Did they exploit me there."

"No. You seemed happier there," said Richards.

"As happy as an eight-year-old can be," added Dr. Leiter.

He thought about that, rocking slowly. "I wonder," he said. "I think I might like to get back in the racing business." He laughed. It was a deep, happy laugh, the laugh of a man who finally knew who he was. "Yes," he said. "I think I'd like that a lot. But maybe not as a groom, okay?"

"And why is that," asked Dr. Leiter.

"You know," he said. "I'm not sure that I—at my age, really—I'm not sure I would enjoy mucking out the stalls. I'm not sure I'd like dealing with all the horseshit." He smiled.

Dr. Leiter smiled and looked at Jay Richards.

Jay Richards slapped his knee. "You know," he said with a laugh, "I can't say I blame you."

Epilogue

HOMER BROWNLEE got a $3 million settlement from the Howard Foundation and went on to become a handicapper and a columnist for the *Daily Racing Form*. He now lives in Arcadia with his young, adoring wife, the former Tiffany Bell.

ELLE MCBRIEN married Foster Kane and became a vice president of Media Unlimited at their corporate offices in Sydney, Australia.

GREMMIE MCBRIEN entered an advanced placement program and won a scholarship to Stanford, where she is now the youngest member of the freshman class.

JAY RICHARDS moved to Washington, D.C., where he became part of a team of investigative reporters under Assistant Managing Editor Dan Morley. Richards still calls himself "a recovering alcoholic."

TOM GREENBERG continues to host the Backstabbers Poker Club every Thursday night.

DAVE BENTON is serving a five-year sentence for computer fraud at the Federal Correctional Institution near Lompoc, California.

NIGEL PARRISH died at the rest home called West of Nirvana at the age of ninety-four.

BETHANY FARNSWORTH is a member of the town council in Altadena, California.

BILLY DWYRE and his foster daughter are still living together in a trailer court in Oxnard.

100147529

Rooney, Mickey
    The search for Sonny
Skies : a novel

DISCARD

100147529

Rooney, Mickey
    The search for Sonny
Skies : a novel

2/95

**YOU CAN RENEW
BY PHONE!**
847-1638

623-3300

GAYLORD M